Eve
Belcher

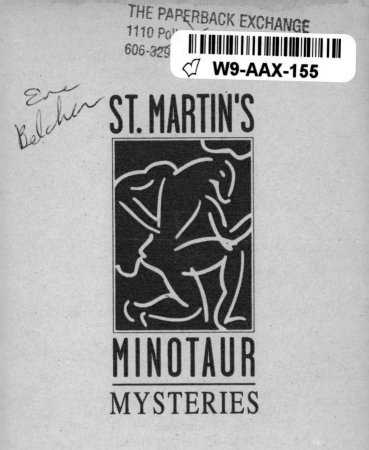

ST. MARTIN'S

MINOTAUR

MYSTERIES

OTHER TITLES FROM ST. MARTIN'S MINOTAUR MYSTERIES

THE HANGING GARDEN
by Ian Rankin
THE MANGO OPERA
by Tom Corcoran
ZEN AND THE ART OF MURDER
by Elizabeth M. Cosin
THE MIRACLE STRIP
by Nancy Bartholomew
THE MURDER AT THE MURDER
AT THE MIMOSA INN
by Joan Hess
BREAD ON ARRIVAL
by Lou Jane Temple
BIGGIE AND THE FRICASSEED FAT MAN
by Nancy Bell
MOODY FOREVER
by Steve Oliver
AGATHA RAISIN AND THE WIZARD OF EVESHAM
by M. C. Beaton
DEATH TAKES UP A COLLECTION
by Sister Carol Anne O'Marie
A MURDER IN THEBES
by Anna Apostolou

Minotaur is also proud to present these mystery classics by
Ngaio Marsh

BLACK AS HE'S PAINTED
TIED UP IN TINSEL
VINTAGE MURDER
WHEN IN ROME

PROPHECY OF DOOM...

"My lord king you'd best come now."

"What is it?" Alexander slurred.

"Three guards have been killed."

All drunkenness seemed to disappear. The king sprang to his feet, snapping his fingers for the others to join him. A cart stood outside the royal tent. Three corpses, foot soldiers, sprawled there splattered with blood. Alexander took a pitch torch from one of the escorts and moved closer. The side of each man's head looked as if it had been smashed in by some war ax or club.

"The men were out on picket duty," the captain explained. "I found one of the shields, then the corpses, as well as this!"

Alexander took the small scroll and handed it to Miriam.

"Doomed," she read aloud. "Oh, lost and damned! This is my last and only word to you. Forever!"

A MURDER
IN THEBES

ANNA APOSTOLOU

St. Martin's Paperbacks

A MURDER IN THEBES: A MYSTERY OF ALEXANDER THE GREAT

Copyright © 1998 by Anna Apostolou.

All rights reserved. No part of this book may be used or reproduced in any manner whatsoever without written permission except in the case of brief quotations embodied in critical articles or reviews. For information address St. Martin's Press, 175 Fifth Avenue, New York, NY 10010.

Library of Congress Catalog Card Number: 98-28727

ISBN: 0-312-97278-4

Printed in the United States of America

St. Martin's Press hardcover edition/ December 1998
St. Martin's Paperbacks edition/ December 1999

10 9 8 7 6 5 4 3 2 1

To Jean and Rick Hewett,
great parents with a love for Greece

LIST OF HISTORICAL CHARACTERS

PHILIP OF MACEDON: king; murdered in 336 B.C.

OLYMPIAS: his widow and queen; Alexander's regent in Macedon

ALEXANDER: son of Olympias; later Alexander the Great

PTOLEMY, NIARCHOS, HEPHAESTION: Alexander's companions

ARISTANDER: Olympias's sorcerer; later in the service of Alexander

DEMOSTHENES: Athenian orator; leader of the anti-Macedon faction

DARIUS III: new king of Persia; Alexander's great opponent

ARISTOPHANES: playwright

ARISTOTLE: Philosopher; tutor to Alexander

SOPHOCLES: playwright; author of the Oedipus cycle of three plays

SOCRATES: Athenian philosopher

ALCIBIADES: pupil of Socrates; later general of Athenian forces

HISTORICAL NOTE

In 336 B.C., Persia, ruled by Darius III, was a world power. Its only rivals were the Greek city-states led by Athens, Thebes, Sparta, and Corinth. They, in turn, were becoming alarmed by the increasing military power of Philip of Macedon, who had forced his will upon them. In 336 B.C., Philip was brutally murdered. Both Persia and Greece thought this would mark the end of Macedon's Power. Alexander, Philip's son, soon proved them wrong. He left his mother Olympias as regent of Pella and, in a brilliant show of force, brought the Greek city-states into line. He was given the title of captaingeneral, and he formed the League of Corinth against Persia.

Alexander, who had dreamed of marching in glory through Persopolis, still had to make sure that all of Greece acknowledged him. He marched into the wild mountain region of Thessaly intent on bringing its tribes under submission. While he was gone, rumors began to circulate in Greece that Alexander and his army were no more and that Queen Olympias had succumbed to a successful coup in Pella. The Thebans rose in revolt, besieging the small garrison Alexander had left in their citadel, the Cadmea. The Thebans, however, were soon proved wrong. Alexander hurried back, leading his bedraggled army, to show all Greece that he would brook no opposition.

THE OEDIPUS LEGEND

Oedipus is a figure from Greek mythology. The son of king Laius and Queen Jocasta, when Oedipus was a child his foot was pierced and he was abandoned, at the behest of his father, because of a warning from the gods that he would kill his father and marry his mother. Unbeknownst to his parents, Oedipus was rescued by a shepherd. He grew to manhood and returned to Thebes to find his parents: by accident, he killed Laius and married Jocasta, and though unaware that these were his parents, he incurred the wrath of the gods. When their identities were revealed, Jocasta committed suicide, and Oedipus, blinded, wandered Greece, a man cursed by the gods and man. Sophocles, the playwright, wrote three brilliant plays—a trilogy that had a profound effect upon Alexander and the world he lived in—based on this legend.

CHAPTER 1

❦

"YE SHALL BEHOLD a sight even your enemy must pity."

"A quote from the *Iliad*, my lord?"

Alexander King of Macedon didn't bother to turn but stared out across the dusty plain toward the soaring gray wall of Thebes. He was studying the Electra Gate, one of the seven great entrances to Thebes. Beyond this rose the Cadmea, the fortified citadel of the city where his men—leaderless, trapped, and besieged—could only look on helplessly at the drama unfurling below. Alexander clawed at his hair. Usually it was styled, cut by his barber so as to imitate the busts and statues of the gods, curled and oiled to cluster round his forehead and fall in layers to the nape of his neck. Now it was dirty, dusty, and far too long. Alexander lowered his hand.

"If mother sees me, she'll moan," he murmured. He shielded his eyes against the light. The Theban army had now deployed in front of the walls: phalanx after phalanx of heavily armed hoplites. In the wings stood the cavalry, their conspicuous blue cloaks ruffling in the strong winds.

"Look." He pointed. "In the center is the Sacred Band,

the cream of the Theban infantry if we break them?" He paused. "What will it matter? The Thebans will simply retreat behind their gates and the siege will continue." He stared back over his shoulder to where his own Macedonians were now deploying for battle. The foot companions in the center, his own cavalry, were held back. Alexander would wait to decide how to deploy those.

"We'll have battle within the hour," Alexander declared. He looked at the man who had spoken, Timeon, leader of the Athenian delegation to the Macedonian camp outside Thebes. "I thought you'd recognize the quotation." Alexander's weather-beaten face creased into a smile, his different-colored eyes crinkling in amusement. "That's not the *Iliad*! It's a quotation from Sophocles' *Oedipus*!"

Alexander strode down the hill, his captains and generals gathering behind him. He paused and stared up at the sky. There was really nothing to see. The clouds had broken, the previous night's storm had ended. Alexander was copying his father. Philip had known all the tricks for keeping people guessing as he acted the role of a preoccupied commander. In fact Alexander didn't have a clue as to how the coming battle should be fought. The Thebans would stay in their positions; his infantry would attack. He would try the usual feint—go for the center, then suddenly switch, sending his crack troops into the enemy's right or left flank, thereby trying to roll up the enemy like a piece of string. He'd force them back, but then what? The Electra Gates would open, the Thebans would retreat, and the bloody siege would continue.

"I'm hungry," Alexander declared. He rested his hands on the shoulders of two of his commanders, tall Hephaestion and Perdiccas. Hephaestion's eyes glowed with pleasure at being touched by a man who was both his lover and his king. Perdiccas, short, wiry, dark-faced, and black-haired as a Cretan, wondered what trickery Alexander was up to.

"We'll break our fast," Alexander declared. He pulled his purple cloak around him and flicked the long hair from his face, a girlish flirtatious movement. "We have the best of stages, gentlemen; the play we are going to present will be witnessed by all of Greece."

Alexander pursed his lips in satisfaction. He liked such lines; his scribes and clerks were taking them down. They would be passed from mouth to mouth: dramatic words before a fateful battle!

I should have been a playwright, Alexander thought. He walked back through the ranks, nodding and smiling at the men standing at ease, their weapons piled before them.

"Will we fight today, my lord?" one of them shouted.

"We fight every day," Alexander replied. "We are Macedonians." He stopped. "That's old Clearchus, isn't it?"

The guard who had spoken shuffled his feet in pleasure. Alexander shook his finger at him.

"That's your problem Clearchus—too much fighting, too little loving. It's time I got you a wife and you settled down."

Alexander moved on, smiling at the ripples of laughter his retort had caused. The men on either side formed a wall of armored flesh. Alexander continued smiling even though he noticed how thin his soldiers were, how dusty and tired. They had marched hundreds of miles in a few weeks, pouring down from the mountains of Thessaly to confront this great danger to his new rule. If we fight, Alexander wondered, are we going to win? Are the men too tired? He passed the horse lines. The ribcages of many of the cavalry mounts were visible, their coats mangy and dull. The baggage carts lay about, the wood was splintered, the wheels cracked. The tents were rain-soaked, weather-beaten, and a hand-picked group of archers guarded their precious stores of food. Alexander snapped his fingers, indicating for his companions to disperse.

"If the Thebans begin to move," he declared, "tell me."

Once inside his tent Alexander let the flap fall and sighed, his shoulders sagging. He took off the leather corselet, threw it on the ground, and slumped down onto a camp stool.

"What's the matter?"

Alexander looked up startled. Two figures sat on cushions at the far end of the tent. Alexander peered through the gloom; one of the figures moved: a woman, rather tall and wiry with a clever pointed face, her oiled hair bound with a fillet. She picked up a cushion, came and knelt beside Alexander.

"What's the matter?" She put a hand on his knee, her fingers pressing the leather kilt. "Alexander, are you ill?"

The king raised his head and grinned at Miriam.

"I had forgotten I had invited you here. . . . I am sorry, Simeon." He gestured at the man still squatting on the cushions. "Come closer."

The man joined his sister. Alexander stared at them. The two Israelites, Miriam and Simeon Bartimaeus, childhood companions who had joined him in the groves of Midas where his father, Philip, had sent him to be educated by the foppish, brilliant Aristotle. Simeon was slightly shorter than his sister, more closed-faced. Miriam, if she hadn't look so sharp, would have been pretty, with her large, lustrous eyes and slender nose, but that determined mouth would put many a man off. She showed a steely determination; this reminded Alexander of his mother, Olympias, now busy ruling in Pella and slaughtering any opposition. He sighed and ruffled his hair.

"I thought I was alone. My men are tired, exhausted, and

now we face a crack infantry that, at a moment's notice, can scuttle behind thickset walls." He grasped Miriam's hand and squeezed it. "Tell me again, Miriam, how this happened! Read the draft of that proclamation I am going to issue."

Miriam leaned back on her heels, head slightly to one side. Alexander was gray with exhaustion. Like all of them, he had hardly bathed or changed. They had been campaigning in the mountains of Thessaly, mandating that the savage tribes accept Alexander's rule. News had come, seeping through like a breeze in the forest, rumors from Greece, that a revolt in the Macedonian capital of Pella against Alexander's mother had been successful. That Alexander himself had been killed, his Macedonian army annihilated. That the League of Corinth, that confederation of Greek cities forced by Alexander to accept his lordship, were plotting revolt, taking gold from the Persian King Darius. Alexander raised his head.

"What are you waiting for, Miriam?"

"If you win the battle," she answered tartly, "there'll be no need for a proclamation. All of Greece will know that you are still alive, that you are king and that you are ever victorious."

Alexander stared at this sharp-spoken young woman. "And if we lose the battle?"

Miriam smiled slightly, "Proclamations will be the last thing on our minds."

Alexander threw his head back and laughed.

"Some wine," he murmured. "Three cups, two-thirds water." Simeon got up, filled the goblets, and brought them back on a tray. The king took one and handed it to Miriam. He waited until Simeon sat down and took his and then toasted them quietly.

"Father has been dead twelve months," he murmured.

"I have troops in Persia and I have taught the Thessalians a lesson they'll never forget. Now I return to find trouble in my own garden."

"It's only Thebes," Simeon murmured.

"It's only Thebes," Alexander mimicked. He jabbed a finger at the entrance to the tent. "Out there, my dear Simeon, throng the delegates from every city in Greece. In their wallets jingle the golden darics of Persia; Thebes' revolt is serious. It's thrown off my rule, killed my officers." Alexander's face grew hard. "That's what I wanted to see you about. It's blockaded my garrison in the fortress of the Cadmea. Now they shout defiance from the walls. If I don't teach the Thebans a lesson, then by this time next week Athens, Corinth, Argos, will all be in revolt, the fires of rebellion breaking out all over Greece."

"Thebes will be defeated," Miriam declared.

Alexander shook his fist and stared above their heads as if talking to someone else.

"I'll not leave one stone upon another," he whispered hoarsely, his eyes half closed. "I'll teach Greece a lesson it will never forget." He blinked and lowered his fist. "Simeon, you've sent my orders out to the commanders?"

"If the city is taken," Simeon repeated Alexander's stark commands, "every house is to be leveled and plunder taken; fighting men will be killed, women, children, and the aged taken to the slave pens. Only the house of Pindar the poet will be spared."

"And the temples?" Alexander asked. "You told them about the temples?"

"You know I did," Simeon replied crossly. "No temple is to be entered, no priest or priestess violated!"

"Especially?"

"Especially," Simeon continued, "the small shrine of Oedipus in the Archon quarter."

"Why is that?" Miriam asked.

"It is a very small and ancient temple," Alexander explained. "It stands in its own olive groves. Father took me there once on a visit to Thebes; it is built out of white marble in a sea of quiet greenness." Alexander closed his eyes. "The path up to it is a dusty chalk. I remember holding father's hand. You turn a corner and the shrine's there: white columns, crumbling steps leading up to a porticoed entrance. The doors are of Lebanese wood reinforced with brass studs. Inside there is a small vestibule; the walls are white and there is a black marble floor. Yes, yes." Alexander's face was like a boy's flushed with excitement. "On the right is a small shrine to the god Apollo. Yes." Alexander opened his eyes. "And on the left. . . . " His eyes were bright. Miriam felt a pang: Alexander was going back to his childhood, when the father he'd adored deigned to show him some love and affection. Cunning, one-eyed Philip with his lame leg and his gruff manner that was interspersed by moments of brilliant charm. Philip could treat an individual as if he or she were the only person in the world. Great Philip, Warrior King, cruelly slain by one of his own bodyguards.

"To the left," Alexander continued, "is a statue of Oedipus. He was King of Thebes." He explained, "*Oedipus* can mean lame foot. As a child Oedipus was abandoned by his parents, King Laius and Queen Jocasta. He was raised by shepherds." He waved his hands. "You know the story from Sophocles' three brilliant plays. Oedipus grew to manhood. He later killed his own father, married his own mother, and the gods turned against him." Alexander paused as he picked at the leather kilt, studying one of the brass embossments that had worked loose.

Miriam held her breath. She knew the story, the legend of Oedipus. In many ways it might also be the story of Alexander. People accused Alexander of having had a hand in his father's murder, and they maintained that the relationship between Alexander and his mother, Olympias, bordered on the unnatural. Both were blasphemous lies. Alexander had been innocent of Philip's death. Miriam knew the full truth behind it. And as for Olympias, no one was more wary of his mother than Alexander. Privately he called her Medea, deeply concerned as he was by her lust for blood, her practice of secret rites, and her constant demands that her authority and status be enhanced.

"You were talking about the shrine?" Simeon broke in.

"Yes yes, so I was." Alexander picked up his wine goblet and swirled it round. Despite the water, it looked like blood. He sipped at it. It was coarse and bitter. He had finished his own wine stores weeks ago and now he was drinking the same coarse Posca as his soldiers.

"The shrine itself," he said, "lies behind heavy bronze doors. The walls are black and gold, oil lamps burn in niches. The floor is of pure porphyry marble. The windows are mere slits. It's very warm; the heat comes from a horseshoe-shaped ditch that runs from one wall around to the other. The ditch is over two yards across and always full of glowing charcoal. On the far side stands a row of spikes and beyond that another ditch full of poisonous snakes." He looked up and smiled. "Mother would like that. Father said there were enough snakes there to even keep *her* happy."

"A ditch full of glowing coals, a row of spikes, and a snake pit?" Miriam asked. "What do they protect?"

"The Iron Crown of Oedipus," Alexander replied. "It lies on top of a stone plinth. Very ancient," he whispered. "There is a legend in Thebes that only the pure in heart can wear it; a god-man guilty of no crimes against his parents. It's guarded by a group of priestesses who take their names from Sophocles' plays. No one can remove the Crown with anything brought into the shrine. Only the high priestess knows the secret."

Miriam studied the king's tired, dusty face. Alexander's looks were a mirror of his ever-shifting moods. Sometimes he could look so young, even girlish, his hair coiffed and his face painted like some Athenian scholar. At other times he looked older, the skin more drawn, the lips a thin bloodless line, the eyes ringed with shadows. When he laughed Alexander reminded her of Philip. And when he brooded Miriam shivered, for it reminded her of her childhood and of watching Olympias bent over a spinning wheel, crooning softly to herself while she planned the bloody assassination of some rival.

Alexander was clicking his finger against the wine cup. He lifted his head. "You know why I want that shrine saved?"

"You will take the Crown of Oedipus?"

"I want the Crown of Oedipus; I want to put it on my head." Alexander was almost speaking to himself. "I want the mark of the gods, the acclamation of the people and their affirmation that I am not a patricide."

"You don't need that," Miriam insisted. "Philip's blood is not on your hands." She glanced sideways at her brother.

They knew the truth and had shared most of it with Alexander. Philip had been murdered by a crazed guardsman, a former lover, just before Philip himself was going to launch a bloody purge on his family and court. Alexander cocked his head to one side as he heard the sound of trumpets from outside.

"I want to wear that Crown," he insisted. "I know I'm no patricide, but I want the gods to sanction me." He grinned. "Just like Achilles."

"Achilles, Achilles, Achilles!" Miriam exclaimed, "Achilles

was your ancestor, but that doesn't mean you have to be like him in every way!"

"We'll take Thebes!" Alexander announced, abruptly changing the subject. "I want that shrine saved."

"It would be a brave man who took on a hundred snakes," Simeon retorted.

"I also want that business at the Cadmea investigated." Alexander put the wine cup down, mood changing as he became more businesslike.

"You remember Hecaetus?"

Miriam pulled a face. Everyone in the Macedonian court knew that Hecaetus was Alexander's spy-assassin—a mincing, lisping fop, more dangerous and venomous than any snake. He and his effete companions were responsible for collecting and sifting information, detecting plots, nipping the poisoned bud of treason before it bloomed full flower.

"How can I forget him!" Miriam retorted. "Once met always remembered."

Alexander nodded. He picked up his cloak and drew it across his lap.

"Before I marched into Thessaly," he declared, "I left a force, a garrison in the Cadmea, the citadel of Thebes, under Memnon, one of my most trusted captains. You remember him, with his grizzled beard, always swearing?"

"And always drunk," Miriam added.

"He was still a good soldier. When I was a boy he used to dangle me on his knee. He made a wooden sword and put a velvet handle on it. I thought it was a gift from the gods. Anyway, Memnon had a lieutenant, another good, ambitious guardsman, Lysander, from Crete. Now, from what I can gather, it seems that the rumors that I had been killed in Thessaly—my army severely mauled—and that mother was facing a serious revolt at Pella were accepted in Thebes as fact not gossip. There was a web of lies. Hecaetus believes that Thebans spread these stories throughout all of Greece." Alexander made a cutting movement with his hand. "You have seen the effect of such rumors. Thebes is in revolt and the other Greek states have adopted a policy of wait-and-see."

"You are sure of this?" Miriam asked.

"As sure as I am that Olympias likes spinning," Alexander caustically replied. "Memnon believed the rumors. He sent Lysander to deal with the Theban leaders and you know what happened to him? He had his throat cut and his corpse was crucified. They erected the cross so that everyone in the citadel could see it. Memnon became frightened. Not of death, but of what was happening. He managed to get a short message out; he claimed that there was a spy in the garrison who was feeding the Thebans all they wanted to know."

"And this is where Hecaetus comes in?"

"Yes, Hecaetus and his darling boys. They sleep together, you know. Do you realize, Miriam, that Hecaetus claims that you are the only woman he'll have near him?"

"That's because I'm flat-chested and my voice is deep," Miriam joked.

Alexander was studying her, his strange, varicolored eyes scrutinizing her face.

"It's curious," he remarked, "isn't it, Miriam, how he has taken a liking to you. Do you know something about him that I should know?"

Miriam moved restlessly on the cushion.

"Keep to the story, my lord," she warned. "I'm not your enemy." Alexander laughed, and leaning forward, he grasped her face between his hands and kissed her lightly on the brow.

"Mother likes you as well, you and Simeon."

"That's because we put on plays for her," Simeon replied. "Like you, she investigated the stories of our people."

"Ah yes, the warring queens," Alexander declared. "Anyway, Hecaetus studied Memnon's message. He was like a boy with a new toy. You see, Hecaetus believes there is a spy in the Cadmea paid by that loud-mouthed demagogue in Athens, Demosthenes, who simply passes on the gold he has received from his Persian paymaster. Hecaetus calls this spy the Oracle, and he would give a bucket of gold to have his head. He believes that the Oracle was a member of the garrison we left in Cadmea. Once I and my army disappeared into the wilderness of Thessaly, the Oracle spun his rumors and lies. Now I know it is not Lysander, as the poor bugger's dead. Hecaetus even thought it might be Memnon, but then, . . . Alexander shrugged, tapping his thumbnail against his teeth.

"Memnon himself was killed," Miriam added.

"We don't know what happened," Alexander declared. "All we've learned is that Memnon was either pushed or that he jumped from the tower of the citadel. His body was found in the courtyard below." Alexander got to his feet and stood in the opening of the tent. His companions and leading generals, Ptolemy, Niarchos, and Hephaestion, caught his gaze and moved to come across. Alexander waved them back and dropped the tent flap.

"I'm going to take Thebes," he declared. "I'm going to take the Crown of Oedipus and put it on my head. I also want vengeance for Memnon and Lysander. I intend to capture the Oracle and to crucify him for all other traitors to see!"

"My lord."

Alexander whirled round. Sly-eyed Ptolemy stood in the entrance to the tent. He winked at Miriam.

"The Thebans have sent you a message: a herald and two trumpeters."

"They wish to surrender?"

"No, no." Ptolemy swaggered across and gave a mocking bow.

He was taller than Alexander and had close-set eyes that, Miriam thought, were always laughing at everything and everybody. A superb horseman, a brilliant general, Miriam suspected that Ptolemy thought he was Alexander's equal. There were even rumors that they shared the same blood, Ptolemy being one of Philip of Macedon's many bastards.

"I'm waiting," Alexander said. "Potlemy, you should have been an actor."

"The Thebans have sent you defiance. They say they'll not bend the knee to a Macedonian barbarian, especially one who killed his own father."

Ptolemy paused and licked his lips, enjoying the fury in Alexander's face. "They bid you to pack your tents and retreat."

"Anything else?" Alexander stepped back. "Anything else, Ptolemy?"

"The men are getting restless."

"Are they now?"

Alexander seized his cloak and threw it over his shoulder. "Miriam you should watch this battle. Pray to your invisible God. Go out and look at the walls of Thebes. I swear, by all that's holy, that you will not see them again." He almost pushed Ptolemy aside as he strode out of the tent. Miriam heard his shouts, followed by the increased bustle in the camp, the braying of war horns and trumpets.

"We should be careful," Simeon murmured. "If the Thebans break through . . ."

Miriam punched him playfully on the shoulder.

"Alexander has never, and will never, lose a battle." She

gazed around the tent and sniffed the sour air. Getting to her feet, she picked up her sword belt. The leather was worn, the scabbard scuffed but the short, broad Macedonian sword was sharp and bright. She pushed it back into the sheath and slung the belt over her shoulder.

"I'll defend you Simeon," she teased, "but I'm not staying here."

They went out into the camp. Soldiers were strapping on armor. A troop of Thessalian cavalrymen thundered by. Cretan archers clustered together, jabbering in their strange tongue; their stout quivers were stocked with arrows, and long horn bows were slung across their backs. Officers swaggered about, canes in hand, pushing and shoving men into position. Of Alexander and his commanders, there was no sign. The Macedonian camp was on the brow of a hill. Down below, the plain was now hidden by a great cloud of white dust as the main divisions marched down to their arranged positions. Now and again Miriam caught a flash of armor, a colored banner, a swirling cloak. The camp became quiet. Only pages, servants, clerks, and scribes were left, as unit after unit hurried after the main divisions. Simeon seized Miriam's arm and pointed farther up the hill, where it rose sharply toward an overhanging promontory.

"We'll get a better view there."

Miriam hurried after him. She felt rather ridiculous—her dress was cumbersome, the scabbard she had so dramatically slung over her shoulder was bruising her. The soldiers called out crudely.

"Do you want me to carry that for you?"

"I've got a better sword than that," another bawled, "long and sharp with a firm point!"

Miriam made an obscene gesture with her fingers and hurried after Simeon. They climbed the hill, the pebble shale shifting under their feet. They grasped onto bushes and the long coarse grass; at last they reached the top where they found others—clerks, camp followers, servants, grooms, and ostlers—also thronging about, staring down at the plain below. Miriam pushed her way to the front and gasped in astonishment.

The dust cloud had lifted. In the distance soared the great walls of seven-gated Thebes; its turrets, towers, and battlements were fearsome. From the walls rose great plumes of smoke where the townspeople had prepared braziers and bronze pots of fire against an attempt to scale the walls: however, the main activity was the two armies now facing each other on the plain below. The Thebans were arranged in a curving line before the main Electra Gate. On their flanks was the cavalry and, between these, great bronze-clad phalanxes ten or twelve lines deep. The Theban gibe had prompted Alexander into action for rolling across the plain to meet them was the Macedonian Army. In the center were the footmen with their long lances, shields locked together, helmets glittering in the sun, horse plumes nodding in the strong breeze.

From where they stood, they could hear the faint cries of officers. Miriam watched spellbound. She couldn't make out individuals but she knew Alexander would be in the center, marching with his companions like any common foot soldier. The tactics employed by both sides were the same as those used at any battle between Greek states: phalanxes of footman against phalanxes of footmen. The two sides were supposed to clash, savage hand-to-hand fighting would ensue. One side would waver and flee the field, yet Miriam knew that this would be different. Alexander had taken the military manuals and torn them up. She had seen that in Thessaly: where foot soldiers were not supposed to go, Alexander would take them. Tactics that would horrify any other commander were used at a moment's notice. Surprise and cunning were no strangers to Alexander but here in the open, in this great dusty plain before Thebes? Miriam watched, grasping her brother so tightly that he winced as her nails dug into his wrist.

"You are hurting me, Miriam!"

"Wait," she said. "Something is about to happen."

The Theban line had also begun to move—marching toward the Macedonians to break their impetus before they charged. Abruptly the Macedonian line changed. Trumpets rang out, banners rose and dipped. The Macedonian army began to turn on its axis. Instead of meeting the Thebans head-on, they were now moving toward the Thebans' right flank. At the same time the Macedonian line began to lengthen.

"They are going to outflank them," Simeon explained. "They are going to push the Thebans back on each other. Roll the line up."

Confusion had broken out among the Thebans. They were unused to this. In warfare, line was supposed to meet line, not shift and turn. The Theban ranks became staggered. Miriam spied gaps, then the armies clashed. Great clouds of dust rose. The sound of trumpets and war horns was broken by faint screams and shouts.

"Can you see what's happening?" she shouted.

A sharp-eyed ostler was peering through the dust.

"Some of the Thebans are breaking!" he shouted. "They are fleeing back to the postern gate. It's been left open and undefended."

CHAPTER 2

IN THE CADMEA, the great gray stone citadel that overlooked the city of Thebes, the spy and assassin whom Hecaetus called the Oracle pulled a military cloak about his shoulders setting the hood firmly around his face. He tapped the hilt of the sword he had taken from the armory and hurried up the steps onto the curtain wall overlooking the city. Other members of the garrison were assembled there, shouting and gesticulating. The spy gazed down the rocky escarpment. The great palisade built by the Thebans so as to hem them in was now deserted. The sound of hideous battle came from the city.

"Alexander has broken in!" a voice shouted. "The king is here!"

Discussion and debate broke out. Should the garrison help or stay in the citadel? There was no Memnon or Lysander to impose order. The spy smiled to himself; that was his doing. What did it matter if Thebes fell? He looked down at the courtyard where the rest of the garrison was milling about. Some were dressed in half-armor, others totally unprepared.

"I can see plumes of smoke!" someone shouted. "They are setting fire to the houses!"

The Oracle stared across at the great high tower of the citadel, which housed the officer's chambers. The windows were all shuttered, a grim, stark place though one where good work had been done. Darius III in Persepolis would be pleased, and the Persian bankers in Argos and Corinth would put aside more silver and gold. He could play this game as long as he wanted, do as much damage as he could, and leave, whenever he wished, with his heart's desire, the love and light of his life.

The Oracle walked down the steps, across the dusty yard, and into the tower: a great square four-storied building. Some people said it had been built when Oedipus was king. The spy stopped, scuffing the dust with his thonged sandal. Oedipus! He knew what Alexander would do if he took Thebes. He'd protect the shrines, particularly the small one in the olive groves that contained the Iron Crown of Oedipus. Would Alexander seize this for himself? Or would that be seen as sacrilege? And what about the harsh-faced Jocasta, the high priestess, she who had negotiated a truce when the news of Alexander's alleged death had swept through the city? The spy leaned against a wall and crossed his arms. Jocasta was old, and that stern face! Those black eyes gleaming beneath the oiled wig she wore over her balding head. The Oracle had been informed that Jocasta would not give up the Crown lightly. It had been in Thebes for hundred of years, so why surrender it to a Macedonian upstart?

The spy rubbed his mouth. He'd be glad to be out of the citadel, to taste a little wine, eat good food. He was eager to plot the escape of both himself and his beloved. He walked up the stairs. On the second floor, he paused outside Memnon's chamber. The old, grizzled captain had spent his last days there. The spy touched the latch; it was locked. From behind the heavy wooden door he heard the dead captain's mastiff, Hercules, whine mournfully. He should not disturb him. There were shouts from below; the spy turned and hurried back down the winding staircase. The courtyard was now a hive of activity. Soldiers were arming, eager to break out and join the plundering. Sharp-eyed scouts on the walls claimed they could already see Macedonian banners. The spy made his decision. When the gates were opened he would slip out and mingle with the rest. As for the Crown of Oedipus? How much, he wondered, would Alexander's enemies pay to have their hands on that?

Jocasta led her priestesses up the white, chalk path that wound through the shadowy olive grove surrounding the sacred shrine of Oedipus. Jocasta moved purposefully. Despite her age she wielded her staff, pulling herself forward. She must get to the shrine! She must be there when the Macedonians broke through. She touched the sacred pectoral resting against her chest, a thick gold crown in its center, then stopped so abruptly that the other priestesses bumped into each other. She gazed at them sharply, dressed from head to toe in white robes, the oiled wigs on their shaven heads slightly askew, their faces dusty and sweat-streaked.

"You should not be worried," she announced. "The Macedonians will not hurt the shrine or its worshipers. But we must be there. We must guard our sacred place."

"Mother . . ." The youngest, Antigone, pushed herself forward. "Mother, we have heard stories. Houses are burning, women and children are being dragged off. The cavalry has fled while the foot soldiers are left unprotected." Tears arose in her eyes.

"We all have kin, menfolk in the army," Jocasta declared tartly. "Soldiers fight and die. Priests and priestesses pray. We each have our place and we must be in ours."

She hurried on. They turned the corner. Jocasta's heart sank. The six guards who manned the sacred doors were gone.

"Cowards," she hissed.

She climbed the crumbling steps, steadying herself on one of the pillars around which ivy tightly curled. The portico was rather shabby and dusty. Jocasta took the keys that hung on her belt and inserted one into the door. She turned it and the door swung open. Jocasta stepped into the darkness and sighed. It was cold but still smelled fragrantly of incense and the salted, perfumed water they used to purify themselves. They now did this hurriedly—dipping fingers into the stoups of holy water and sprinkling themselves before taking small pinches of salt, which they rubbed between their hands and around their lips. Jocasta pulled the white linen hood over her wig. She joined her hands, fingers pointing upward, and tried to compose herself. She turned and bowed to the statue of Oedipus, it was of white marble, though now cracked and dusty with age. The body was sinewy, that of a soldier—one hand holding a club, the other a shield. His bandaged eyes gazed toward the bronze doors that shielded the shrine. Jocasta stared up at the face. Was this really the likeness of Oedipus? The fleshy cheeks, the jutting lips, and prominent nose? Was this the man-god who had married his mother and killed his father, and yet, if Sophocles was to be believed, still had the courage and favor of the gods to confront such sins?

Jocasta, followed by the other priestesses, moved across the dark vestibule to the small shrine of Apollo, the hunter. The high priestess gazed up. The god's features were smooth, girlish, the hair neatly massed, falling down around his brow and ears. The sculptor had dressed Apollo in a simple chiffon and hunting boots, a girdle slung round the slim waist. In one hand a bow, in the other an arrow. Jocasta's eyes filled with tears. A true god's face! She had been brought here by her own mother, and though she had never confessed it, had fallen in love with this statue. It represented the brother she had always wanted, the husband she so vainly pined for, and the son she . . . Jocasta clutched her stomach. Her womb was shriveled, her breasts merely dry sacks of skin. She watched the oil lamps in the niches dance from the draft that seeped through the open door.

"We must lock it," she declared.

The two priestesses hurried off. The door was closed. Jocasta inserted the key and turned the lock, which had been intricately and cunningly wrought by a locksmith hired by the temple. The priestesses then made themselves ready and moved toward the inner shrine. The bronze doors were unlocked and opened. The priestesses stood on the threshold behind Jocasta and gazed into the sacred place of their city. All was in order. The black marble floor glinted in the light from the alabaster oil lamps located in niches around the white marble walls. Jocasta bowed her head. She intoned: "How great are you, oh Lord Apollo!" / Mighty in war, mighty in peace! / And you, Oedipus, true son of Thebes! / Be with us at this dangerous hour!"

As if in answer to her prayer, the sun, which had slipped behind the clouds, now moved out, and its rays came through the narrow window, bathing the shrine in light. Jocasta moved slowly forward, eyes fixed on the white pillar at the far end of the room. On its sharpened end was the Crown of Oedipus, the sacred relic of Thebes. The Crown was of gray iron, small in circumference but broad-rimmed. In the center a blood-red ruby glowed. It was fixed to the post with iron clasps. Jocasta smiled and touched the sacred pectoral around her neck. Only she, the chief priestess, knew how these clasps could be removed. She stared at the charcoal pit that glowed behind the black iron curtain bar; a sea of fire, it gave a blast of heat stirred up by the drafts blowing in from under the door. Beyond that was a small rim of marble, spiked, as if dozens of spears jutted up from under the floor; behind these, around the pillar that bore the Crown, the snake pit, which teemed with venomous vipers specially collected from the hills around Thebes. The snakes could curl in the darkness and slither away beneath the floor but they never left the pit.

The priestesses knelt on the dark brocaded cushions specially laid out. Jocasta gazed at the Crown. This was a symbol of Theban might. A sacred place where the generals and leaders of the council took their oaths to defend the city. Only a few weeks ago this shrine had been thronged as the leaders of the revolt, hands outstretched, swore the most binding oaths to free themselves from Macedonian tyranny. Jocasta had been their witness, even though she quietly despaired at their male arrogance; such hubris would surely bring down the anger of the gods. She had not believed the rumors; she believed that Alexander had the makings of greatness. She had quietly warned the leaders of the rashness of their course of action, but who was she? They dismissed her as a garrulous old priestess. True, she'd had her dreams, but what had one called her? A silly Cassandra? They should have believed their Cassandra that Thebes, like Troy, was about to fall. She'd heard of insults shouted at Macedonians from the city walls; she'd also listened to the travelers and merchants who came here to make votive offerings. How Alexander would brook no opposition, determined to prove that he was a better general than his father. Indeed, that he was a god incarnate. Jocasta bowed her head and led the praises to Apollo and the other guardians of Thebes. Her sisters, the other priestesses, answered, but their words were faltering. At the end, Antigone who, despite her youth, was impetuous in her speech, leaned back on her heels.

"Mother what shall we do?" she pleaded. "The Macedonians are in the city."

"Alexander will spare the shrine," Jocasta snapped.

"He will take the Crown, Mother," Antigone declared. "He knows the legends."

"It can only be worn by the pure of heart," Jocasta retorted, lifting her head, "and one who is touched and blessed by the gods. If the Crown is to be Alexander's then it will be Alexander's."

"Shall we help him?" another asked. "Mother, shouldn't we take the Crown and offer it to him?"

"That would be blasphemy and sacrilege," Jocasta said. "The Crown is removed only once a year, worn by the chief priestess, blessed, and returned. If Alexander wishes it, he must take it according to the ritual."

"But that would be easy," Antigone said. "He'll clear the burning coals and destroy the snakes. He'll build a bridge across the pits and simply seize it."

"No, not Alexander." Jocasta shook her head. "Alexander is dutiful and pious. If the Crown is to be his then he will not take it by force but by ancient custom and human cunning."

"Then how will it be done?" one of the older priestesses asked. "Mother, shouldn't you tell us how the Crown of the man-god Oedipus can be removed, without danger from, the pits?"

"It's a temple secret." Jocasta tried not to sound patronizing. She spread her hands out in prayer and closed her eyes. "This place is sacred," she intoned. "The Crown is holy. According to legend it can only be worn by he or she whom the gods wish to hold it."

"And if blasphemy occurs?" Antigone asked.

"According to the legend of Thebes," Jocasta explained,

"if the Crown is taken through blasphemy and sacrilege, Oedipus will return to his city. He will come, carrying his club and shield, and destroy the profane." She paused.

The temple was so quiet, and she tried to hide her own inner turmoil. Were the other priestesses right? Shouldn't she curry favor with the conqueror by taking the Crown and offering it herself? She recalled her oath taken so many years before. She was about to repeat this when she heard a terrible pounding on the door outside. She took off the key and handed it to her favorite, Antigone.

"See to it," she said quietly. "Offer no resistance."

Antigone got up, sandals slapping on the marble floor. The inner bar on the bronze door was lifted, the outer ones unlocked. A murmur of voices broke the silence.

"Mother."

Jocasta turned. A man stood in the doorway, in one hand he carried a sword, in the other what looked like a seal. Jocasta could tell from his dress that he was a Macedonian. He walked slowly into the shrine and stood staring about. Jocasta couldn't see his face because of his helmet but she knew he was studying the pits and the Crown on its pillar. She rose to her feet.

"I am Jocasta, high priestess of the this shrine."

"And I represent King Alexander and the power of Macedon."

The officer bowed. He walked back to the door and placed the seal on the floor.

"Show that to all who come. You have nothing to fear!"

Miriam followed Alexander and his entourage up through the Electra Gate and along the highway into the center of Thebes. A gray, dull day. Miriam stared around in horror. She had never visited Thebes but she had heard the stories about this great city. Now it looked as if it had been consumed by fire from heaven. Houses, shops, council chambers, barracks stables, taverns, and storehouses had all been reduced to feathery black ash. Wooden buildings had disappeared. Alexander's soldiers were now finishing off those built of stone, dragging down walls. The air was thick with dust, smoke, the smell of burning, and the stench of cooked flesh.

"Not one stone left upon another." Alexander had sworn the ancient oath of destruction against the city. The only people they passed were the occasional priest and priestess, the rest were Macedonian solders combing the ruins for any plunder or for Thebans who may have hidden away in the cellars. Six days had passed since the destruction had ended. The Theban cavalry had fled. The foot soldiers had fought to the last man; then the city had been given over to wholesale destruction. Only the temples and the house of the poet Pindar had been spared, as well as the occasional sacred cypress and olive grove. The survivors had been rounded up. Men, women, and children were marched off to the slave markets. Even Alexander's hardened commanders, now that their blood had cooled, were quiet in the face of such savage destruction. The king himself looked stricken: his face white, his eyes constantly flickering about. Hephaestion, his close companion and lover, started to speak but Alexander made a cutting movement with his hand. Miriam looked at Simeon; his face was so pallid and sweat-soaked, he would surely vomit. They passed a crossroad, Miriam pulled the cloak up over her nose and mouth. Here the corpses had been collected and burned in a great funeral pyre, and the air still stank from the horrid smoke. In places, the ash was ankle deep on the cobblestones; Miriam was pleased she had worn leather riding boots beneath her tunic. She felt a little nauseous, giddy and she grasped her walking cane more firmly. She bowed her head. She felt ashamed—of Alexander, his army, of what had happened here. It brought back memories of her father's description of the destruction of Jerusalem.

They crossed a square, past the ruined mansions of the wealthy, and began the climb toward the broken palisades that had once surrounded the Cadmea. The silence was broken only by the sound of their footsteps crunching the ash and the clink of armor from Alexander's bodyguard. No one dared bring horses here. Fires still burned, sparks shot up, and the stiff hot breeze pricked the flesh. At the top of the hill Alexander stopped and turned.

"Thebes has been destroyed! Leveled to ash! It is my decree." His face was harsh, reminding Miriam of his father, Philip.

"It is my wish," he repeated, "that it never be rebuilt. It rose in rebellion against my father and was defeated at Chaeronea. It played a hand in my father's murder. It rose in rebellion when I was elsewhere. They called me an assassin, a patricide. I did not destroy Thebes. The gods did!"

He glared at Timeon, the Athenian delegate, and beside him at Aristarchus, the representative from Corinth.

"Let the word go out," Alexander said quietly. "All of Greece is to be united under Macedon. All the world is to see the glory and power of our might. Yea," he stared at the skies, "even to the ends of the earth."

"If the gods destroyed Thebes," Hephaestion spoke quickly, "then all of Greece was party to it." He glanced out of the corner of his eye at the Athenian delegate.

Timeon—a small, thickset man with a balding pate, a luxuriant mustache and beard, watery eyes, and a bulbous nose—blinked and forced a smile. Hephaestion was reminding everyone that Thebes had rebelled not only against Macedon but against the League with Corinth. The League, too, had voted for Thebes' destruction, recalling stories of how Thebes had helped Xerxes and his Persians during the Great War, citing all its other petty infidelities and treacheries. Alexander had used the League to legitimize the destruction, but in the end, he'd simply delivered a stark warning to all of Greece. Alexander was their captain-general. Any revolt would be ruthlessly crushed.

Alexander took a breath, rubbed his face, and walked on through the palisade built by the Thebans to hem in his garrison in the Cadmea. He stopped at a cross thrust in the rocky earth. He touched the wood still stained with Lysander's blood.

"I have avenged him," Alexander murmured. "I'll avenge all who died here." He gestured at Simeon and Miriam. "Follow me! You, too, Hephaestion. The rest of you," he gave a lopsided smile, "show our delegates around Thebes. Let them see how a city burns."

Alexander walked on up the rocky path, through the gatehouse and into the courtyard of the Cadmea.

The garrison was assembled in full armor, breastplates and shields gleaming. Their officers stood in front of them, their helmets, adorned with bright horsehair plumes, held under their arms. Alexander's mood changed as it always did when he moved among soldiers. He walked slowly along the ranks, stopping to chat and joke, slipping silver coins into the men's hands. He clasped them by the shoulder and kissed them on the brow, calling them his companions and friends, praising them for their valor in holding Cadmea against a hostile Thebes. The soldiers responded: guffaws of laughter broke out as Alexander shared some private joke. Miriam noticed he had no words for the officers. These four were left standing in front, eyes ahead. Alexander gave them no order to relax or stand at ease. When he had finished his inspection, Alexander simply clicked his fingers. The men were dismissed and the four officers followed Alexander up into the tower along a stone-vaulted corridor and into what must be their mess hall. Tables stood around the room. These and the floor had been carefully scrubbed and washed. Servants had laid out bread, cheese, meats, bowls of fruit, and a jug of watered wine. Unceremoniously Alexander sat on a bench and gestured for the others to join him. He took a bunch of grapes from the bowl and began to pop them into his mouth, like a child, cheeks bulging as he slowly chewed. He nodded at Hephaestion who ordered the officers to introduce themselves. All four were Macedonians, grizzled veterans who had fought in Philip's armies. Patroclus was the youngest: blond-haired, one eye half closed due to an old wound, front teeth missing, nose slightly broken. He reminded Miriam of a boxer. Alcibiades was thin and swarthy-faced; his hair was cropped close to his head and he wore a brass ring in one earlobe. Slightly foppish, Miriam thought, with an ornamental bracelet that he kept shaking. Demetrius was gray-haired, cruel-faced, with sharp, deep-set eyes, and a thin nose above thick lips. He kept scratching at a scar that ran from the top of his right ear down beneath his chin. The fourth, Miletus, was bald, fleshy-faced; his eyes were almost hidden in rolls of fat; he had pursed lips and was clean shaven. He reminded Miriam of a eunuch, an impression greatly enhanced by his rather high-pitched voice. Nevertheless, despite their appearance, Miriam recognized that all four were skilled fighting men, though now very nervous. Alexander had praised the defence of the citadel against the Thebans but they must have expected to be closely questioned on what had happened to cause the deaths of two favorite officers, Lysander and their commander Memnon.

Alexander finished the grapes. He filled the cups himself, chattering about the citadel, how thick its walls, and idly wondering if the tower they now occupied had been built

during the time of Oedipus. The soldiers replied perfuncto-
rily. Alexander leaned back, tapping his hands on the table.

"There's someone missing, isn't there?" He winked down
the table at Simeon, who had already taken out a sheet of
papyrus, ink, and stylus; where ever Alexander went, he always insisted on keeping some record of what was said, particularly his own pronouncements.

"There's someone absent, isn't there?" he repeated.

"I'm here, my lord."

They all turned. The thin young man who stood in the
doorway, moved nervously from foot to foot, scratching his
black hair, rubbing his hands together.

"Come in! Come in!" Alexander smiled. He leaned forward. "You are Cleon? Memnon's aide-de-camp?"

The young man nodded. "Yes, my lord," he stammered.

"I was at the jakes, my stomach . . ." He chewed the corner of his lip nervously. "I apologize."

"Dysentery is no respecter of persons," Alexander
laughed. "Come on, sit down, but don't drink the wine or
eat the fruit." He pushed the bread basket forward. "Take
some of that and a little honey in water mixed with candle
grease. It might not taste too pleasant but it will bind the
bowels. Now you've got the ingredients."

Cleon sat on the bench opposite Miriam and nodded.

"Well, come on, man," Alexander declared. "Repeat it."

Cleon did, his harsh Macedonian voice slightly stumbling
as he listed the king's own recipe for the cure of diarrhea.
His reply caused a little laughter. The four officers relaxed.
They picked up their cups and sipped. Hephaestion rose and
closed the door, bringing down the bar.

"I won't detain you long," Alexander began. "My two
good friends here, clerks and scribes Miriam and Simeon
Bartimaeus, have my authority to continue this inquiry and
question you closely."

"A woman." Miletus's lip curled. "An Israelite?"

"Mother likes her," Alexander replied.

Miletus's face fell as he thought of Olympias.

"Good." Alexander sipped from his own cup. "Outside, Thebes burns! It is no more. I left you along with Memnon and Lysander to hold this citadel and keep and eye on the city. You held the citadel but what happened to the city?" His face became grave. "Above all what happened to my commanders? Just what occurred while I was chasing bare-arsed Thessalians through the forest?"

The officer looked at Demetrius, apparently their leader. He slurped greedily from his goblet.

"I'm waiting," Alexander snapped.

"It's as you say, my lord." Demetrius glowered down the table. Miriam recalled that among the Macedonians kingly rank and status was no defence against blunt speech.

"You went off chasing your Thessalians and we poor buggers were left in Thebes. Now, at first . . . nah . . ." He scratched his chin. "No, from the very beginning they hated us, though they didn't move against us for weeks. Two of our lads went out to the brothels; they have not been seen since. After that, Memnon became more cautious. He allowed us to bring in stores and whores but he forbade any of us to leave the citadel. The Thebans responded; they built the stockade, sealing us in."

"Even though we were at peace?" Hephaestion asked.

"The Thebans said it was for our own protection. Then the stockade was replaced by a stouter, higher one. You've seen the remains. Memnon and Lysander objected. After two weeks of siege, they went out to meet representatives of the Theban council."

Alexander looked at Cleon. "Were you there?" he asked.

"Yes, Memnon, Lysander, and myself. Usually." Cleon rubbed his stomach. "We kept well away from the palisade.

Memnon even gave orders to shoot any who approached it since it was not unknown for the Thebans to try and jab a sword or spear through the slats."

Miriam watched Simeon's stylus racing over the smooth piece of papyrus, using a code only he could decipher.

"Anyway," Cleon sighed, "it was a shouting match. Memnon and Lysander were in full armor. The Thebans jeered at them, asked if they were frightened. Memnon demanded to know why the palisade had been built. 'For your own protection,' the Thebans replied; then bricks were hurled over the palisade."

"I've never seen our old commander move so fast," Alcibiades lisped. "He and Lysander fair scurried back."

"So would you, you wine-soaked fop!" Cleon shouted.

Alcibiades colored, his hand dropping to the dagger in his belt.

"That's enough, boys," Alexander murmured. "Then what happened?"

"Memnon became anxious, withdrawn," Patroclus replied, his voice abrupt. He beat his knuckles on the table. "He met us all in here. He said that he didn't like the mood of the Thebans. During the exchange of insults, the Thebans had . . ."

"What?" Alexander asked impatiently.

"I was there," Cleon blustered. "My lord king, the Thebans seemed to know all about us and the fortress, as if they had a spy, someone sending them secret messages."

"What did they know?" Miriam asked before she could stop herself. The soldiers looked down the table at Alexander.

"I'd have asked the same question," he said languidly.

"They knew everything," Demetrius declared, "including about the two soldiers we'd recently lost; they'd slipped out under the cover of darkness but the Thebans had been waiting for them."

"And you?" Alexander asked.

"I agreed with my commander," Demetrius retorted. "Old Memnon was right; there's a spy in the Cadmea." He gazed bleakly round the table.

"And, as far as I am concerned, he's still here!"

CHAPTER 3

DEMETRIUS'S REMARKS CAUSED consternation; his fellow officers had been taken unawares.

"If you have suspicions," Patroclus snapped, "name them!"

"He tells the truth." Cleon spoke up. His voice was so loud that it calmed the dissension. Cleon's eyes filled with tears. "Memnon believed this. He claimed the Thebans had a spy in the citadel."

"Did he say who?" Alexander asked.

"No." Cleon shook his head. "He never openly voiced his suspicions." He smiled. "Well, my lord king, you know Memnon. If he spoke three sentences it was surprising."

"Old Memnon was as thrifty with his words as a miser is with gold," Alexander agreed. "But continue, Cleon."

"Memnon spoke to me on a number of occasions. They were more grunts than speeches. "The Thebans know too much,' he declared. 'They know about our stores, our men!'"

"If there was a spy," Miriam broke in, "how on earth would he communicate with the enemy?"

The patronizing smile that spread across Demetrius's face told her she had made a mistake.

"An arrow fired at night," Cleon kindly explained. "A message wrapped around the shaft. It could be easily done. There are parts of the citadel where an archer could loose and not be seen. The arrow would clear the stockade." He shrugged. "And the Thebans would know everything."

"I'm confused." Miriam smiled apologetically. She brought her hands together.

"You were besieged in the citadel?"

"Yes!"

"For how long?"

"About two months, until news of Macedon's advance ended all rumors."

"So," Miriam thanked Demetrius with her eyes, "during that time, the spy must have acted secretly."

"Of course!"

"But, by then, the damage was done surely? The rumors had begun, the Thebans were in revolt."

"Ah, I see." Demetrius scratched his head. "Yes, before the siege began, we had about six to eight weeks of relative freedom."

"Ah yes, my supposed death." Alexander asked, "The rumors about a catastrophe in Thessaly—these changed everything?"

"The Thebans became more arrogant." Demetrius rubbed his face. "Crowds would stand by the stockade. They'd jeer, shout, throw bricks. One day a herald approached under flag of truce. Memnon went upon to the gatehouse and asked what he wanted. The herald said that news had come to Thebes. That you, my lord king, had been trapped in a gully in the mountains of Thessaly. That you, Hephaestion, Perdiccas had all been killed. That the army was routed during a revolt in Pella."

"But surely," Hephaestion broke in, "you must have thought he was bluffing?"

"Memnon said as much," Cleon replied. He stared around at his companions. "You were all there. Memnon started laughing. The herald went away and Memnon held a meeting here."

"He wasn't laughing, then." Melitus spoke up, his fat jowls quivering. "You see, my lord king, how did the Thebans know that Hephaestion and Perdiccas were with you? How did they know that your mother was ruler of Pella?"

"Continue." Alexander now cupped his face in his hands, his eyes half closed.

"The following day," Demetrius continued, "the herald returned; he brought a Thessalian with him who described, in great detail, your death and defeat. The herald was more courteous. He pointed out that if you were dead and the Macedonian army defeated, the League of Corinth was dissolved. Thebes could withdraw its loyalty and we should leave the citadel." He paused and stared at Cleon.

"From that moment," the aide-de-camp continued the story, "Captain Memnon became depressed, more withdrawn than ever. He stayed in his chamber drinking, talking to Hercules."

Simeon raised his head. "Hercules?"

"His great hunting mastiff. He adored Memnon. Where the captain went, Hercules always followed. If Hercules didn't like someone, they wouldn't be allowed anywhere near the captain."

"Lysander took over most of Memnon's duties," Demetrius explained.

"He said that we should accept the Theban's offer to negotiate, to try and establish what was really happening. Memnon agreed; he sent Lysander out alone."

"That's not true," Patroclus interrupted. He pointed at Cleon.

"You offered to go?" Miriam asked.

Cleon nodded. "But Memnon would have nothing to do with it. You see . . ." He looked questioningly at her. "Miriam?"

She replied, "My name is Miriam Bartimaeus."

Cleon bowed deferentially. "My lady, my father is Macedonian but my mother is Theban. Her family always supported my lord king; twenty years ago my parents were murdered on a visit to Thebes. Our whole family was marked for destruction because of its loyalty to King Philip."

"So Memnon ruled against you going out?" Miriam asked.

"Yes, he did." Demetrius picked up the wine jug and filled his goblet. "We were all concerned. However, the herald returned under a flag of truce. He was accompanied by the high priestess from the shrine of Apollo, which houses the Crown of Oedipus. What was her name?" he asked. "Ah yes, Jocasta. She came dressed in her oil-soaked wig, her face painted white, black rings of kohl under her eyes. She gave solemn and sacred promises that Lysander would be treated properly."

"But he wasn't." Alexander took up the story.

"No, my lord! He was barely beyond the palisade when the Thebans closed in. From the gatehouse and tower you could see their dagger-work. Two hours later they put up a cross near the stockade; Lysander's corpse was nailed to it."

"But the priestess?" Miriam asked.

"She objected," Demetrius replied. "I believe she spoke the truth. When Lysander was gibbeted, she came forward, her hands extended. She swore by heaven and earth that what the Thebans had done was blasphemous and sacrilegious and that she had had no part in it."

"Memnon grew worse." Cleon got to his feet. He took out his dagger and placed it on the table. "Whenever I went into his chamber, . . ." He sat down again, ". . . Memnon grasped his dagger like this, pulling it out. He believed the spy was one of his officers—indeed, that they were all plotting against him."

"He'd lost his wits," Alcibiades drawled. "My lord king, we are Macedonians. I fought at Chaeronea. I would rather die than betray my lord and my companions."

A growl of approval greeted his words.

"True, true." Alexander forced a smile. "But there is still a spy here. You say you are Macedonian." He rubbed his hands together. "But, with the exception of Cleon, all of you have been garrisoned in Thebes for some considerable time. Before I left, before the citadel was besieged, you were allowed to walk through Theban streets, drinking Theban wine, lying with Theban women."

"You have no proof," Demetrius spoke up hotly, "of treason!"

"I will get it!" Alexander snapped. "My two good clerks here, the Israelites, they will dig it out. We were talking about Memnon?"

"He stayed in his chamber," Cleon declared. "He did not wash or shave. He was constantly dressed for battle, Hercules beside him. And then, ten days ago, his body was found at the foot of the tower. He'd either fallen, been pushed, or jumped from his chamber."

"Why should Memnon commit suicide?" Miriam asked. "Yes, yes, I know his wits may have been disturbed but he was a soldier."

"Was it murder?" Alexander asked.

"How could it be?" Demetrius cried. "Melitus here was on guard outside his chamber."

"Is that right?" Alexander asked.

Melitus nodded. "It must have been suicide," he replied thickly. "The door was bolted and locked on the inside. He had Hercules to guard him. I never heard any sound from the room, nor did Patroclus who took over from me just after midnight. The next morning his corpse was found at the foot of the tower."

Alexander pushed back his stool and got to his feet.

"Let us see this chamber," he said.

Demetrius went first. Outside the hall two page boys dressed in ragged tunics were playing in the small entrance-way. Alexander went over to look. One of them had a magnet and was seeing how close he had to push it before the iron filings stuck to it.

"You enjoy that?" Alexander asked.

One of the pages looked up, eyes squinting.

"My lord king, it's a good way of earning money."

"Money?" Alexander asked.

"They gamble," Demetrius explained, pushing his way through. "It's a game popular with the soldiers. Better than dice game of hazard." He pointed to the twigs laid along the ground.

"There's a sack of magnets; one is pulled out, and we lay odds as to which twig it must reach before it can attract the iron filings. It's a popular game in Thebes. The men often played it to while away the boredom of the siege."

"It takes me back." Alexander smiled over his shoulder at Miriam. "Do you remember the groves of Midas? And Aristotle lecturing on the property of things? How like attracts like?" He tossed two coins on the floor. "Continue with your betting lads." He ruffled the hair of one of the pages. "Now, lets see Memnon's chamber."

This was at the top of a winding spiral staircase entered by a small recess in the stairwell. The brass-studded door hung slightly ajar, the great key in the lock.

"It shouldn't be open." Demetrius drew his sword and kicked the door back.

The great wolfhound was lounging on the floor allowing himself to be stroked by a man who crouched with his back to them. The animal lifted his great shaggy head and growled, his upper lip curling in a display of sharp, white teeth.

"There, there my beauty!" The man turned and smiled.

Miriam recognized Hecaetus, Alexander's master of spies and keeper of all secrets. A human viper who could curl and twist his way through the court. She was always amazed at how Hecaetus's foppish appearance could disarm people: his cropped, curly hair; his thin, clean-shaven face; his eyes ever merry; his lips always smiling. The languid way he walked, the rather girlish movement he deliberately cultivated were no different now. He patted the dog and got to his feet, adjusting the green-edged robe thrown over his shoulder.

"My lord king." He bowed.

"What are you doing here Hecaetus?" Miriam asked.

"Why Miriam, the same as you, searching out my lord's enemies." He pushed his head forward. "I was told you were in council, my lord, and were not to be disturbed." He sighed. "So I came up here and . . . He gestured at the dog who had now risen, brushing against him. "I thought I would make acquaintance with Hercules. Isn't it a pity that animals can't talk?"

Alexander walked into the room. He stretched out his hand and the dog approached and licked his fingers. The rest fanned out around him in this austere gray-stone chamber.

"He's friendly enough," Alexander observed.

"He always is," Cleon declared. "He wouldn't hurt a child."

"But he protected Memnon?" Miriam asked.

Cleon nodded. "If he thought Memnon was under attack, if you raised your voice or made any threatening gesture, Hercules would change."

Miriam crouched down. The great war dog was a beautiful animal: iron-gray fur, lean body, long legs. She patted him, feeling the muscle ripple under the smooth soft skin. The hair around his neck was bunched and more coarse, the head perfectly formed. She noticed the powerful jaws. The dog now started licking at her so vigorously that she got to her feet, wiping her cheek with the back of her hand. Alexander laughed and stared around the chamber.

"It's not much, is it?"

Miriam had to agree. A truckle bed in the corner, a chest at the foot of the bed, a large table with a camp chair before it. Some shelves bearing cups and pots, pegs driven into the wall on which to hang belts, armor, and cloaks. In one corner a statue of Aphrodite, small, perfectly carved. Alexander pointed at it.

"Memnon stole that from a house. He called it his good-luck charm."

Followed by Miriam he went across to the window, nothing more than a wooden square. The shutters had been pulled back. Miriam leaned over and looked down into the cobbled courtyard below. She studied the rough gray-stone walls, the plaster ceiling, the heavy reinforced door. There was no secret passageway into this room.

"What's above this?" she asked.

"An empty garret, a storeroom," Demetrius explained. "Memnon kept it locked. He hated anyone going in there."

"Why?"

"Oh, it's empty enough," Cleon replied. "It was a personal foible. Memnon once fought as a mercenary and had to hide in a cellar. He couldn't stand hearing footsteps above him, it brought back memories."

"He often told us the tale," Alcibiades drawled. "He would send us up to check that it was empty, no rat droppings on the floor. It's nothing more than a dingy loft."

"How did he die?" Hecaetus wondered.

"It must have been suicide," Alexander declared. He went across the room and tapped the great bolt on the door. "How did you get in? I mean, this has not been forced!"

"Memnon's corpse was found just after dawn," Demetrius explained. "We came up here; well, you've seen the door— it would take a siege to batter it down. So we went up to the tower, tied a rope around one of the battlements and lowered down one of the Cretans, an archer. The shutters were open; he slipped into the room. It's almost as you find it now: the bolts were drawn, the key turned in the lock. Hercules was lying on the floor asleep. We gave the archer some meat so the dog proved to be no trouble. He pulled back the bolts, turned the key, and we came in."

"What about his papers?" Miriam asked. "As commander of the Cadmea, he must have kept records?"

"I seized them immediately," Demetrius explained. He went across to the chest, opened it, and took out a roll of papyrus, coarse string binding it together; it was tightly knotted and had been carefully sealed.

"I've been through them myself," said Demetrius. "There's nothing really, just lists of provisions and arms. A family letter; I believe he has a son in the guards regiment at Pella?"

Miriam put them into her leather writing satchel. Alexander walked carefully around the room. He touched the statue of Aphrodite, sat on the bed, then went to the window and stared out.

"Miriam Bartimaeus," he spoke absentmindedly, "you will investigate this matter."

"My lord!" Hecaetus objected, his voice strident.

"You, my lovely boy," Alexander turned, "will search among the Theban prisoners, see if there is anyone who can help us here."

"I doubt it!" Hecaetus snapped. "The Thebans who were in power, those members of the army council, are either dead or have fled."

"Do as I say," Alexander declared quietly.

Miriam could see that the king was annoyed that Hecaetus had come to the Cadmea without his permission.

"Hephaestion, stay here and ensure that all is well with the citadel. Miriam and Simeon, come with me."

"My lord, you need a guard," Hephaestion objected.

Alexander clapped him on the shoulder.

"Not here, Hephaestion," he murmured. "Not any more."

They left the citadel. In the end Hephaestion had his way: when Alexander stopped and turned, two hoplites in full armor were trailing like shadows behind them. He squinted his eyes against the strengthening sun.

"Hephaestion worries too much."

"Be sensible," Miriam replied.

She gazed around at the blackened devastation: whole quarters leveled to the ground, nothing more than steaming ash. Hordes of scavengers—kites, hawks, crows, and buzzards—had flown in searching for plunder. The stench was still offensive: smoke and the sickly sweet smell of burning flesh. Occasionally the cry of a woman came from the ruins, and soldiers still sifted among the ashes. Others sat in groups sharing wineskins.

"In ten years," Alexander breathed, "this will be nothing! People will talk of seven-gated Thebes as they do about Troy and the palaces of Midas."

"Was it necessary?" Miriam asked.

"It was necessary!" Alexander retorted.

They walked on a bit farther, passing the occasional cluster of trees that marked some shrine or small temple. Alexander entered one of these and stopped to look at the gnarled branches of the olive trees. Miriam was pleased to be in the green coolness where the stench of burning was not so strong. Birds still fluttered and sang, it was an oasis of life in this city of the dead.

"Hecaetus may be right," she remarked. "There must be Thebans still alive who knew what happened, and who might barter for their freedom."

"Hecaetus didn't say that," Alexander retorted. "He said that the search would be a waste of time. Most of the Theban leaders are dead. Those who survived have fled." He glanced at her brother.

"What do you think happened in the Cadmea?"

"There's undoubtedly a traitor," Simeon replied, hitching his writing bag over his shoulder; he stared curiously through the trees at the white path that must lead to the shrine.

"Miriam?" Alexander asked.

"I agree." She played with the clasps on her cloak, wishing they would move on. She felt weak, slightly nauseous from the destruction, the burning, the wholesale slaughter, that grim citadel with those soldiers whose moods shifted between insolence and fear. Alexander picked up an olive shriveled brown; he squeezed it between his fingers. A barber had cut his hair, but apart from the rings on his fingers and the gold-embossed sword hilt, Alexander looked like a young officer from the army rather than the conquering victor of Thebes.

"Mother will be here soon," he groaned. "She'll want to see the sights. She'll also want vengeance for Memnon."

"Why is that?" Miriam asked.

"When father divorced her just before his . . ." He

blinked, ". . . well, just before his death, he asked his drinking companions what they thought. Of course, they all agreed. Memnon was standing on guard duty. 'Memnon,' my father shouted, 'what do you think?' Memnon bawled back, 'That you are a bloody fool.' " Alexander smiled and shook his head. "Well, you know father, he bellowed with laughter. He even asked Memnon if *he'd* like to marry Olympias; that's when the old soldier really warmed the cockles of my mother's heart. 'Men like me,' he replied, 'mere mortals, do not marry goddesses.' Mother sent him a ring. A pledge of eternal friendship. And, as you know, Miriam," he hitched up his military cloak for it had turned cold, "when mother gives an oath for life or death, she keeps it. I don't think . . ." he threw the shriveled olive on the ground and squashed it under his foot, ". . . Memnon committed suicide. He was an old soldier, he wouldn't have had the imagination."

"But you saw the room," Simeon objected. "The walls, the ceiling, the floor were of stone. The door would need a battering ram!"

"The assassin could have entered by the window," Alexander said weakly.

"Oh, come!" Simeon grasped his dagger hilt. "I'm a clerk, I'm a scribe, my lord, but even a mouse like me would fight. Did Memnon, one of your father's heroes, just sit there and allow someone to pick him up and throw him through a window? 'Oh, good morning,' Memnon must have said, 'what are you doing here?' 'I've come to kill you, throw you out the window.' "

"And there's the dog," Miriam added. "He may be friendly but I doubt he would just sit there. If it turned nasty he could be savage; Hercules has the strength and cunning of a panther."

"Ah, well." Alexander moved a ringlet of hair from Miriam's brow. "Investigate this matter but, remember, they don't like you, Miriam. Aye, and don't tell me it's because you're flat-chested with a deep voice. They've heard of my two Israelites spies. Do you know that mother wanted to keep you at Pella. To protect her? Would you have liked that, Miriam? Sitting by Olympias while she spins that bloody wheel of hers?" He made to brush by her but Miriam stood her ground.

"If you want to send us back, my lord . . ."

"Oh don't be stupid, I'm only teasing. You, Ptolemy, Niarchos, and Simeon were all with me when I was at the academy in the groves of Midas. I wonder what Aristotle is going to write when he hears about my destruction of Thebes."

"The Athenians and the rest demanded that it be leveled."

"Ah yes, Athens. Strange isn't it, that there are so many connections between Thebes and Athens? In the legend, Oedipus fled to Athens. Sophocles died in Athens, his tomb is near the city gates. But come, let's see the shrine."

They left the olive grove and took the white chalky path. Miriam looked around; the two soldiers still followed them. They turned a corner. Miriam stopped and gasped. The temple or shrine was small, of white stone; the trees around it heightened the atmosphere of serenity and coolness, it was as if Thebes still lived. Four soldiers lounged on the steps, an officer and three guardsmen. They scrambled to their feet as Alexander approached, desperately strapping on war belts, looking for shields and lances.

"Oh, for the love of Mother," Alexander bawled, "what do you think I am, a Theban war party?"

The captain threw his belt away and came down the steps. He genuflected and kissed Alexander's ring.

"Everything is in order here?"

"Yes, my lord," the soldier replied, getting up. He glanced at Miriam and Simeon then back along the path to where the two soldiers stood.

"They are inside, my lord."

"Who are?"

"The priestesses, sir. They have been here most of the time."

"They haven't been hurt?"

"Of course not, my lord. Two of my lads are in the vestibule."

"And the keys?" Alexander asked.

"The old-bi- . . . the high priestess refused to hand them over."

"Ah," Alexander sighed; he rubbed his eyes. "I've got a feeling Jocasta and Mother would get on very well."

They walked up the steps through the half-opened doors. Alexander paused to admire the club-bearing statue of Oedipus and the graceful form of Apollo the hunter. The soldiers inside were busy playing dice; they, too scrambled to their feet.

"Are the doors locked?" Alexander asked.

Miriam stared at the huge bronze-plated doors.

"I think the old woman has barred it behind her," the soldier replied. "She said animals were not allowed in the shrine."

Alexander walked up, drew his sword, and hammered. There was a faint sound of footsteps, of a bar being raised. The door was opened by a pale-faced and frightened young priestess dressed in white.

"You are not allowed in here." She stumbled on the words.

"I am Alexander of Macedon, and I go where I wish!"

"Then enter, Alexander of Macedon!" a voice called out.

The young priestess moved aside. Miriam followed the king into the shrine.

She was aware of marble walls and floor, a white stuccoed ceiling. No ornaments, just niches in the walls where oil lamps glowed in pure alabaster jars. A wall recess to the side and, at the far end, glowing in the light of the sun whose rays shot like spears through the narrow windows, a long white pillar, an Iron Crown on top. Only then did she become aware of the two pits: The one around the pillar was simply a dip in the floor but she saw the glowing charcoal, the spikes at the far end. The women, who stood in line near a black iron bar that ran along the rim of the charcoal pit, were dressed from head to toe in white linen. Miriam glimpsed leather sandals, rings on fingers, a gold armlet. One of the women came forward, pulling back her cowl. Her wig was oil-drenched, her face old and raddled and coated in thick white paint, her eyes ringed with black kohl. Despite her age the woman carried herself with a certain majesty, her old eyes scrutinizing Alexander. She stopped and bowed.

"My lord King, I am Jocasta, chief priestess of the shrine." She gestured at the other four. "This is Antigone, Merope, Ismene, and Teiresias."

"All names," Alexander said, "from the plays of Sophocles."

The high priestess nodded. "Who we really are is no matter. We serve a god and guard his shrine in what was 'Thebes, the City of Light.' "

" 'And what am I?' " Alexander replied, " 'the shedder of blood? The doer of deeds unnamed?' "

Miriam recognized the quotation from *Oedipus Rex*.

" 'Who is this man?' " Jocasta answered, also quoting from the play, " 'the son of Zeus, who needs to destroy?' Welcome to our temple, Alexander, son of Philip."

Miriam caught the sarcasm in her voice: Jocasta had pointedly described Alexander as she would any other man, as the son of a human father. Alexander brushed back his hair. " 'Greatest of men,' " he quoted, staring at the Crown, "He delved the deepest mysteries! Was admired by his fellow men in his great prosperity. Behold, what a full tide of misfortune swept over that head.' "

" 'And none can be called happy,' " Jocasta finished the quotation, " 'Until that day when he carried his happiness down to the grave in peace.' "

Alexander seemed not to be listening. He knelt on one of the quilted cushions in front of the iron bar, eyes fixed on Oedipus's Crown. His hands came up, fingers curling, as if he wanted to stretch out and take it immediately. Jocasta came up behind him. The other priestesses, more nervous, clustered about her.

"Behold," she said in a singsong voice. "Behold, Alexander, king of Macedon: the Crown of Oedipus, king of Thebes, beloved of the gods!"

"Slayer of his father!" Alexander finished. "Lover of his mother!"

"None can wear that Crown except the pure and those touched by a god."

"I am king," Alexander retorted. "I am conqueror and victor of Thebes. By divine decree that Crown is mine!"

"Then take it Alexander." Jocasta's voice was softly mocking. "What are you going to do? Empty the pit of fire? Crush the serpents under your boot? Unlock the clasps and take the Crown? And who can stop you? An old priestess and her acolytes? How all of Greece will laugh," she taunted, "at the lion of Macedon."

Alexander got to his feet, his face flushed. "It cannot stay here."

"Look, look, Alexander." Jocasta seized his elbow. "There is the Crown; it rests on top of the pillar. Look at the iron clasps. They can be loosened, the Crown lifted up and brought to your head.'

"How?" Alexander demanded.

Miriam closed her eyes. Alexander's petulance had come to the fore. The old priestess had cleverly trapped him, like an elderly aunt reproving a recalcitrant nephew. All Alexander had to do was stamp his foot and shout, "I want! I want!" and the picture would be complete. Miriam stared at the pit of fire. It must be at least three to four feet deep and about two yards across. The spikes were ugly and gleaming, and in the dark pit beyond, what horrors existed! She had seen snake pits in the chambers of Olympias, the serpents writhing and coiling so that it seemed as if the whole floor were moving! All to protect that Iron Crown, the ruby in its center glowing like a small ball of fire. It was kept in place by two clasps at the front, like those on a chest, but how could they be pulled down without crossing the pits? Did the priestess have some kind of bridge that could lowered and extended across? And what would it rest against? The fire would burn any wooden structure, and the snakes would strike; even a man wearing thick military boots would be in great danger. So, if it was to be removed, it would have to be by subtlety and cunning rather than brute force. Miriam grasped Alexander's arm, pinching the skin. The king moved away, walking the edge of the pit, his eyes fixed on the Crown.

"How do you remove it?" he asked.

"That is a mystery, my lord king. If the gods and the shade of Oedipus believe it is yours, the way will be shown to you," responded the high priestess.

Alexander's fingers drummed on his sword hilt. He

smiled bleakly at her, and Miriam realized that this cunning old priestess had cleverly trapped him. Alexander might be conqueror of Thebes but now all of Greece would learn whether the Crown of Oedipus was still to be withheld from him.

CHAPTER 4

"THERE IS ANOTHER matter." Alexander walked determinedly toward Jocasta in an attempt to reassert himself.

"The death of Lysander?" she asked. "My lord king, it had nothing to do with me. Pelliades, leader of the Theban council, asked me to mediate. I swore sacred oaths that your envoy would be safe. He'd hardly stepped beyond the palisade when the daggers were drawn."

The old priestess blinked away the tears.

"I cursed them," she continued. "I told them that they had broken their most sacred oaths, that the gods would respond. They just laughed. Pelliades said that you were dead and the power of Macedon shattered." She lifted one shoulder. "I cursed him; the rest you know. Lysander's body was put on a gibbet." She stared down at the black marble floor.

"And Pelliades?" she asked.

"Dead," Alexander replied. "Killed with the rest in the final stand beyond the Electra Gate." He stretched out his hand. "I may not take the Crown of Oedipus, not yet, but I will take the keys."

"We have to worship here." Jocasta's lower lip trembled. She clasped the pectoral on her chest. "We have to tend the shrine."

"The officer outside," Alexander replied kindly, "will hold the keys. He will hand them back whenever you wish."

The high priestess sighed but took the keys off the girdle around her waist. They were large, their brass heads shaped in the form of a snake. She thrust them into Alexander's hand. Alexander gestured for the soldiers to withdraw from the door. When they did so he stepped closer.

"There'll be a password. I'll tell the officer in charge."

"What is it?" Jocasta asked.

Alexander stared across at the Crown.

"Why, *Oedipus*." Alexander smiled. He grasped the keys and walked to the door. He went down the steps, Miriam and Simeon following. Alexander called the officer over.

"Four of you will guard the outside," he declared. "Leave two others in the shrine itself." He handed the keys over. "These are only to be given to the old priestess or to me; the password is *Oedipus*." He grasped the young man's arm. "You are well armed?"

"With everything, my lord king: bows, arrows, spears, swords."

"You have a hunting horn?" Alexander asked.

"No, my lord, but I know where I can get one."

"If anything untoward happens," Alexander declared, "sound the alarm." He stared around at the dark olive trees. "But you are safe enough. No fighting men remain in Thebes and the Macedonian army guards all the approaches. Eat, sleep, but be vigilant." He wagged a finger and smiled.

"You are Meriades, aren't you?"

"Yes, my lord king." The young man beamed with pleasure at being recognized.

"Your father was in the guards regiment. He died at Chaeronea. Be worthy of your father's name." Alexander spun on his heel and walked back along the white chalk path. He entered the olive grove, leading Simeon and Miriam deeper into the trees to a small clearing where he sat down on a stump, staring up at the greenery. He gestured for Miriam and Simeon to sit next to him. Simeon sighed and looked at his sister. This was one of Alexander's favorite customs. He loved to walk away from the throng and the bustle, then sit and talk, turning over some problem. Miriam suspected he daydreamed. A great deal of the time Alexander was anxious; he even had anxiety attacks, periods of panic when he'd sit tense. Afterward he'd abruptly stir himself into action, issuing orders, dictating letters so fast the scribes and clerks could hardly keep up with him. He'd charge around the camp inspecting equipment and munitions, sharp-eyed for failure: a harsh word to a defaulter, lavish praise for those who pleased him.

"Jocasta does remind me of Mother." Alexander scratched his head. "The way she walks. Why do women do that?"

"Do what?" Miriam asked.

"They seem to grow taller," Alexander replied. "All of their spirit seems to come into their eyes when they look down at you rather disapprovingly. Mother always does that. Even Father confessed he felt frightened whenever Olympias played the royal Medea."

"You could take her head," Simeon replied. "She had a hand in Lysander's death."

"Don't be bloody stupid!" Alexander kicked at Simeon's knee with his foot. "How my enemies would love that! Alexander, the lion of Macedon, killer of ancient priestesses! From what I can gather she spoke the truth. Pelliades was a treacherous piece of work. They simply used her to lure poor Lysander out."

"But why?" Miriam asked. "Why kill Lysander, gibbet his corpse?"

"They must have truly thought I was dead." Alexander undid his sword belt and placed it between his feet. "Somehow this spy, the Oracle, convinced the Theban elders that I and my army had perished in Thessaly. They took their fury and hatred out on poor Lysander and, by executing him, sent a defiant message to Memnon. He was expected to surrender, to capitulate and withdraw from the citadel."

"But he didn't," Miriam continued. "He was an old soldier, tough and loyal, but he became wary of this officers. He believed one of them was a traitor. He locked himself up in his chamber and, if the accepted story is to be believed, committed suicide by throwing himself out his window. But that's not the Macedonian way is it? Why didn't Memnon drink poison or fall on his sword? How was he dressed?"

"According to reports," Alexander replied, "he was wearing a cuirass over a leather tunic, he had his marching boots on and his sword belt strapped about him. Oh yes, he was also wearing his military cloak."

"And he fell during the middle of the night?"

"Apparently so."

"But why?" Miriam persisted. "Why should this old soldier dress himself up for war, open the shutters of his window, and throw himself out in the dead of night? And, before you say it, Simeon," she poked her brother, "no fabulous tale—about him being drugged or someone entering through the window—that simply doesn't make sense. If any assassin had come into that chamber, Hercules would have torn him apart." She sighed with exasperation. "We know who was on duty. I like to know where the rest were?"

"Why?" Simeon asked.

Miriam shrugged. "I don't know why. On the one hand Memnon's death looks like suicide, but on the other the captain was a veteran—tough, used to sieges. Why should he dress himself up in the middle of the night and jump out a window?"

"And yet if he was murdered," Simeon insisted, "how could someone attack a hardened warrior faithfully guarded by his huge hunting dog?"

"We've got an even more pressing problem." Alexander lifted his head. "You've seen the shrine and the Crown of Oedipus? Can either of you Israelites devise some subtle stratagem for bringing that Crown fairly into my hands?"

"Oh, just take it," Simeon grumbled. "You are king, conqueror."

Alexander chewed on his lower lip. "No, there must be another way. Ah well." He got to his feet, picked up his sword belt and slung it over his shoulder. "You don't believe in any of this, do you?" He helped Miriam to her feet. "The God of Israel is not confined to temples or shrines. You don't believe in relics or legends of the past?"

"We have our stories," Miriam replied, "but our God is in all places."

"Is he now?" Alexander teased. "I wonder what he thinks about Thebes burning to the heavens?' Or about the legends, the ghost stories? Look around you," he whispered.

Miriam did so. The trees grew close together, old and gnarled, twisted with age; their branches spread out and interlaced like old people leaning forward to grasp one another.

"They say Oedipus still walks here. The men are superstitious. They have talked to the Theban captives. Oedipus has been seen dragging his swollen foot, club in hand, around the streets of Thebes."

"But didn't he protect them?" Simeon scoffed.

"No, they said he'd come to wreak vengeance. The Thebans have forgotten the old ways, and I," he added, "am that vengeance."

Miriam pulled her cloak about her a little closer. If the truth be known, she didn't like this devastated city or that strange shrine, with its painted priestesses, marble floors, fire and snake pits. Miriam wondered if the Iron Crown, with its blood-red ruby, would trap Alexander, rob him of the fruits of his victory.

"We should be going," she murmured. "I would like to go back to the citadel. Ask a few more questions."

Alexander agreed. "I'll walk you there." A twig snapped and Alexander whirled round, hand to his sword hilt, but it was only the two soldiers now tired of waiting on the edge of the grove.

"You've been good guard dogs," Alexander called out, "and the day is drawing on."

They left the grove and entered the sea of devastation and destruction around the citadel. Alexander's companions were waiting, crouched in a circle sharing a wineskin, their war belts on the ground beside them. A short distance away a woman crouched, her arms around two children who were white-faced and had black rings around their eyes; they gazed in terror at the soldiers.

"What's this?" Alexander asked.

Miriam's heart sank at the fear in the woman's face, at the way the children clung to her—probably some Theban mother who had hidden in the ruins with her children only to be discovered by the soldiers. But why hadn't she been dragged off to the slave pens? Despite her terror, the woman now stood, one hand on the shoulder of each child. She would have been beautiful, but there was a bruise high on her cheek, and her face was streaked with dirt and ash; her gown and tunic were soiled and one sandal was missing.

"She's guilty of murder," Niarchos the Cretan declared. He gestured across the ruins with his hands. "Some of our lads found her in the cellar of a house."

"And?" Alexander asked.

Niarchos put his hands on his hips and clicked his tongue. "Well, the officer who found her was a Boeatian; he roughed her up a bit."

"You mean, he raped her?" Miriam asked. "In front of her children?"

Niarchos's monkeylike face creased into a smile. "You always did have a tart tongue, Miriam; even in the groves of Midas we felt the lash."

"With people like you?" Miriam retorted, "no wonder!"

Niarchos just pulled at his oil-drenched hair. Alexander was staring at the woman.

"What happened?" he demanded.

"Well, the Boeatian, after he had his pleasure, wanted to know where her treasure was hidden. She said it was down a well in the garden at the back of the house."

The woman was now blinking, her lips moving wordlessly.

"She took him there," Niarchos continued. "Er, he had been drinking."

"And she pushed him down, didn't she?" Alexander finished the story.

"Snapped the bastard's neck," Niarchos declared. "The rest of the squadron would have killed her on the spot." He pointed to Perdiccas. "But he heard the clamor." He moved from foot to foot. "What shall we do, my lord king?" he asked sardonically, "a thousand lashes and into the slave pen, or shall we crucify the bitch as a warning to others?"

Alexander put his hand on Niarchos's shoulder, his fingers near his neck, and he squeezed. Niarchos winced with pain.

"By all that's holy! . . ." Alexander used his sacred oath. "She's a mother Niarchos. The blood lust is over."

One of the children began to cry. Miriam glanced away. There was a cruel streak in Alexander, and if it surfaced, the woman and both her children would die.

"For pity's sake, she killed one of my officers!" Niarchos shouted.

The woman clutched the children closer. "He was drunk," she declared defiantly. "He was an animal. He deserved to die." She gestured at the black sea of ash around them. "You all deserve to die. You are Alexander, lord, king of Macedon. Why not kill us? The great conqueror, the victor!"

Alexander narrowed his eyes. "You are free to go."

Niarchos made to object.

"Shut your mouth!" Alexander snapped. "You are free to go! Simeon write out a pass! I'll seal it myself. Niarchos, that money pouch! Come on, it's so heavy you can't even walk straight!"

The Cretan handed it over. The rest of the officers were now laughing, their mood ever fickle. They knew about Niarchos's love of money; he was a brave fighter but he had combed the ruins looking for anything that glittered. Niarchos sullenly handed it over. Alexander threw it, and the woman deftly caught it.

"My scribe will write out the pass," Alexander declared. "You will also get new clothes, horses, saddlebags, food, wine, and a soldier to guide you to wherever you wish to go." He glanced away. "My blood has cooled. Alexander of Macedon does not make wanton war on widows and children. And, as for the officer, he shouldn't have been drunk on duty. He deserved what he got."

The woman now crouched down to comfort her children. Simeon found a place to sit cross-legged, his writing tray resting on his thighs. Niarchos was glowering at Alexander, but the king chucked him under the chin.

"I've got a present for you Niarchos."

The Cretan's eyes glowed.

"It's a cup of pure gold." He put an arm round the Cretan's shoulders. "Come, lets drink." Alexander sauntered off. Niarchos had now regained his good humor, and the rest joined in the banter.

Simeon finished the letter. Miriam made a move toward the woman.

"Thank you." The woman held a hand up. "But leave me alone. I and my children shall soon be gone from here."

Miriam turned away and walked up the incline, through the ruined palisade, and into the Cadmea. The place was fairly deserted now. There was no city to guard, no attack expected. Most of the garrison had drifted back toward the main Macedonian camp. Only a few soldiers remained, lounging against the wall, playing dice or sleeping off a day's drinking. A guard came across; Miriam showed him the royal seal and the man hastily withdrew. The tower was also deserted though in the mess hall Miriam glimpsed the two pages still using the table to play with their magnets. They looked up as she entered.

"Do you have breasts?" one of them called.

"Aye, and a brain," Miriam retorted. She sat on the stool and watched. They were gambling for coins. One held the magnet, the other pulled out iron filings from a bag and wagered how far they would have to be before the magnet pulled them close. The game *did* remind her of the lectures in the groves of Midas. Aristotle had been fascinated by magnets. He'd expanded his teaching to talk about the properties of the earth, and did it contain a magnetic force?

"Do you want to wager?" one of the pages abruptly asked.

Miriam got up, closed the door, and came back. She opened her own purse and shook a few coins out onto the table.

"I'd like to ask you some questions."

The boys immediately ceased their game.

"You are pages of the royal court?"

"Oh no! We are Thebans."

Miriam looked nonplussed.

"We are orphans," the elder one said.

"Before things turned sour, Memnon took us in. We don't know who our father and mother were. We might be Thebans. Someone told us that we were bastards."

"Do you know what that means?" Miriam asked.

The older one, thin-faced and cheeky, nodded. He looked tough; the younger one was more sly-eyed. Street children, Miriam thought, who hang around soldiers' camps.

"Anyway, Memnon took us in. He was a crusty old bugger but fair. We cleaned the slops, ran messages."

"But the Macedonians destroyed your city?" Miriam asked.

"Not our city," they both chorused.

"What are your names?"

"Memnon called us Castor and Pollux. We asked him why, and he just laughed. We thought he liked bum boys."

"And?"

"Then we heard one of the serving wenches squealing in his chamber. But you can't say the same about the rest."

"His officers?" Miriam queried.

"Bum boys the lot of them," the elder one said.

"You are?"

"Castor."

"What do you mean they are bum boys?"

"By Apollo's cock," Pollux retorted, using a soldier's favorite oath, "they were always clinging to each other in the stables or in their chambers. Demetrius and Alcibiades, Melitus and Patroclus. If they were dogs you'd throw a bucket of water over them."

"They were lovers?"

"We didn't say that," Castor declared, his eyes fixed on the coins. "They just like each other's bottoms."

Miriam hid a smile. Sodomy amongst the Macedonian soldiers was common; many of them were bisexual. In her youth she had been shocked, but now she glanced away; if the truth were known, she really didn't care about Macedon or its army. Alexander was different.

"And Cleon?" she asked.

"Oh, he was fair enough Memnon's man. He protected his captain like an old woman would her solitary chicken."

"And the night Memnon died?"

"No one knew about it," Castor replied. "Not till first light and the poor bugger's body was found at the foot of the tower. I think Patroclus was on guard. Cleon was furious. They had a meeting here in the hall, Patroclus swore he heard nothing from the captain's chamber."

"Why do think Memnon died?" Miriam asked.

"He was lonely," Castor replied. "He thought there was a traitor among his officers. It was common gossip. To be blunt, mistress, everyone was terrified! They thought the Thebans were going to attack, break in, and crucify us as they did poor Lysander."

Miriam pushed two coins down the table.

"And do you know who the traitor was?"

"It couldn't have been Cleon or Memnon."

"Why is that?" Miriam asked the younger one.

"One night Cleon was in his captain's chamber. I came up with some wine and a bowl of fruit. There were voices raised."

"And what was said?"

"Cleon was talking to his captain. He agreed there was a traitor in the garrison. Cleon was terrified that this traitor would open the gates and allow the Thebans in. He was begging Memnon to double the guard, which the captain did. Anyone who went near the gate at night would have had an arrow in his gullet. And then Cleon said 'If they break in, sir, you'll not let them take me alive? You'll kill me won't you?' Memnon scoffed, but Cleon insisted. I paused on the stairway. I love hearing conversations. Cleon asked Memnon if he had his suspicions about who was the traitor? Memnon said. 'Who ever it is must be an archer, that's right!' Cleon asked why. Memnon replied that he had been on top of the tower late one night and had seen a fire arrow shot from the yard below. It went across the palisade. I thought I had heard enough," he stammered, "so I brought in the wine."

"But you left hurriedly?" Miriam asked.

"They closed the door," the page replied cheekily.

"But you listened at the keyhole?"

"Memnon begged Cleon to discover who the spy was. Cleon agreed, though he said something strange. . . ." The page looked at the small pile of coins near Miriam's elbow. She pushed two across the table.

"Go on," she said.

"Cleon said that if the assassin struck, he'd strike at Memnon. Cleon thought that the Thebans hoped Memnon would join Lysander; they then would have killed the two principal officers, and the garrison would have surrendered. Memnon agreed. Cleon told him to bar and bolt the door and to stay well armed. 'They'll try to kill you here,' Cleon warned. Memnon pointed to that bloody dog he kept."

"Where is he now?" Miriam interrupted.

"Oh, he's been taken into the camp by that other bum boy, the one with dyed hair."

"Ah, Hecaetus."

"Yes, that's right, Hecaetus. Anyway Memnon pointed at that great bloody mastiff and said he would take care of any assassin."

"What else do you know?"

Both boys shrugged.

Pollux looked toward the window, where the light was beginning to fade.

"We'll be going now."

"Where?" Miriam asked.

"Back to the camp; that's where the best food and wine are kept."

The pages pushed back the bench, grabbed the coins, and scampered out.

Miriam sat until she heard their voices fade. She sighed and, taking her writing satchel, walked out into the corridor. Now that darkness was falling, she realized what a gloomy, somber place the citadel was. She put her hand out and felt the cold granite walls. It wouldn't remain long. When Alexander left, this place would be destroyed. She took a pitch torch from its bracket and climbed the steep, spiral staircase. The tower seemed deserted, a ghostly hollow place. She paused on the stairwell and peeked into the chambers. The doors were open, the rooms were ransacked. She went farther up. The door to Memnon's chamber was ajar; she pushed it open and went in. The air smelled stale— of dog, oil lamp, sweat, and leather. She placed the torch in a holder, and groping in the darkness, found some oil lamps, which she lit.

The shutters were closed. Miriam went to open them but felt a cold draft seeping through the cracks and decided to leave it. She opened the satchel and took out Memnon's papers; she undid the cord and laid them on the table. In the light of an oil lamp, she began to leaf through the greasy, well-thumbed pieces of papyrus. In her time she had helped Simeon with army records, and these were no different. Typical soldiers' entries, the writing crude and large. Stores, provisions, arms, a rough drawing of the Cadmea, a votive prayer to Apollo, drafts of orders. She found a copy of a letter Memnon must have intended for his son. Apparently written during the early days of his command of the Cadmea, the letter depicted Memnon as a jovial, bluff man, proud of Alexander's trust in him, full of advice on how his son was to act. The letter, however, had never been sent. The scribbles of graffiti on the bottom half of the page were interesting. Probably done during the last days of his life, Memnon had written out promises: he would travel to this shrine or that, make votive offerings to the gods if he was safely brought through the present dangers. One phrase, however, was repeated: the name *Oedipus,* or the literal translation of the ancient Theban king's name, swollen foot. "I have seen him tonight," Memnon had scrawled. "I have heard him on the stairs, his club rattling against the wall."

Miriam went cold. What had Memnon been talking about? The ghost of Oedipus? The accursed king of Thebes dragging himself through this ancient citadel? She continued reading, the same entry was repeated time and again. She found another dirty piece of parchment with the same remarks beneath a crude drawing of Oedipus carrying his club. Miriam raised her head. The citadel was very quiet now. She stared round the chamber.

Was Memnon's shade here, she wondered? Did the old captain stand in the shadows and peer out at her? Or had he gone to Hades? She grasped her torch and went out to the stairwell. She heard a door close and turned around but there was no other sound. She went up the steps and passed the small garret, its door flung back; she peered in: nothing but a dusty cubicle. She climbed on. The staircase became narrower and led to a wooden door. Miriam raised the latch, and a buffet of cold air made her torch splutter. She went out onto the top of the tower, her feet crunching on gravel deliberately strewn there so that no one could miss their footing. The wind was strong, and Miriam shielded her face. She walked to the edge and stood with one hand resting on the crenellations. She lifted the torch and gazed down. It was now pitch dark. Yet she was aware of the dizzying height. Fires still burned in the city, and beyond, she could see the lights of the Macedonian camp. Memnon must have stood here when he'd seen the fire arrow loosed into the night sky. She once again stared at the ruins of Thebes and repressed a shiver. This was truly a necropolis, a city of the dead. She heard a sound; a group of soldiers were leaving, their torches mere pinpricks of light. Behind her the door to the tower clattered and banged. Miriam went back and, carefully closing the door behind her, went down the steps. She reentered Memnon's chamber, and her stomach pitched. Someone had been here. The oil lamps had been moved. Her hand went to her girdle and she realized she had brought no weapon. But surely the garrison? Men were still here? She hurried to the chest at the foot of the little truckle bed and opened it. It smelled of stale sweat. She fumbled through the contents and sighed with relief as her fingers clutched a dagger. She pulled this out, threw away the battered sheath, and went to the door.

"Who is there?" she called. Her own voice echoed down the stairwell. She heard a door opening and closing. "Castor, Pollux!"

Someone was coming up the stairs. Her blood chilled, yes she was sure, one foot dragging after the other; something smacked against the stone wall time and again as if a drum were being beaten.

"Who is there?" she called.

"I am the shade of hell!" A voice echoed, hollow, up the steps.

Miriam's mouth went dry. What could she do? She felt the thickness of the door and stepped back into Memnon's chamber. The key was gone but she drew the bolts across. Outside, though more faintly, she heard the sound of the intruder, lame foot dragging after him, as he climbed the stairs. The awful drumming against the wall grew louder. Miriam recalled the words about Oedipus, the swollen foot, ancient king of Thebes. And what had Alexander said? That Oedipus's ghost had been seen in Thebes. The sounds grew nearer. Miriam drew in her breath, grasping the dagger more firmly. The door was tried. A loud rapping and then a crashing, as if someone were beating it with a club. Miriam stood transfixed, torch in one hand, dagger in the other. She heard her name being called but this came from the courtyard below. The crashing grew louder; the door was shaking.

"Who is it?" Miriam screamed. She hurried toward the shutters, pulled off the bar, and threw them open. The cold night air rushed in. Miriam was only aware of that terrible crashing against the door. She turned, dagger in hand, and then the knocking ceased.

CHAPTER 5

"Miriam! Miriam!" Simeon called. "What is the matter?"

She moved to the door. Was it Simeon? she thought. Or someone mimicking his voice?

"Go away," she called.

"Miriam Bartimaeus, it's your brother. I was concerned about you."

She drew back the bolts. Simeon stood there on the stairwell; behind him she could make out the shadowy outlines of two soldiers.

"Miriam, what is the matter?"

She backed into the room, throwing the dagger onto the bed.

"There was someone else," she declared, "someone with a lame foot. He came up the stairs. He was banging at the door." She brushed by him; outside, the soldiers were smirking.

"It's a mausoleum of ghosts," one of them remarked. "Mistress, there's no one here."

"I know what I heard and saw," Miriam retorted. She

stared down the stairwell. Of course, it could have been a ghost. But, then again, if the intruder had heard her brother calling her name, he could have slipped down the stairs into another chamber and, when Simeon and the guards passed, slipped quietly out.

"How many are here?"

She went back into the room.

"Just the three of us. I was in the camp," Simeon replied. "Alexander asked where you were? I realized the soldiers had come in from the citadel. I asked these two to follow me. We found the Cadmea deserted; we'd passed the last of the guards on the road. I saw the shutter open and glimpsed the light."

Miriam closed the door and sat down on a stool.

"There was someone here," she whispered, "and I don't think they meant me well." She then described what she had read in Memnon's manuscript. Simeon whistled under his breath.

"The specter of Oedipus!" he joked. His face became serious; he stared owl-eyed at his twin sister. She was so different from him, tall and resolute. Simeon liked the comforts of life. He felt at home in the writing office, sifting through parchments, drafting letters, listening to the gossip, reveling in the excitement that always surrounded Alexander. Miriam, that determined look on her thin face, was always wandering off to places where she shouldn't.

"Come on," he urged. "You haven't eaten. Let's leave this benighted place. Alexander is holding a banquet."

By the time they reentered the camp, the revelry had already begun. They were stopped by cavalry patrols and sentries in the iron ring Alexander had placed round his sprawling camp. Alexander was cautious. A small portion of the Theban army, including the cavalry, had escaped.

Alexander was wary of the silent assassin, or the madman who might try his luck in delivering one blow, one knife thrust.

They found the king in a banqueting tent, a huge pavilion of costly cloths, now turned into a drinking hall. All around, shaped in a horseshoe, were small banqueting tables, cushions, and other costly chairs and stools looted from hundreds of Theban homes. Torches burned brightly on lashed poles or spears thrust into the ground. Huge pots full of burning charcoal sprinkled with incense provided warmth. The tent flaps were open allowing the cold night air to waft away the smoke.

Alexander lounged at the top of the tent on a makeshift couch, his household companions on either side. Perdiccas, Hephaestion, Niarchos, Ptolemy, and the principal commanders of the different corps. Food was being served: lamb, beef dressed in different sauces, great platters of stone-ground white bread, bowls of fruit. A makeshift banquet but the unwatered wine was copious and flowed freely. A page led them to a table on Alexander's right. The king lifted his head. He had bathed, his hair was cut and oiled, his face closely shaven. In the torchlight Alexander's face had a burnished look. Miriam smiled and winked. Alexander loved to imitate the appearance of a god and now he posed as a victorious one. He had deliberately donned his dress armor; a gold-wrought breastplate, where snakes writhed and turned; silver armlets on his wrists; a thick military cloak fastened around his neck by a silver clasp.

"Greetings, Miriam, health and prosperity! And you Simeon?" He drank from the cup and went back to whisper to Hephaestion.

Miriam groaned. "It's going to be a long night," she whispered.

Dancing girls, accompanied by a dispirited group of musicians were ushered in, but the revelers were not interested in dancing or music. Some of the guests started throwing scraps of food at them. Alexander clapped his hands and wearily dismissed the dancers. His commanders were intent on eating and drinking their fill, reveling in their victory, boasting of their own prowess. And, of course, the toasts began.

"To Alexander, lion of Macedon! To Alexander, captain-general of Greece! To Alexander, conqueror of Persia!"

Miriam leaned back on her cushions and smiled across at Eurydice, Ptolemy's mistress, a beautiful, olive-skinned young woman with oil-drenched ringlets framing her perfectly formed face. Her gray eyes had a glazed look, and there was a petulant cast to her mouth.

"She's like us," Simeon whispered. "She'd prefer to be elsewhere."

Miriam absentmindedly agreed. She was settling down, slowly drinking her cup of very watered wine. Alexander was now in full flow.

"We will wait for Mother," he declared, "and then take counsel."

"Not return to Macedon?" Perdiccas asked.

Alexander shook his head. "We shall not return to Macedon," he slurred, "until we have marched in glory through Persia. By the spring we shall be across the Isthmus. I shall sacrifice to Achilles among the ruins of Troy."

"Oh no!" Miriam whispered, "not Achilles!"

"And then," Alexander lurched to his feet, swaying tipsily, cup in hand, "we will march to the ends of the earth."

His triumphant shout was greeted by roars of approval. Alexander sat down.

"For those who wish to," he smiled, "you may retire! But those who drink can stay!"

Some of the women left, followed by some of the lesser

commanders who had duties to carry out. Miriam excused herself, but Simeon said he would stay. She put down the cup, slipped out of the tent, and stood allowing the night breezes to cool her. She collected her writing satchel from the groom she had left it with and made her way back to the tent she shared with Simeon.

The camp was noisy, fires glowing in every direction. Soldiers staggered about, but officers dressed in full armor and horsehair-plumed helmets, kept good order with stout ash canes. Soldiers lurched up from the campfires and staggered toward her. When they recognized who she was, they mumbled apologies and slipped quietly away. The camp followers were doing a roaring trade in different tents and bothies and she could hear the hasty, noisy sound of lovemaking. Somewhere soldiers were singing a raucous song. From another place she heard the piping tunes of flutes. Horse neighed. Servants hurried through with bundles on their backs. Miriam looked up. The sky was clear, the stars more distant than in the hills of Macedon. She recalled Alexander's words. He would never go back there. She wondered about his boast to march to the ends of the earth. Sometimes Alexander, in his cups, would talk of leading his troops to the rim of the world, of creating an empire dominated by Greece that would make the world gasp in surprise. He wants to be greater than Philip, she thought; he wants to outshine him in every way.

She pulled back the flap of her tent and went in. Someone had lit the oil lamp on the table; it still glowed weakly. She picked up the scrap of parchment lying beside it. She made out the letters in the poor light.

"Doomed, oh lost and damned! This is my last and only word to you for ever!"

Miriam's heart quickened. She fought hard to control her trembling. She recognized the quotation from Sophocles and recalled the mysterious intruder outside that lonely chamber in the Cadmea. She was being warned, and if Simeon hadn't come? She sat down on the thin mattress that served as a bed.

"Miriam." She started. Hecaetus poked his head through the tent flap, smiling sweetly at her like a suitor come to pay court.

"You shouldn't crawl around at night, Hecaetus. It doesn't suit you!" she snapped.

"May I come in? I have a visitor."

"I can't very well stop you."

Hecaetus entered. He pulled his great cloak more tightly. "It's so cold," he moaned. "Why doesn't Alexander march somewhere warm, where the sun always shines. By the gods, where is he?" He went back and pulled up the tent flap. "Come on man," he said pettishly, "the lady's tired and I'm for my bed."

The man who lumbered in was small and thickset; a scrawny mustache and beard hid the lower part of his face. His hair was unkempt and oil-streaked. He moved awkwardly, nervously staring around the tent.

"This is Simothaeus." Hecaetus made the man sit. "He's a soldier, served under Memnon. Come on. Do you want some wine?" Hecaetus spoke to the man like some disapproving aunt. The man shook his head, eyes fixed on Miriam. She smiled and he grimaced in a show of broken teeth. Hecaetus sat between them and patted the man's bony knee.

"Simothaeus likes drinking, and he's been rejoicing at his king's victory. Do you want some wine, Miriam?"

"I drank enough in the king's tent."

"Yes, I'm sure you did." Hecaetus's womanish face became petulant. "Always the servant, never the guest." He waved his hand foppishly. "Alexander needs me but never invites me to drink with him."

"He knows you are a skilled hand at poisons."

Hecaetus, eyes crinkled in amusement, wagged a finger. "You are very naughty, Miriam; I only remove the king's enemies."

"Or those who get in your way. Do I get in your way, Hecaetus?"

"I am the king's searcher-out of secrets," Hecaetus replied defensively. "But no, my dear, I like you. I've watched those eyes of yours, sharp and shrewd. You mean me no ill. You don't mock me like the others do."

"And your friend Simothaeus?" Miriam asked.

"Well I've spent the day . . ." Hecaetus began. He waved his hands; the fingernails were gaudily painted. "Some of these soldiers are such bitches," he lisped. "You share a cup of wine with them and they want their hand in your crotch. And no, I don't enjoy it. They are far too rough; not like my boys." Hecaetus turned and looked over his shoulder.

Miriam knew all about Hecaetus's "boys": effete but courageous; where their master went, they always followed. It would be a foolish soldier, indeed, who tried to take liberties with Hecaetus.

"Do you want to bring your boys in here?" Miriam asked. "Though it could get rather crowded."

"Don't be such a minx!" Hecaetus mewed like a cat. He patted her hand. "You are far too hard, Miriam; I am your friend, I always will be. We should share what we know, shouldn't we?"

Miriam stared at the light-blue eyes so innocent, so child-like. How many men, she wondered, had he trapped with that pleading slightly hurt look?

"I'm waiting Hecaetus."

"Oh, go on!" Hecaetus tapped Simothaeus on the shoulder. "I spent the whole day, Miriam, drinking with him and his companions, and they couldn't tell me a thing. But then Simothaeus, in that dark dim area he calls his brain, remembered something very important." He fished beneath his cloak, brought out his purse, and shook two coins into the palm of his hand.

"Go on, Simothaeus."

"I was on guard duty." The man spoke like an actor who had repeated his lines time and again but really didn't understand the importance of them. "Yes, I was on guard duty."

Hecaetus sighed noisily.

"Old Memnon came out of the courtyard. He was slightly tipsy. He was dressed in full armor, hand on the hilt of his sword."

"When was this?" Hecaetus interrupted. "Tell the lady."

"Why, the day before he fell from the tower. It was late in the afternoon. We had heard rumors that the king and the Macedonian army were marching on Thebes. Most of the men were celebrating. Memnon came over to me. He gripped me by the shoulder and asked my name. 'Simothaeus,' I replied, 'my father tilled the land north of Pella.' "

"And?" Hecaetus asked testily.

"The captain was a hard bugger, but he was blunt. 'Simothaeus,' he said, 'whatever Hades and the Thebans throw at us, we will stand fast, we will welcome our king into the citadel.' Then he leaned closer. 'You are going to see all of Thebes burn!' "

"Did he say anything else?" Miriam asked.

Simothaeus shook his head.

"Right," Hecaetus said testily. "Here is a coin, Simothaeus. Go and get as drunk as the other pigs."

The soldier lumbered out of the tent.

"Do you see the importance of Simothaeus's evidence?" Hecaetus asked, raising his eye brows. "Here we have old Memnon supposedly drunk and brooding in his chamber, his mind has turned and he attempts to fly like Icarus from his tower."

"But it doesn't make sense," Miriam interrupted. "In the last days of the siege, a Macedonian army was marching on Thebes though, even then," She added, "Didn't the Thebans think Alexander had been killed and that the troops were being led by one of his generals?" She held her hand up. "But true, true Hecaetus, I follow your drift. Memnon expected to be relieved, so why commit suicide?"

"See, Miriam, I am willing to share what I discover."

"But how did Memnon know that?" Miriam asked. "How did he know that a Macedonian army was marching to his relief? After all, the Thebans had him tightly controlled."

Hecaetus grinned. "They may have spies in the citadel but I had spies in Thebes. Arrows can go both ways. So, Miriam, . . . He played with the bracelet on his wrist, ". . . tell me what you have discovered. One of my pretty boys saw you return to camp. You looked agitated."

Miriam told Hecaetus everything. Her visit to the citadel, Memnon's manuscripts, and the attack on her. Hecaetus, eyes half closed, heard her out.

"It's strange," he mused. "Rumors are sweeping the camp that Oedipus's shade has been seen. I just wish the king would take that bloody Crown and march away from here. But he's such a showman. He should have been an actor on the stage. In fact, he is, and all of Greece is the audience. He's taken Thebes by storm, and now he wants some god to come down from Olympus and hand the Crown to him."

"These spies of yours . . ." Miriam began. She was wary of talking to Hecaetus about Alexander. She didn't trust the man as far as she could spit but she didn't want him to be her enemy.

"Oh a few merchants, tinkers, travelers."

"Anyone in particular?"

"I am looking for a lovely boy, by the name of Meleager. He was a scribe in the service of the Theban council. He was close to their leader Pelliades."

"But he has disappeared?"

"Yes, Miriam, the boy has gone, vanished. He may have fled, he may be in hiding, or he may be one of the corpses lying beneath that sea of ash once called Thebes." Hecaetus paused, head half-cocked, listening to the sounds of the camp. "I tell you this, Miriam, I don't think Memnon jumped. He was murdered, but how or why, well that's a mystery." He got to his feet. "I'm going to continue searching for Meleager. He could well be in one of the slave pens. He can protest about how much he helped Macedon, but in the eyes of Alexander's soldiers, one Theban's like another." He leaned down and kissed Miriam on the top of her head, and pointing to the piece of parchment bearing the quotation from Sophocles, he said, "If I were you, young woman, I would walk very carefully."

And then he was gone. Miriam picked up the piece of parchment and stared at it. Was it to frighten her?

"No," she exclaimed. She was supposed to show this to Alexander! The king was as brave as a lion in battle but, like Philip, highly superstitious, wary of omens, portents, and warnings.

"Miriam."

She turned, startled. Simeon was crouched in the mouth of the tent.

"It's busier here," she quipped, "than anyplace in the camp."

Simeon just blinked and crawled in on all fours.

"I don't feel well," he murmured. "They are drinking fit to burst."

"You are an Israelite," Miriam retorted. "Never try to imitate Macedonians in their cups."

Simeon got to his feet. Miriam took a jug of water and quickly prepared an herbal drink.

"It will settle your stomach. You should be asleep."

Simeon shook his head. "The king wants me back at his tent."

"Oh no." Miriam groaned.

"It's the Crown of Oedipus. He also wants you." He stumbled on his words. "Well, you'd best come."

Alexander's banqueting tent was not as stately as when she had left. The ground littered was with scraps of food. Tables and chairs were overturned. Two of his commanders were lying flat out, snoring like pigs. The musicians and dancing girls had fled. Alexander had changed the seating arrangements. He had moved his couch farther down the tent—one arm around Niarchos, the other round Perdiccas. At the far end he had set up a makeshift pillar, a huge wooden stake planted in the ground, with iron clasps on it. These had been bent and held a crown Alexander must have taken from his treasury. He had laid out cloaks in front of the stake to imitate the pits in the shrine; now he was challenging everyone, all comers, to remove the crown without standing on the cloaks. Miriam groaned and closed her eyes. Alexander flush-faced and bright-eyed, was shouting abuse at Hephaestion, who stood before the cloaks staring blearily at the crown. Alexander staggered over, put his arm around Hephaestion's shoulder and kissed him on the cheek.

"You are supposed to be a bloody engineer!" he bawled in his ear. "How do you get that crown off that bloody pillar without standing on the cloaks? Remember . . ." Alexander lifted one finger up as he swayed backward and forward. He blinked.

"What must I remember?"

"He must take the crown off," Niarchos yelled, "without touching the cloaks. One's a fire, one's a snake pit, and in between them is a row of spikes. Nor must he use anything brought into the shrine."

Hephaestion blinked owlishly at his king and stared at the wooden stake.

"I could go outside," he said, "go around the tent, lift the flap, and take it."

The rest of the company roared with laughter. Alexander caught Miriam's eyes.

"Come on Israelites!" he gestured. He went and took Niarchos aside. "Sit down Miriam, you are the only sober man among us!"

His quip raised a few sniggers. Miriam blushed slightly. She had heard the secret jokes about her being more man than woman. Alexander must have seen the hurt in her eyes as he squatted down beside her.

"I'm sorry," he slurred, "but it all started when I told them about our visit this morning. And do you know, not one of these drunken buggers can give me any advice."

Miriam stared at the red cloaks that stood for the burning charcoal, the spear in between that stood for the spikes, and the long cloak of blue that represented the snake pit. She had been so frightened about what had happened in the citadel that she hadn't given any thought to this problem. Niarchos had now sprung to his feet. He yelled at one of the bodyguards to bring him a long lance or pike, but when he did so, Niarchos realized that it was far too short to reach. Alexander sat, gnawing his fingernails.

"There must be a way," he muttered, "to take that crown."

"Do it by force?" Perdiccas clinked his cup against that of the king. "Burn the temple and take it by force."

"And all of Greece will see that."

The speaker at the far end of the semicircle stood up. Miriam recognized Timeon, the Athenian delegate.

"My lord Alexander, if you take it by force, all of Greece will know of it."

"Thank you, Timeon." Alexander forced a weak smile. "And before you leave, I'll have words with you . . ." he scowled, "about the traitor Demosthenes."

"He is no longer in Athens," Timeon declared. "He has fled; we do not know where. All of Greece now has its eyes on Thebes."

Miriam gripped Alexander's wrist. She could feel him beginning to tremble with anger. One of those terrible rages that swept him, particularly when he was deep in his cups. What had begun as a drunken joke was now turning ugly. She looked along the line of Alexander's commanders for a sober face, but they were all drunk. Some were half asleep, others were now glaring at the Athenian envoy. Niarchos, stung by Timeon's hidden taunts, walked along the cloaks. He forced back the metal clasps on either side of the crown, took it off, and tipsily put it on his head.

"That's the way we take Crowns in Macedon!" he yelled at the Athenian. "We just move in and take them!"

"Of course," Timeon purred, "whether it's Macedon or anywhere else."

His remark stilled the clamor and noise in the tent. Alexander sprang to his feet. He ran and picked up the spear that separated the different-colored cloaks. Miriam thought his anger was directed at Timeon but it was Niarchos he confronted.

"You stupid Cretan bastard!"

Niarchos stared fearfully back. Alexander brought the

spear up. Miriam jumped to her feet, ran forward, and caught his arm.

"My lord king," she cried, "you know this is only a charade. Niarchos acts the fool. Don't reveal our secret."

Alexander's arm remained tense.

"Put it down," she whispered. "Alexander, put it down!" She felt his arm relax.

"Miriam is right." Alexander stuck the spear into the earth.

"What do you mean?" Timeon, eager to create more trouble, stepped forward.

"We know how to remove the Crown of Oedipus, but it will take time." Miriam blurted the words out before she could stop. "Yes, I swear by the holy name of the God of Israel, that it will not be by force but by human cunning and divine favor. Alexander of Macedon shall wear the Iron Crown of Thebes!"

A murmur of approval broke out from the king's companions. Timeon look puzzled. Niarchos came forward. Alexander grasped him by the shoulder and kissed him on each cheek.

"Do that again," he whispered, "and I'll have your bloody head." And with one arm around Niarchos and the other around Miriam, Alexander staggered back to his cushions. He wiped his flushed, sweat-soaked face with a wet rag and clapped his hands.

"The night is still young."

Servants came in bringing more bowls of food and fresh jugs of wine. Alexander deliberately turned his back on Miriam and began to tease Hephaestion. Only when he was sure his guests were diverted did he turn back.

"You know what you've done, Miriam?"

"I know what you would have done," she hissed. "You showed all Greece that a Macedonian could not solve a problem. And, in the presence of the envoys, you almost killed one of your generals. Alexander, when you drink, keep your hands away from your weapons."

"I thought Niarchos was going to pee himself," Alexander grinned.

"So would anyone," Miriam countered.

"Do you know how to remove the Crown?" Alexander taunted.

"No!" Miriam hissed. "But if my lord . . ."

"My lord king."

Miriam looked around. A captain of the guard had entered the tent—one hand on the hilt of his sword, the other covered in blood.

"My lord king you'd best come now."

"What is it?" Alexander slurred.

"Three guards have been killed."

All drunkenness seemed to disappear. The king sprang to his feet, snapping his fingers for the others to join him. A cart stood outside the royal tent. Three corpses, foot soldiers, sprawled there splattered with blood. Alexander took a pitch torch from one of the escorts and moved closer. The side of each man's head looked as if it had been smashed in by some war ax or club.

"The men were out on picket duty," the captain explained. "To the south on country roads. I went to check that all was well but couldn't find them. I thought they had gone drinking or even slipped back into the camp; I found one of the shields, then the corpses, as well as this!"

Alexander took the small scroll and handed it to Miriam.

"Doomed," she read out aloud. "Oh, lost and damned! This is my last and only word to you. For ever!"

"I received the same." She handed it back. "Earlier this evening; it's a quotation . . ."

"I know," Alexander broke in, "from Sophocles." Alexander strode away from his companions, now gathering round the cart; he gestured at Miriam and the captain to follow.

"There's something else isn't there, man?"

The captain nodded, his face pale and sweaty under the great Corinthian helmet.

"When I crouched down to examine one of the corpses, I heard a whistling. I looked up. In the moonlight I glimpsed a figure on top of small hill. In one hand he carried a club."

"And when he walked," Miriam intervened, "he had a limp?"

The captain nodded. "I hurried toward him, but by the time I reached the top, he'd disappeared into the night. The men are now saying that we have been visited and punished by the shade of Oedipus."

Alexander sobered up. It was as if he hadn't touched a drop of wine; there was a thin, mean twist to his lips, his eyes were hard and unblinking.

"I conquered Thebes," he declared. "And now they are going to argue that Oedipus has conquered me. Perdiccas," he shouted, "I want officers to check all the pickets and sentries. Send out cavalry patrols at first light! Scour the countryside for any Thebans. Miriam come with me."

They walked out of earshot of the rest.

"I'm begging you, Miriam." Alexander held her wrists tightly.

"What my lord?"

"To get a good night's sleep. Tomorrow morning do two things: hunt down the Oracle and find a way for me to secure that bloody Crown!"

CHAPTER 6

MIRIAM RETURNED TO the citadel just after dawn, ruefully realizing she had broken Alexander's first request because her
sleep had been plagued by dreams and nightmares. It was a
cold gray morning, and a mist had seeped in over the
charred remains of Thebes, reminding Miriam of some
image of Hades with the black and twisted timbers, the
ankle-deep ash, the occasional smoldering fire. She found
some of the soldiers had drifted back to the citadel, and
drew some comfort from their presence. She had to kick her
heels while a servant went looking for Memnon's five principal officers. Cleon was the first to arrive, bright-eyed and
clean-shaven. He insisted that Miriam join him for breakfast.
He took her to the mess hall and brought out two dishes of
fragrantly smelling meat and some rather stale bread, for
which he wryly apologized, and a jug of beer.

"It's Theban," he declared, "but it tastes fresh and tangy.
Best thing to clean the mouth in the morning." He sat on a
bench opposite and offered Miriam a napkin. The meat was

hot to the touch. Miriam had to blow on it as well take hasty sips of beer.

"You are a good cook," she teased. "You'll make someone a wonderful husband."

"Captain Memnon was a stickler," Cleon replied between mouthfuls. "He said he had starved enough during sieges and had eaten his fill of army rations. So, in a place like this, he would demand all the luxuries."

"Was he a good officer?" Miriam asked.

"Excellent. Loyal, brave. A kindly man, I never saw him hit anyone. Oh, he could curse and he'd rant, but unlike his dog," Cleon grinned, "his bark was infinitely worse than his bite!"

"Did he know that Alexander was marching on Thebes?"

"Yes, we all did," Cleon replied. "Shortly before Memnon was found at the foot of the tower."

"And Memnon was happy with this news?"

"He said he had it on good report, though he was still worried that Alexander had been killed. He was also terrified that the Thebans might suddenly launch a surprise attack and take the citadel before the Macedonian army arrived."

"And that was possible?" Miriam asked.

"Yes certainly! If the spy among us had opened the gates, we would have been massacred."

"And why didn't that happen?"

Cleon narrowed his eyes and wiped his fingers on the napkin.

"To have achieved that the Thebans would have had to mass behind the palisade. Our guards would have seen them."

"Was there a guard at the top of the tower when Memnon died?"

"No." Cleon shook his head. "It's far too high; it only serves as a lookout post during the day. Our sentries were on the ramparts along the curtain wall."

"I am sorry for my interruptions," Miriam apologized. "you were talking about a sudden attack."

"The Thebans would have had to mass," Cleon declared. "And that would have become apparent. The spy or traitor, whoever it was, would have had to open a gate. Now, the citadel has two gates, the main one you came through this morning and a small postern door."

"And both were closely guarded?"

"Oh, yes. Footmen in full armor, archers; the garrison was on full alert. If the Thebans had broken in they would have shown no mercy." He cleaned the bowl with a piece of bread and popped the bread into his mouth. "And don't forget that the spy or traitor would have been worried. If the Thebans had broken in they wouldn't have known friend from foe; he might have been killed along with the rest."

"And Memnon's state of mind?" she asked.

"He was very anxious, worried." Cleon's voice dropped to a whisper. "He really did believe the spy was one of his officers."

"Not you?" Miriam asked.

"The Thebans have no love for me!"

"Then, who?" Miriam asked.

"I don't know." Cleon shook his head. "I really don't. You see, Miriam . . ." He pushed the bowl away. "All of us could be described as secretive or lonely men."

"What do you mean?"

"We were in a siege. Tension in the Cadmea was palpable. We all tried to look for some refuge for ourselves. One person would go off here, another there."

"But did you see anything suspicious?"

"Nothing." Cleon made a cutting movement with his hand.

"But Memnon did?"

"He might have, though he never mentioned it to me. All

he could talk about was the traitor. Someone who knew the strength of our garrison." Cleon licked his lips. "He did become a little suspicious toward me."

"Why?" Miriam asked.

"Memnon had two great fears. One was the spy, but the other?"

"Was a mutiny?" Miriam asked.

"Yes, a mutiny. Memnon was concerned that his officers, would believe that the Macedonian army had been destroyed and killed. And that they might murder him and open negotiations with Thebes for some sort of honorable surrender."

"So this worry could have caused him to commit suicide?"

Cleon picked up the napkin and dabbed at his mouth. He smiled at Miriam from under his eyebrows.

"I would like to say yes. I would like to put my hand on some sacred object and swear that Captain Memnon's mind was turned, that his wits were as wandering as flies in summer. But that wouldn't be the truth. I don't think Captain Memnon committed suicide." He leaned his arms on the table. "But only the gods know how he was murdered."

"I ask the same question myself."

Miriam started and turned. Alcibiades stood in the doorway. He sauntered across, picked up a piece of stale bread, and sat on the bench next to Cleon. He had been drinking, and his eyes were red-rimmed, his pale face sweaty; the tunic he wore still bore stains from the previous night's feasting. He scratched his unshaven cheek.

"Don't worry. I am going to have a bath."

Cleon wrinkled his nose. "And not before time," he whispered.

Alcibiades playfully nudged him back but his eyes held Miriam's. She saw the malevolence, the sneering look.

"You don't like me, do you?" she asked.

She moved the writing satchel from the table on to the bench beside her.

"It's not that, my dear. I just don't like women in general. And I don't like those who come snooping into men's affairs." He chewed noisily on the bread, deliberately opening his mouth so Miriam would look away.

"Do you like Israelites?" Miriam asked.

"You are the first I have met. So, no."

"Hush," Cleon intervened, "she's from the king's writing office."

"I couldn't give a donkey's fart where she's from!" Alcibiades retorted. "I am a Macedon, I can speak my mind. I was loyal to Philip and I'll be loyal to his son. I have marched through freezing snow. I have had the sun burn my arse! I have stood in battle line with the rest and I've never retreated." He turned and spat the bread out of his mouth onto the floor. "I was a loyal officer of the garrison." His voice became strident. "As is Cleon and the others! I saw no treachery. We should be rewarded not treated with suspicion."

"I fully agree." Demetrius, clapping his hands, came in with Patroclus and Melitus. They bowed sardonically at Miriam and then wandered into the kitchen looking for food. They came back talking noisily about the feast the night before—like boys in a school room determined to antagonize their master through dumb insolence rather than direct insults. They sat on the bench, scraping their bowls with their fingers, slurping beer from their cups.

Miriam sat patiently. She had been raised among men like these, coarse but brave. Soldiers who believed women had a certain place in the scheme of things but it certainly wasn't in their mess hall asking questions. Nevertheless, beneath all their bluster, they had a deep personal loyalty to the Macedonian crown. She was here on Alexander's orders, and by their very presence, they were acknowledging that. Demetrius cleaned his bowl, running his tongue round the rim.

"Well, mistress, you sent for us? More questions, eh?"

"More questions," Miriam replied. "But I assure you, they won't take long."

She asked the same questions she'd asked of Cleon, and they responded in similar vein. They were terrified of a Theban surprise attack. Memnon was surly and withdrawn. He was personally worried about Alexander but relieved at the approach of the Macedonian army. He feared a mutiny and, in the last days before the Macedonian attack, kept to himself. Of all the men, he seemed to trust Cleon the most; they also declared that it was difficult to accept that a man like Memnon would commit suicide.

"So, why did you put a guard on his door?" Miriam asked. "I mean, the night he died, two of you took turns?"

"It was to reassure the old bugger!" Alcibiades drawled. "We were his officers. We had pledged loyalty."

"And you heard nothing untoward that night?"

"Not a flea's fart," Melitus declared.

Miriam rolled the goblet between her hands. The men were politely attentive but she caught a look of sardonic amusement in Alcibiades' eyes.

I am making no progress, she thought, and they know it.

"Tell me how Memnon was dressed." She said.

"I have told you, in battle drill."

"He was wearing a sword?"

"Yes, he was."

"Did anyone see him fall?"

"No one," Cleon replied. "We heard and saw nothing. You must remember, apart from fires and lights on the gates, the citadel was in darkness."

"But surely," Miriam persisted, "even when a man commits suicide, he very rarely falls to his death without a scream or a yell?"

"He may have screamed," Alcibiades retorted. "We are simply saying we heard nothing."

The way he said, "we" pricked suspicion in Miriam's mind. Was it possible that all four, even all five, were conspirators? But that didn't answer how they would have managed to get through a locked door, take an old veteran, silence his dog, and throw him through a window. Memnon would have fought for his life; he would have shouted and screamed.

"Who took his food up that night?" Miriam asked.

"I did," Alcibiades declared. He blinked. "And before you say it, Mistress . . ."

"Say what?"

"That the wine or food could have contained a potion."

"How do you know it didn't?" Miriam asked. "I am not," she added hastily, "saying you are responsible."

"The food was prepared in the kitchen," he explained.

"Alcibiades took it up."

"I was there," Demetrius added. "We knocked on the door. The dog growled. This must have been early in the evening. Memnon opened the door, took the bowl and cup, then locked and bolted himself in."

"And how do you know it wasn't drugged?"

"Because when we entered the chamber," Demetrius answered, "the food and the wine had been untouched; everyone who was there saw that, not just us."

"But he must have been hungry." Miriam said.

"Yes, that's what I thought," Cleon replied. "However, earlier that day he had come down to the mess hall here; he was rather sullen and withdrawn but he ate well."

"And the ghost story?" Miriam asked, quickly changing the subject.

"The ghost story?" Cleon asked.

"Oedipus," Miriam explained. "Didn't Memnon say he had heard or seen the shade of Oedipus in the citadel?"

"Yes, and in the week before he died," Demetrius declared, "he complained that sometimes he'd hear a man with a lame foot climbing the stairs, the sound of a club being struck against the brickwork."

"And?"

"None of us saw anything." Demetrius turned to his companions. "Did we?"

They all shook their heads.

"You must remember," Cleon declared, "that sometimes Memnon was the only one in the tower; during the day we had our own duties to carry out, while before the siege began, we could go where we wished."

"Didn't Memnon go out into Thebes?"

"Never! It was too dangerous."

"So this ghost could have been a figment of Memnon's imagination?"

"No," Demetrius snapped, "we didn't say that. We have heard, mistress, what happened last night in the camp. In fact, I saw . . ." He blew his cheeks out. "Well, both Melitus and I saw something." He looked shamedfacedly at his companion.

"One night we were on guard duty." Melitus took up the story. "I was on the parapet walk. Now beyond the stockade the Thebans had set up, we always glimpsed torchlight, camp fires. One night Demetrius called me over; a figure was standing in the glow from a fire. He was tall, long-haired; you could make out the outline; in his hand he carried a club. The rest of his body was shrouded in a cloak but when he moved it was with a limp. We watched him for some time."

"You didn't loose an arrow?" Miriam asked.

"Why should we? He posed no threat. And we didn't wish to antagonize the Thebans any more than we had to."

"So," Miriam mused, "we have Memnon believing he hears the shade of Oedipus in the citadel. You also see him in the wasteland between the citadel and the city; meanwhile, the same creature, specter, ghost, whatever, may have been responsible for the death of the camp guards last night."

"Rumors are sweeping the army," Patroclus declared. "The men don't like the city; it reeks of death. They want Alexander to march away."

"But not before he's taken that bloody Crown!" Alcibiades groaned.

"Are you all right, Miriam?" Simeon stood in the doorway, pale-faced and heavy-eyed.

"Yes, Yes, I'm fine."

"Are there any more questions, mistress?" Demetrius got to his feet. "We still have duties to perform."

"What will the king do with this citadel?" Miriam asked.

"When we march, he will burn it. Gut it with fire."

Miriam thanked them and, picking up her writing satchel, joined Simeon in the passageway outside.

"Did you discover anything new?"

"Hush." Miriam pressed a finger against his lips. "Not here, Simeon."

She led him up the stairs and into Memnon's chamber. The shutters were still open; the room was freezing so she hurriedly closed them. Simeon went out, got a torch, and tried to light the charcoal brazier. Miriam sat on the edge of the bed and watched him. At last Simeon was successful. The charcoal glowed red. He pulled the brazier over and sat beside it.

"Two more guards have been found," he declared, "their heads staved in. What do you think it portends?"

"I'd like to say its Oedipus," Miriam retorted. "That the old king has come back to curse the destroyers of his city. But, I don't believe in ghosts, Simeon. It's human trickery."

"Why?"

"Alexander is the Conqueror of Thebes." Miriam paused. "Yes, he has shown how he will deal with rebels but our noble king always likes a challenge. Never since the Spartan war has a Greek city been leveled with such cruel barbarity. Oh, all of Greece will hail him, as victor and captain-general. They've got little choice; Alexander's boot is firmly on their necks! We all know what's going to happen next. Alexander is going to march to the Hellespont. He'll demand that some Greek states send troops and that Athens send its navy. Those war triremes will be essential for any attack on Persia."

"You should have been a general, Miriam."

"Brother, I sit and listen to Niarchos and Perdiccas argue with Alexander about tactics and strategy. Which ships should go first? What formation should be adopted? Alexander is like a dog with a bone; he knows that, once he crosses the Hellespont, he must leave a united and quiet Greece behind him. Now there are many who will whisper behind their hands that the destruction of Thebes was a mistake. How Alexander is guilty of hubris and will rightly incur the wrath of the gods. They will look for some sign."

"The Crown of Oedipus?"

"Precisely. If Alexander takes it by force then Greece will say he has lost divine favor; meanwhile these stories about a lame-footed specter killing Macedonian soldiers will make the story more juicy, the scandal more alluring."

"So it's the work of the Oracle? This master spy here in the citadel who passed secrets to the Thebans?"

Miriam scratched the side of her head. "I think so. But there's the rub. There's no secret entrance or passageway here. The citadel is built on a rock. It would be a hard nut to crack. I suspect Alexander will have some trouble destroying it." She held out her hands. "On the one hand, we have Memnon babbling about the shade of Oedipus within the citadel. On the other, we have two of his officers claiming they saw the same specter beyond the walls. The obvious conclusion, the force of logic, as Aristotle would put it, indicates this must be a ghost. How else can he move through thick brick walls and heavily guarded gates? Or wander around the camp at the dead of night and kill Macedonian veterans?"

"But you don't believe in ghosts?" Simeon grinned.

"No, I don't. I would like to know why the same specter trapped me in this chamber last night? Above all, I would like to know why dear old Memnon, who had about as much imagination as his dog and twice as much courage, should dress in full battle gear, clasp his sword around him, and throw himself out of this tower at the dead of night. Just think, Simeon." She pointed to the door. "No one could come through there." She banged her foot on the hard ground. "Or through the floor, or the roof, the walls while the window, well, we've reflected on that." She glanced at Simeon. "Old Memnon would have drawn his sword. Hercules would have launched an attack. They would have heard the outcry in Thebes. I wish Aristotle were here," she added. She got to her feet and raised her hand languidly.

"My dear," she mimicked the foppish but brilliant philosopher, "it's all a matter of logic." She minced up and down, one hand on her hip. Simeon laughed.

"Don't laugh, Simeon. You only show your stupidity! This is the problem. You can't find a solution," her voice became even more languid, "because you are looking at it, my dear boy, the wrong way." Miriam relaxed and clapped her hands together.

"And then there's the Crown," Simeon said impishly. "All

the camp knows about Alexander's outburst last night. How he nearly pinned Niarchos with a spear, how you intervened and said there was a way." He rubbed his stomach. "Is there one, dear sister? Alexander was bleary-eyed this morning, but he was all full of it: 'Miriam will have an answer,' he declared."

"And I can imagine what his companions said."

"Oh yes, they all began to chant: 'Miriam will have an answer! Miriam will have an answer!' Niarchos has already laid a wager with Perdiccas that you have got nothing of the sort; Perdiccas has accepted it."

Miriam went and looked out the window. Two soldiers were emptying the stores and placing them on a cart. She could hear their laughter on the breeze. She recalled the shrine of Oedipus, the Iron Crown resting in the clasps on the stone pillar, the bed of fiery charcoal, the spikes, and the dark shadowy pit where serpents writhed.

"Do you have any ideas, brother? You are always the more practical one?"

"There must be a way. The high priestess removes the Crown at certain times. We could bribe her?"

"Not someone like Jocasta," Miriam declared. "She's the sort who would rather die than give up her secrets. She is full of the mysteries, proud of what she guards."

"What about a long pole?" Simeon offered.

"It would have to be a very long one," Miriam countered, "but go on."

"You'd stretch it across, knock down the iron clasps, loop the Crown and pull it up toward you."

"It would have to be a very long pole," Miriam repeated. "And I don't think it could be done. I can't see how the clasps are pulled loose."

"Well, it might be possible. Why don't we try?" Simeon asked. "And what about those grappling hooks?" he added.

"You know, the sort sailors use when they try to come to grips with an enemy ship?"

"No. It would be like taking a hammer to smash a nut. Go down to the stores, Simeon. See if you can find one of those long sarissas the phalanx men carry. Let us visit our reverend Jocasta."

Miriam found it strange to leave the destruction of Thebes and enter the cool olive grove around the shrine. The sweet scent of leaves, the bittersweet tang of their fruit brought back memories of the groves around Pella, the Macedonian capital. The shrine itself was deserted. Three soldiers and their officer were squatting on the steps. The officer rose as Miriam and Simeon approached; he watched in amusement Simeon's difficulty with carrying the long spear.

"It takes years of practice," he declared, coming down the steps. "Put it down, man, you'll do someone an injury."

Simeon dropped it gratefully on the white chalk path. The soldier loosened his neck cloth and wiped the sweat off this throat.

"Before you begin mistress, I know who you are." He gestured toward the door and tapped the great bronze key that hung on his belt. "You can't go in."

"On the king's orders?"

"Mistress, the king's orders are quite explicit. I am to allow no one in unless they are accompanied by the priestess. I and three lads are on guard outside; the other two are in the shrine itself. We take turns." He hawked and spat. "I'm glad to be out here. Have you heard the stories?"

"We've heard them," Miriam declared. "What do you mean about two being inside?"

"Well, we are here," the officer explained. "I have the key to the vestibule. Beyond the bronze doors are two of my lads; they have locked themselves in the shrine. I did the dawn watch this morning. It's a sinister, eerie place, that char-

coal glowing in the middle of the floor, the spikes like dragons' teeth coming to bloom. I thought the snakes were simply a bluff but I saw three, long and slimy, slithering out."

"And the priestess Jocasta?" Miriam asked.

"She comes down here as do the others, with faces
painted, eyes darkened."

"Where do they live?" Miriam asked.

The captain pointed to his left. "The grove runs deep; follow the path round. They have a house there."

Miriam thanked him and followed his directions. The
path snaked between the trees and brought them into a large
glade or clearing. At the far end was a typical family house:
red-tiled roof, white walls with a small courtyard in front,
bound by a wooden palisade. The gate was open. Miriam
glimpsed chickens and a goat tethered to a post. The courtyard was empty as she entered. In the middle was a shrine to
some unknown god and beneath it a large tank to collect
and store rainwater. The small porter lodge was empty, but
smoke curled up from a hole in the roof at the back. Miriam
smelled cooking odors, cheese and spices that made her
mouth water. She looked around.

"Not even a guard dog," she muttered.

Jocasta appeared in the doorway. The old priestess's face
was clean of paint and she had hurriedly pulled a hood across
her balding head. She glanced at the sarissa or lance that
Simeon carried, and her age-seamed face crinkled into a
smile.

"I can guess why you are here," she called out. "Do come
over. You, young man, I think you had better leave the lance
outside; you might do yourself or someone else a damage."

She led them into the main room of the house. The floor
was tiled in black and white, a small brazier had been lit;
there were tables, a couch, chairs, and some Samian earth-
enware pots along the wall.

"My sisters are in the kitchen or in their chambers above."
She saw that Miriam was distracted by the beautiful piece of
linen pinned to the wall just inside the door: hoplites surrounded a king in his chariot who was talking to a dark-
haired man whose right foot was bandaged and whose left
hand held a club.

"That's Oedipus," she explained, "meeting his father,
Laius—a simple accident that led to murder."

Miriam stared at the painting. The Oedipus depicted here
was not frightening: a young man, his black hair curled and
oiled.

"I did that," Jocasta spoke up, "when I was young, but
now my eyes fade. I cannot execute the stitches as well as I
should. Sit down! Sit down!"

She made them sit side by side on the couch and hurried
out. She brought back two bowls of barley pottage, some
bread soaked in wine, and figs covered in goat cheese. She
put this on the table and served them herself, passing out the
food in small wooden dishes. She sat quietly and watched
them eat. Miriam did so quickly, rather embarrassed by the
way the old priestess just sat and stared at them.

"You said you knew why we were here."

"You've come to ask me about the removal of the
Crown?"

Miriam nodded.

"And you brought that wooden lance." She smiled. "It is
not long enough and, even if it was, you couldn't possibly
wield it over such a long distance. I'd be frightened that
you'd totter onto the charcoal." Her face became severe.
"Nor do you know the ritual: the Crown cannot be removed
by any tool or weapon brought into the shrine. Such an action would be blasphemous."

"Why can't you tell us?" Simeon demanded, "how it can
be removed?"

The old priestess's face grew even harder.

"Young man, there are ceremonies and rituals; the Crown of Oedipus is a sacred relic. If the gods wish Alexander to wear it, the gods will reveal it. And, as for your ridiculous pole, you'll either do yourself damage or possibly wreck the shrine." She saw Miriam staring up at the black beams. "Our house was spared," she murmured, "as was the shrine. A Macedonian officer told us not to worry and Alexander has kept his promise. However," she added softly, "I cannot help him in this matter."

"Do you believe that the shade of Oedipus now prowls the deserted city?" Miriam asked. "You've heard the stories?"

"Oh, yes," Jocasta said. "But it's not his shade. It's the old king himself."

Miriam got to her feet. "How do you know this?"

"I have seen him myself. Here among the olive groves, just standing, staring up at the house."

"You've seen him?" Simeon exclaimed.

"It's no shade or ghost," Jocasta added triumphantly, "but Oedipus himself! Who knows, he may even claim the Crown himself?"

Miriam was about to answer when there was a sound of footsteps outside, a woman's voice raised. Jocasta gestured at them to remain. She left and immediately came back. "It appears your king needs you back at his camp," she declared. "His mother, Queen Olympias, is about to arrive."

CHAPTER 7

IN THE END, Olympias did not arrive until just before dusk. Alexander had been almost beside himself with preparations. The camp was cleared, particularly the principal path to his pavilions and the small park containing the shrine to his favorite god. A guard of honor was prepared dressed in bronze cuirasses; white-and-red-leather kilts; burnished greaves; shields polished until they caught the light; and great Corinthian helmets that concealed most of the face, their red horsehair plumes thick and luxuriant. Rank after serried rank was drawn up. Alexander had a dais prepared, draped in purple and gold, to receive the woman whom he publicly called the best of mothers. Privately he confided to Miriam that Olympias charged too a heavy rent for his nine-months stay in her womb.

A squadron from the cavalry was sent out—the best horsemen in the army—along with musicians and standard bearers, to greet the queen. At last she entered the camp in a blare of trumpets and with men flanking her chariot on either side.

"Just look at her!" Alexander whispered. "By all that's holy! Just look at her! For Olympias, everything has to be dramatic; Mother never changes."

Miriam stared down at the lustrous chariot pulled by two white horses, their harness and strapping of burnished gold. The chariot itself was ceremonial—plated with silver, a gold rail along its high top. Olympias now clutched this with one hand, the other raised in salute. As she passed, the guardsmen clashed their spears against their shields and sang a poem of praise. Olympias was dressed in purple-and-gold robes over a snow-white tunic. Her reddish hair shiny, thick; the silver crown on her forehead was gold, encrusted with the most precious jewels: her beautiful, imperious face was hidden behind a silver mask that covered all but her eyes and mouth.

"Oh no," Alexander groaned, "she's in one of her Medea moods. The 'tragic queen' returns to Thebes." He pushed back his own cloak, stepped off the dais, and helped his mother out of her chariot. She bowed, almost a nod, and then let her son escort her onto the dais to receive the acclamation of the army. She did this, smiling, one hand raised, and all the time talking quickly to Alexander.

"That chariot's bloody uncomfortable!" she hissed. "I nearly fell off the damn thing! I want it mended!"

"There's nothing wrong with the chariot mother!" Alexander snapped. "It's built to go along smooth paths, not rocky ground!"

"Don't contradict me," Olympias retorted. "And don't scowl, Alexander; I've told you before, it reminds me of Philip."

Alexander forced a smile. Once the acclamation was over Olympias was led off the dais and into the pavilion. Simeon, Miriam, and the other companions followed. Olympias was given a seat of honor. Alexander on her right, Hephaestion on her left. Olympias now removed her silver mask and looked daggers at her son, her sea-gray eyes blazing with fury, her beautiful smooth face twitching in annoyance.

"She hates Hephaestion," Miriam whispered to Simeon, "and Alexander knows that."

The servants brought in wine bowls and water jugs. The cooks had surpassed themselves; animals had been hunted and killed and the fresh meat dressed in sauces. Each dish was presented first to Olympias but she was more interested in the silver-and-gold plate and cups looted from Theban treasuries.

"Don't worry Mother," Alexander rubbed his hands and stared round the tent, "I've put your portion aside to take back to Pella. When are you going?"

"I've just arrived," Olympias hissed. She picked up a cup and admired the pattern around the rim. "Don't be insolent, Alexander. I came to see Thebes but you've burned it. I also brought my troupe of actors."

The grin faded from Alexander's face. Olympias rolled back the sleeve of her gown.

"I have decided," she declared for all the tent to hear, "to stage the great trilogy of Sophocles—*Oedipus the King, Oedipus at Colonus,* and *Antigone.* In the first two I will play Jocasta, in the third Antigone. Ah, Miriam." She smiled dazzlingly down as the Israelite desperately tried to hide behind her brother. "You are an actress. You and your brother. You are both to join. I've heard about the play you put on, about the stories and traditions of your people. Niarchos, stop smirking; you can be Cleon. Perdiccas you can be Haemon. And of course," she glanced over her shoulder at Aristander, her old necromancer, "you can be Teiresias, the soothsayer."

"But he was blind!" Aristander moaned.

"If you don't play your part well, I will personally arrange that!" Olympias rapped. "Now, son, let us eat, and tell me all that has happened to you."

The evening remained tense. Alexander's companions always felt wary when Olympias was near. Sharp of eye, tart of tongue, and quick of wit, Olympias could be as vicious as one of her vipers. As the feast went on, she shifted from one mood to another. Miriam quietly confessed to Simeon that she could sit and watch Olympias all evening, provided she didn't have to sit too close. Sometimes Olympias was a tearful mother complaining about Alexander's officers back in Pella. Other times she was flirtatious, a young girl, or a doting mother with her only son, and when this didn't work, she became imperious, snapping out orders or poking Alexander's chest.

"I still miss your father." She now moved to the role of mourning queen.

The tent fell silent. No one dared say the truth: When Philip was alive he and Olympias had fought like cat and dog. Now Philip had gone to the gods, and his new wife, whom Olympias regarded as a deadly rival, had disappeared together with her baby son. Miriam caught the watery eyes of Aristander. Only he and she knew about that terrible graveyard behind the palace in the old capital of Aegae. The secret crypt and graves in which Olympias's victims had been quietly and secretly buried.

"And Memnon?" Olympias voice carried. "Poor Memnon! Alexander have you discovered what happened to him?"

"We have that matter in hand, Mother."

"If it was murder," Olympias narrowed her eyes, "I want to see the man crucified." She picked up her wine cup. "Now come, tell me about the shrine of Oedipus and his Crown. I heard rumors during my journey here. Why haven't you taken it? Where is it?"

Alexander began the lengthy explanation. Everyone else turned to their drinking and conversations. Miriam, whose eyes had grown heavy, leaned her head against her brother's shoulder and quickly fell asleep.

Jocasta, high priestess and custodian of the shrine of Oedipus, pushed back the stool on which she was sitting and walked to the window. Her chamber stood at the back of the house, overlooking an olive grove. Onto the small curtain wall below, torches had been lashed. Jocasta watched the pool of light intently. She was about to turn away in disappointment when she saw the figure slip out from the shadows and stand in the faint pool of torchlight. The figure moved unsteadily, dragging one foot as if lame. She could see he was dressed in goatskins, a rope girdle around his waist. His hair was shaggy and matted, his features hidden behind a leather mask, a cloth around his eyes. In his right arm swung a knotted club.

"It's the same every night," she whispered. "It's the same as before." Now she felt a thrill of excitement. The figure drew closer. She could almost feel the eyes glaring through the terrible mask. Jocasta leaned on the windowsill.

"What do you want?" Her lips mouthed the words.

"Mother, I have seen it!"

She turned. Antigone, her eyes heavy with sleep, stood in the doorway.

"I, too, have seen him," Jocasta snapped. She felt slightly disappointed that a junior priestess had also been given the opportunity to gaze on this mystical figure. Nevertheless, Antigone was her favorite, the daughter she'd never had: a wayward, slightly fey girl, with her dreams and desires to wander by herself. Jocasta turned and stared down. She thought he had gone but there was a movement in the shadows and again he stepped into the pool of light, one hand lifted.

"He's beckoning you," Antigone whispered. "Mother, he's beckoning you!"

Jocasta felt her stomach flutter with excitement. She had *her* dreams. She had seen omens and into visions of the night but this was real. Again the hand was raised, this time more urgently beckoning her to come.

"I must go!"

"No, Mother!" Antigone gripped her wrist. "It could be some form of trickery." Jocasta threw off her hand.

Then Jocasta picked up her cloak and wrapped it around herself. She returned the oiled wig to her shaven head, hung the sacred pectoral around her neck, and slipped her feet into her sandals. She sat on the edge of her bed and fastened the thongs.

"You stay here," she ordered. "Do not tell your sisters! If the god calls, I must respond." Jocasta blew out the oil lamp and, leaving Antigone standing in the darkness, hurried down the stairs, out through the back entrance, and across the small courtyard. She was about to undo the wicket gate but stopped at the voice, which sounded hollow, sepulchral.

"Come no further!"

"Who are you?" Jocasta whispered into the darkness. She could see nothing. She caught the smell of goatskin.

"Come no further!" the voice ordered, "until I tell you to!" Jocasta was trembling with excitement.

"Who are you?" she urged, "please."

"I am Oedipus, King of Thebes! Beloved of the gods! I have come to my city and it is wasted. In the shrine my Crown awaits!"

"Will you take it?" Jocasta asked.

"It is mine by right," the voice replied, "and not the plaything of a Macedonian prince. Come with me, Jocasta!"

She opened the wicket gate but stopped. The pool of light only stretched a little way; beyond, the olive grove was dark. Jocasta felt the cold night wind cool the sweat on her brow and neck.

Was this trickery?

"Come!" the voice ordered.

Jocasta stepped into the darkness. "I can't see you," she stammered. A warm hand caught hers and gently pulled her closer.

"Do not be afraid, Mother. We must be gone."

And Jocasta, thrilling at the voice of her god, followed his dark shape into the trees.

A few hours later the beggar known as Paemon came out of his hiding place among the pile of rocks in the olive grove and walked toward the shrine. Paemon was used to begging in front of the temples of Thebes but all of these were gone. When the city had been stormed, Paemon, who knew the streets and alleyways of Thebes, had fled like the wind. He had escaped the fury of the Macedonian phalanx, the wholesale plunder and looting that had taken place. Indeed, Paemon himself had indulged in some petty pilfering: a cup, some coins, some food. He had sheltered in the groves around the priestesses' house and had come out to sell his ill-gotten gains to the soldiers who guarded the shrine. They had been kindly enough, giving him coins, scraps of food, bread, cheese, and wine.

Now Paemon felt agitated. He had been roused from his wine-sodden sleep by two people moving through the grove. He watched them go and then he heard what sounded like sobbing, groaning, but he dared not leave his hiding place.

Now, curiosity had gotten the better of him; Paemon trotted like a dog. His bare foot caught on something and he stumbled. Falling headlong he scrambled about. The old woman's body lay there, her gown torn; the oiled wig had slipped off, revealing the wound, a savage blow that had cracked her skull like an egg. Paemon felt the corpse, cold and stiffening. Those old eyes stared out as if her soul had not gone to Hades but still lurked in the crumbling flesh. Despite the poor light Paemon caught their look of terror.

He peered around. What monstrosity now walked this grove? He looked at his hands. They were sticky with blood. Paemon got to his feet and ran to a nearby spring to wash himself. What could he do? Where could he go? What happened if the soldiers came? Would they arrest him? Would they put him on a cross to hang and writhe for days? The soldiers? Paemon's tired mind raced. He was innocent. The gods knew he was innocent! The full horror of what had happened dawned on him. The old woman was a priestess. Whoever had killed her was guilty of sacrilege and blasphemy!

Paemon stared up at the lightening sky. The Furies would come, sent by almighty Zeus to pursue the killer to the ends of the earth. Paemon found that he couldn't stop his teeth from chattering; his sore gums flared in pain. He scratched his crotch. Soldiers, men in armor would throw him about, joking and laughing, before they crucified him. But what about the soldiers in the temples? The captain of the guard was a kind fellow. He'd go there, tell him what he had seen.

Paemon ran, blundering out of the grove and onto the white track. Dawn was now breaking. He ran head down, and so he noticed them: small red blotches. He crouched down, touching one with his fingers. More blood. Paemon's heart thudded. He heard a sound and turned. The specter standing behind him seemed to have come out of the earth, from the dark halls of Hades. A cloth mask covered his face, around the eyes was a bloody bandage. Some wild animal skin covered his head and draped his body. Was it a goat? A lion? The specter just stood there. Paemon backed away;

the specter did not follow, but he brought one hand up. Paemon watched the club, knotted and gnarled. The ghastly figure then held up his other hand, clutching the Iron Crown. The ruby in the center gleaming like a fresh spot of blood in the morning light.

"Tell them all!" a voice grated. "Tell them that Oedipus has come to Thebes and taken his Crown!"

Paemon turned and fled. He didn't care now. He must reach the soldiers. He tried to scream but his mouth was dry. He found himself at the foot of the steps. He wiped the sweat from his face and stared round. Something was wrong. The four soldiers lay there, sprawling in pools of blood that was seeping out of the hideous wounds to their heads. Paemon climbed the steps and stared in horror.

"You are dead!" he murmured, "all of you are dead!" He banged on the doors. No answer. He saw the corpse of the young officer and went over to it. The key still hung on his belt. Paemon went to touch it, but, no, he'd seen enough! And, turning, he fled like the wind toward the Macedonian camp.

Miriam was roused by Simeon shaking her shoulder.

"Get up!" he hissed. "Miriam, something dreadful has happened!"

She threw back the rough horse blankets and dressed hurriedly, slipping on sandals, wrapping a cloak around her, pulling up the hood. She splashed water on her face, grabbed an ash cane and followed her brother out of the tent. Alexander was there. Perdiccas was beside him—he was captain of the guard for that day. He grasped a tattered beggar man by the shoulder. The fellow looked as if he were about to swoon with fear; his lined face was red and sweat-soaked. His straggly mustache and beard were drenched with perspiration.

Alexander talked to him soothingly, stroking his hair. Perdiccas released his grip. Alexander took a golden daric out of his purse and held it before the man's eyes. The man took it, his lips moving wordlessly.

"What are you saying?" Alexander asked.

"Your majesty, your worthiness, some wine and cheese."

Alexander, though his face looked severe, smiled and nodded at Simeon who went back into the tent, bringing out a wineskin and some cheese in a linen cloth. The man ate these, gnawing at the cheese and drenching his mouth in spurts from the wineskin.

"There," Alexander took the wineskin from him, "we need you sober."

A figure loomed out of the morning mist: Olympias, garbed as if she were about to enter Athens in triumph, her hair dressed and pinned with a silver jeweled crown. Her red cloak was of pure wool with a gold fringe, though in her haste, she'd pulled on a pair of army boots.

"I've heard the news," she snapped. "Alexander, what has happened?"

"I don't know, Mother. But now we are assembled, we'll all find out."

Miriam rubbed her face. She wanted to ask questions but she knew Alexander. He hated to waste time in useless banter. Through the morning mist came the clink of armor.

"That's my lads," Perdiccas declared. "Every one a guardsman in full armor." He resheathed his sword. "I also sent some of our Cretans into the grove. I've told them to go nowhere near the shrine."

"The temple?" Olympias gasped.

"This gentleman," Alexander patted the beggar gently on the shoulder, "has brought us a strange and horrid story. He stumbled across the corpse of a priestess in the grove. I think it's Jocasta, her head smashed in. He ran for help to the guards at the shrine."

The beggar man was now nodding. Miriam pushed her way forward.

"What's your name?"

"Paemon." He liked this woman. She had a severe face but the eyes were kindly.

"What happened at the shrine, Paemon?"

"I saw Oedipus."

"Oedipus is dead," Miriam said gently.

"Then the gods have sent him back. Terrible he was, a bloody rag around his eyes, his face covered by a mask. In one hand he carried a blood-encrusted club, in the other a crown."

"A crown?" Olympias's clawlike hands would have grasped Paemon's shoulder but Miriam gently intervened.

"I ran to the temple," he gabbled. "They are all dead!"

Alexander was marching away followed by Perdiccas. Miriam grasped Paemon by the arm and hurried after. They went through the camp, now silent except for the cries of the sentries or the occasional soldier wandering about, still recovering from the drinking and feasting of the night before. Fires had burned low. At the edge of the camp, ostlers and grooms were up, heavy-eyed, making their way down to the horse lines. They passed sentries and pickets. Word seemed to have spread: A small crowd of soldiers was now following the guardsmen who had formed a protective ring around the royal party. Perdiccas shouted at them to go away. They crossed the deserted quarter of the city. The tower and walls of the Cadmea could be seen faintly through the mist.

At last they reached the olive grove and then the white path. Paemon pointed to the ground, and Miriam saw the patches of blood. The scene on the temple steps was terrible.

The beggar man had described it correctly. All four soldiers sprawled there, great wounds in their heads. Two were armed; others still grasped their wine cups. The young officer was wearing his war belt. He lay there, eyes closed, as if asleep, face white as chalk and streaked with lines of blood. Perdiccas hammered on the doors with the pommel of his sword. Miriam took the key off the belt of one of the officers and opened the doors.

Inside, the vestibule was cold and deserted. Miriam, going ahead, pushed at the bronze doors. They swung open. Inside, the lamps and torches still glowed. An eerie place full of dancing shadows. She glimpsed the bed of charcoal glowing fiery red; then she saw the two guards, dark shapes huddled on the floor. The blood from their split heads snaked out across the gleaming marble. All were armed, but they looked as if they had died without a struggle.

Miriam looked toward the far end of the shrine. The iron clasps were down. The Crown was gone! Alexander swore. Olympias just stood there, her face pale, glaring at that empty pillar as if she had been cheated of something. Perdiccas and Miriam examined the corpses.

"They didn't even draw sword or dagger," Perdiccas murmured. "Look, Miriam, there are no wounds, no cuts, nothing."

Miriam felt the throat of each soldier, the skin was cold and clammy.

"They have been dead for some time," she said.

She went across to the corner. Here the soldiers' shields and lances were piled, wine cups and wineskins, linen cloths that contained stale bread, cheese, and bruised grapes. Alexander was still staring speechlessly at the empty pillar. Miriam took a wineskin and poured some into an empty cup. She sniffed and tasted it.

"Why that?" Perdiccas asked. Ever practical, the captain of

Alexander's bodyguards was more concerned about dead soldiers than a missing crown.

Miriam offered him the cup. "I wondered if it was drugged, but? . . ."

Perdiccas took it and sipped it. "Cheap and watery!" he replied, handing it back. He smiled thinly. "Niarchos could drink three of those wineskins and still do a dance."

Helped by Miriam, Perdiccas searched the shrine but they could find nothing amiss. No secret entrances or passageways. She went and crouched before the great rim of the charcoal pit. The fire was still glowing red hot. She stared carefully. She couldn't see any disturbance.

"What are you doing?" Olympias asked imperiously.

"The Crown is gone," Miriam replied. "I just wondered if someone had crossed the pits."

"It would have to be a long plank," Olympias scoffed.

"I know," Miriam replied, "and the shrine would reek of burned timber. . . . Perdiccas!"

"What are you going to do?" Alexander came up beside her.

"I want Perdiccas to clear a path through the charcoal. I want to look into the snake pit.

"Why?" Olympias asked.

But Alexander was already shouting out orders. Perdiccas brought in some of his guards; using their shields and pieces of wood, they sifted the charcoal, throwing the red hot pieces on top of the marble floor. Miriam calculated that the charcoal pit was at least one and a half feet deep. Beneath it lay a thick layer of white dust from previous fires. The shrine began to fill with smoke, which made them cough and made their eyes water. Now and again the soldiers had to break off and go out for fresh air. Meanwhile Perdiccas removed the corpses to the recess, covering them with their cloaks.

At last a small path began to form through the pit, the soldiers banking up the charcoal on either side. Miriam ordered a shield placed on each side of the banked charcoal, another one in between. She walked tentatively across the makeshift bridge and felt the blast of heat. At last she reached the edge where the iron spikes jutted up from the marble floor. She quickly looked over. One glance was enough: a host of snakes writhed there! She hurriedly went back, climbing over the black guard pole.

"Full of snakes," she declared.

"Then how was it done?" Alexander exclaimed. "What, it must be over two yards across the charcoal; the spikes and snake pit cover another four."

"How was it done?" he repeated.

Miriam was mystified. No one could have crossed those pits, not unless they had wings. Alexander crouched beside her, Olympias behind him, eager to catch every word. Simeon went out to help Perdiccas with the corpses on the temple steps.

"Here we have a shrine," Alexander began. "Its walls and floor are of marble. The Crown could not be reached by any secret tunnel or passageway. There's certainly no way to cross, what, about six yards of dangerous pit? And no one could stretch over it with a pole or a lance."

"I thought of that myself," Miriam murmured.

"No one could fashion a bridge," Alexander continued. "But that's only the beginning of the mystery. I have four of my best guards outside, their brains smashed in. They didn't even have a chance to draw their swords or offer any resistance. Think of that, Miriam."

Miriam closed her eyes. She thought of the soldiers squatting out on the steps. How could anyone approach and kill them in such a barbaric fashion without the alarm being raised?

"The officer carried a horn."

Alexander nodded. "If any war party, anything strange occurred, he was under strict orders to sound the alarm, but he didn't."

"So they are killed," Miriam continued. "We don't know whether their attacker took the keys, but he opens the doors and enters the shrine. Inside, two more soldiers are waiting. They are veteran guardsmen. Yet they, too, die in the same barbaric way. The intruder, or intruders," she added, "then manage to cross the charcoal and the serpent pit, release the clasps, take the Crown, and walk back through locked doors. . . . The beggar man claimed he saw Oedipus."

"He must have," Olympias whispered. "Oedipus has come back to his city!"

CHAPTER 8

"THAT IS NONSENSE!" Alexander exclaimed. "Oedipus is dead!" He sighed. "But I agree, 'I learn in sorrow upon my head the gods have rendered this terrible punishment they have struck me down and trod my gladness under foot.'"

" 'Such is the bitter affliction of mortal man.'" Olympias finished the quotation from Sophocles.

"It's strange," Miriam interrupted. Both the Queen and her son glanced at her.

"What is it?" Olympias snapped.

"Here we are, in a devastated Thebes," Miriam continued. "And what is happening? Echoes of Sophocles' play."

"Explain," Alexander insisted.

"Well, the city was founded by the hero Cadmus, whom misfortune had befallen even before the city was established: he was ravaged by a fierce dragon, which he killed. However, heaven was still against him and the dragon's teeth were sown on the site of Thebes. From these sprang a tribe of giants. Now, Oedipus was one of Cadmus's descendants." Miriam stared at the empty pillar. "Oedipus solved the mystery posed by the Sphinx but ended up killing his father, Laius, and marrying his mother, Jocasta, bringing down the judgment of the gods."

"And how does this apply to my son?" Olympias fumed.

"Well, Oedipus has returned. The city is devastated once more. Alexander, in a metaphorical way, has sown dragons' teeth. The Sphinx is represented by the riddles surrounding Memnon's death—the spy in the citadel, the dreadful murders, and the theft of the Crown."

"And so what do you suggest?" Alexander asked quietly.

"That we act quickly," Miriam replied. "Word of this will spread. It will be in Athens within a week. Alexander may have destroyed Thebes, but Thebes is destroying Alexander. His men are being mysteriously killed, the Crown wrenched from his grasp, the displeasure of the gods made manifest for all to see."

Alexander now forgot the Crown as he realized the implications of such propaganda.

"So what do you suggest," he teased, "woman of Israel?"

"All those who know about this," Miriam declared, hoping she was saying the right thing, "should be sworn to secrecy: the guards, everyone. This temple should sealed, the dead quietly buried."

"Continue," Alexander demanded.

"I don't believe in ghosts," Miriam declared, but she looked at the corpses, the blood coursing along the floor, and she repressed a shiver. "That poor beggar man saw flesh and blood. If Oedipus had been sent by the gods, why should he kill the poor priestess? Or the soldiers? Why not do something more dreadful, like call fire from heaven? A true immortal," she gibed, "could pass through marble walls and take the Crown."

"You don't take our legends seriously, do you?" Olympias, arms crossed, sauntered toward her. "You think they are children's fables. My son called you a woman of Israel, you with your hidden God, whose name cannot be mentioned!"

Miriam looked over Olympias's shoulder at Alexander, who had a warning look in his eyes. Olympias's face was full of rage, not at Miriam but at being cheated of the Crown. And, as was her wont, Olympias vented her rage on anyone and everyone around her.

"Yes, I think your stories are legends and fables," Miriam replied quickly, "but behind them are hidden truths; that is what we have here. Truth and lies. The truth is that Alexander conquered Thebes, which rose in rebellion."

Olympias's face softened. "And?"

"The lie is that someone wants to mock that victory. I don't think it's Oedipus's wraith or specter but flesh and blood. He is here to weaken Alexander's victory, to snatch a great prize from his hands. The theft and murders committed in the shrine are somehow connected to the death of Lysander and Memnon's fall from the tower."

"The Oracle?" Alexander asked.

"Yes, the Oracle. But I cannot see how he works. I discovered, my lord, that Memnon thought he had seen the shade of Oedipus in the citadel, yet two of his lieutenants saw him beyond the walls."

"Treachery?" Olympias asked. "Hidden doors and passages?"

"No," Miriam shook her head. "The citadel was well-fortified and guarded. Now this Oracle, dressed as Oedipus, terrorizes lonely sentries on the outskirts of the Macedonian camp. Tell me, my lord, imagine yourself as a sentry on the lonely heath land, a mile away from the camp. Someone approaches you."

"I'd call out to him to stop."

"But these don't," Miriam insisted.

"It could have been done by stealth."

Perdiccas had come back into the temple, and was standing behind her.

"One sentry, perhaps," Miriam replied. "Even two, but three or four? And the sentries here? If they'd seen someone approach they'd have issued a challenge. If the officer had thought it was threatening, he would have immediately raised the alarm, but that didn't happen."

"What are you implying?" Perdiccas snapped. "Some form of bribery and corruption among my men?"

"No, no, Perdiccas, don't stand on your honor," Alexander declared. "Miriam is trying to reach a conclusion."

"It's not much of one," she confessed. "But the murderer of these soldiers came alone. They saw him as a friend; therefore, he must be a Macedonian."

"Agreed." Alexander kicked at a pile of cold charcoal ash. "But," he continued, "let's say a Macedonian did approach the temple steps. He's welcomed by an officer and three guardsmen, the best my regiment can provide. What happens then? Does he start running about with a club? He may kill one but how can he slay three others and face no opposition?"

Miriam pulled a face. "I don't know. That's where my hypothesis fails."

"And once in here," Olympias snapped, "the soldiers welcome him with open arms?"

"That's a real mystery," Alexander declared. "The assassin has killed four of my soldiers; he takes the key and goes into the vestibule. Now the doors to the shrine are locked from the outside, but they are also barred from within." He pointed to the doors and the bronze bar hanging down.

"The soldiers inside will only lift that if the password is given by either their officer or the high priestess but we know that, by then, both of them are dead. Moreover, the two soldiers have heard nothing of the violence outside." He flailed his hands. "Yet the doors are unbarred, the assassin enters, quietly dispatches fighting men, and steals the Crown. How?" he demanded angrily.

"Again, I don't know," Miriam declared, her cheeks growing hot with embarrassment. "I can only describe what I think is logical."

Alexander patted her gently on the shoulder.

"But what now?" Perdiccas asked. "If I accept your conclusion, Miriam, this Oedipus is one and the same as the Oracle spy. He now has the Crown. Why doesn't he just flee?"

"Oh, he will, eventually," Miriam agreed. "But not too soon; that would arouse suspicion. True, he has the Crown, but what's he going to do with it? Now we go back to Sophocles. The playwright went to Athens; his tomb can still be seen outside the city gates."

"Of course!" Olympias exclaimed. "And in the second play, *Oedipus at Colonus,* the blinded king goes to Theseus, king of Athens for succor."

"Demosthenes!" Alexander exclaimed. He began walking up and down, rubbing his hands together as he did whenever he became excited. Now and again he would curl his fingers into a fist.

"He'll sell the Crown to Demosthenes. Oh, how the Athenians will laugh."

"That's why you must act quickly," Miriam insisted. "Issue a proclamation that we have the Crown."

"What good will that do?"

"It will cause confusion," Miriam declared. 'I am sure our ironsmiths could fashion a Crown with a red ruby in the center. If our suspicions are correct, if this Oedipus is going to sell the Crown to the Athenians, our action will cause chaos. Demosthenes does not want to buy a fake and proclaim himself a fool throughout the length and breadth of Greece." Alexander stopped his pacing. He smiled dazzlingly at Miriam and then, going forward, wrapped her in a hug. She smelled the sweat from his body—wine mingled with olives.

"You are choking me!" she gasped, although Miriam was more concerned by the viperish look in Olympias's eyes.

"I always said she was a clever girl," the queen declared. "Alexander," she purred, "you really should leave Miriam with me in Pella when you march against Persia."

"And I'll be dead within a week," Miriam whispered.

"Nonsense, Mother!" Alexander stood away but he held on to Miriam's hand. "Where I go, my companions always follow. Perdiccas, clear up the mess in here! Have the corpses quietly removed! Tell the guards to take an oath. Oh I, know some of them will chatter, but give them a gold piece each and tell them that if they blab, they could end up on crosses."

"And the beggar?" Perdiccas asked. "Shall two of my lads take him into the trees and cut his throat?"

"No, no please." Miriam gripped Alexander's fingers. She could see that Alexander was about to confirm Perdiccas's order. "Please!" she added, "there's been enough killing!"

"He's my prisoner," Alexander declared. "He's to be kept in honorable but very comfortable confinement. Mother, I suggest you go back to the camp. Miriam, where's Simeon?"

"Outside," Miriam replied. She was going to add that her brother could never stand the sight of blood but she bit her tongue just in time. They went out onto the steps; the corpses had been removed.

"We checked the wine and food, or what was left of it," Simeon declared. "There's no sign of any potion or philter. No evidence the guards were drugged."

Alexander nodded and snapped his fingers at Perdiccas.

"I want this shrine closed." He paused halfway down the steps. "How could they?" he whispered.

"What?" Miriam asked.

Alexander didn't reply but, shaking his head, walked down the steps and strode into the grove. Miriam followed. Cretan archers now squatted among the trees; they rose as the king approached.

"Where's the corpse?" he asked their commander, "the priestess?"

"There's no corpse, my lord."

"What?"

"We have searched, sir."

"Where's that beggar man?"

"He led us to the spot, sir, but there was no corpse. The earth appears to have been disturbed, kicked and scuffed. Something happened there. Come and see!"

The captain led them to the spot deep in the grove, a small clearing with a spring nearby. The patch of grass where the corpse must have lain had been brushed as if someone had tried to hide all signs of the priestess's murder. The light was poor; Miriam squatted down. Dried flecks of blood were still visible, and she could see where someone had brought water from the spring to wash away the rest.

"Have the grove searched," she demanded. "The assassin apparently came back, took the corpse, and hid it elsewhere." She lifted her head and sniffed the breeze. At first she thought she must be mistaken. She smelled not only the acrid wood smoke but something else, the stench of fat left in a pan over a burning fire.

"In that direction." She pointed deeper into the trees where the grove stretched beyond the shrine.

"I smelled it, too!" the Cretan replied.

"Didn't you investigate?" Alexander asked.

"Sir, all of Thebes smells of burning."

Alexander snapped his fingers and the Cretan hurried off. Alexander squatted down next to Miriam, poking at the earth with his dagger.

"Why burn the corpse?" he murmured. "That's what's happened isn't it, Miriam?"

She agreed.

"But why?" Simeon echoed Alexander's question.

"I don't know."

Alexander got to his feet and, not waiting for them, strode off, following the Cretan into the trees. Miriam, wrapping her cloak more firmly around her, looked at Simeon, shrugged, and followed. The olive grove apparently ran beside the shrine and then around to the back. The deeper they went into the trees, the stronger the offensive stench grew. At last, just behind the temple, the tree line broke and they reached the edge of a small glade. The Cretan commander was standing in a spot where small rocks thrust up from the earth. He was squatting down, hand over his mouth and nose, staring at a great patch of burning black remains. The smoke was still rising in spiraling gray wisps. Miriam approached. The corpse, or what remained of it, lay in a smoldering bed of ash. No distinguishing elements remained. The flesh had shriveled and bubbled; the bones were charred and had snapped.

"She must have been drenched in oil," the Cretan declared. "Drenched in oil and set afire." He drew his dagger and, poking through the ash, pushed the tip through the eye socket of the skull and lifted it up. He pointed to the great hole on the side.

"That's her death wound," he declared. "Her skull was shattered!"

"That's why the beggar man met Oedipus," Miriam declared. "He was going back into the grove to dispose of her corpse."

The stench was so acrid that Alexander had to pinch his nostrils and walk away.

"Clear up the remains!" he shouted back. "Put them in a jar! The priestesses have a house here, haven't they?"

"Yes," Miriam replied.

"Then hand the remains to them." Alexander went back into the trees, squatted on the fallen log, and put his face in his hands.

"Our killer has been busy," he murmured. "And it's my fault. I should have put guards in these trees. I issued a decree. All temples and their sacred groves were to be protected. I just didn't want any of my men to give offence to the priestesses."

"The killer had a free hand," Miriam declared. "He could wander the grove, plot mayhem, and carry it out under the cloak of darkness. True, more soldiers may have prevented it, but, there again, I suspect the assassin would have only changed his plans."

"In what way?" Alexander said crossly.

"He always intended to seize Oedipus's Crown," Miriam replied coolly. "By fair means or foul, probably the latter. He was determined to wreak havoc and destruction. However, let's not concentrate on what might have been and what should be. By the way, your mother's right, my lord, being cross doesn't suit you."

Alexander chuckled. "I haven't eaten and I can still taste yesterday's wine."

"What is more important," Miriam persisted, "is possibly the mistake our Oedipus made in burning that corpse. Why not just leave it out in the grove for all to see? I believe that the poor old woman was tortured for the password and for the instructions as to how the Crown was to be removed."

"But she was a stubborn old thing."

"Stubborn is as stubborn does," Miriam replied. "But can you imagine being enticed into a grove by some horror from Hades who then binds you and begins some subtle torture."

"Someone would have heard her scream," Alexander objected.

"Not if she was gagged. Eventually she would have broken. Whatever, Oedipus or the Oracle did not want us to see the signs of his destruction. Indeed, I wager her murder will be placed at your door."

Alexander cursed and got to his feet.

"Her death will have to remain a secret," he declared. "I'll send orders to guard the priestesses' house. They'll not be allowed out to spread rumors."

"Let me go there first," Miriam requested. "I haven't washed or changed, but those unfortunates had better be informed of what has happened." She stared up at the entwined branches; the sky looked threatening with lowering gray clouds. We should be gone from here, she thought. Oedipus, horrors of the night, a devastated city, and a shrine that seems set to sour Alexander's great victory. She glanced at her brother.

"Simeon, what will you do?"

"He'll come back with me," Alexander offered.

Miriam watched them go, listening to the crackle of bracken; then the grove fell silent. She stayed still and listened. No sound of birdsong. Was this place cursed? She had talked so rationally, dismissing all fanciful notions! She swallowed hard. This was a sacred place, to Thebans as well as to all of Greece. A great sacrilege had occurred. And what if Oedipus, that shadow of the night, still lurked among the trees? Miriam grasped her walking cane and hurriedly left the clearing. The Cretan archers were assembled, their captain calling out orders. Miriam approached him and made her request. The fellow nodded.

"Two of my lads will go with you."

"They must not enter the house," Miriam declared. "The priestesses will be frightened enough."

The archers went before her, one of them claiming he knew in which direction the house lay. Miriam had visited the place the day before but she was still glad of the archers' company. Images teemed in her mind: blood-splattered corpses in the shrine, the blackened, burnt remains of the old priestess. A killer was prowling Thebes, and he had already attacked her, trapping her in Memnon's chamber. It would only be a matter of time before he struck again. When they reached the priestesses' house, Miriam told the archers to be vigilant and walked into the courtyard. The door was off its latch. She pushed it open and walked into the sweet-smelling atrium. A young priestess appeared from out of the kitchen. She was dressed in a white linen shift, her feet bare. She wore no wig, and her face looked white and anxious.

"Where's Mother?" she demanded.

The other priestesses sat in the kitchen, clustered around the table. From the smell, Miriam realized that they had been cooking.

"We were to have a feast today."

"You are Antigone, aren't you?"

The young priestess nodded.

"We were to have a feast today." She continued as if Miriam hadn't interrupted. "Jocasta said we should celebrate our deliverance."

"Deliverance from what?" Miriam asked.

The young woman waved her forward.

"Your master Alexander, he has been most kind to us. He has kept his word. The shrine and this house have not been troubled."

"But you are Thebans, and your city is destroyed."

"Jocasta thought differently," Antigone murmured.

"When Pelliades killed Lysander and put his corpse upon a cross, Jocasta cursed him. If Alexander had been beaten off by Thebes, who knows what might have happened to us?"

"Why?" Miriam asked.

"Pelliades, leader of the council, was very angry with Jocasta. He accused her of being pro-Macedonian. In the city, so great was the hatred of Alexander that such an accusation carried the death sentence."

"But you are priestesses?"

"Pelliades wouldn't have cared. He was ruthless."

Miriam nodded. She wondered if Hecaetus had any luck among the Theban prisoners. What a pity they couldn't have laid hands on Pelliades. What a song he would sing, what information he could give. A man who had lost everything might reveal the name of this spy. She looked at the other priestesses and recalled the reason for her visit.

"I'd best come in," she murmured. "I have something to tell you."

"You should really wait until Mother returns."

Miriam took her gently by the elbow and led her into the stone-paved kitchen. She stood at the end of the table.

"What time did Jocasta leave?" she asked.

"It must have been very late last night," Merope, a middle-aged priestess replied.

"Why?"

"She is high priestess," Antigone declared. "She may have visited the shrine, sat and prayed there; sometimes she did that.

"She didn't visit the shrine," Miriam declared. "Your shrine has been violated. The Crown has been stolen. And, I am afraid, Jocasta has been killed."

The priestesses looked at her in stunned silence. Antigone's hand went to her mouth. She sat like a frightened child.

Merope was the first to recover. She sprang to her feet, kicking the stool aside, her face contorted with rage.

"You did that! You and your bloody-handed masters. You've murdered Jocasta and stolen the Crown. You've committed blasphemy and sacrilege. All of Greece will know!" Her eyes filled with tears. "Jocasta was our friend, our mother. Consecrated to Apollo." She paused gripping her stomach. "Jocasta was also your friend, a brave woman. She tried to save your envoy Lysander."

The other women were now weeping. Miriam stood her ground. Merope picked up the stool and sat next to Antigone, putting an arm around her shoulder.

"I swear on my life," Miriam declared quietly, "by any oath you wish me to take—by Apollo, by land and sky, by the name of my unknown God—Alexander of Macedon had nothing to do with this sacrilege."

A wail of protest greeted her words.

"No, no listen!" Miriam held her hands out. "I have come here on my own. Two archers stand outside, but they are forbidden to enter. Please!" Her voice rose at their cries of protest. "Please listen to what I say. I can produce proof!"

Merope was about to object but Antigone clutched her wrist.

"Let the Israelite speak," she declared. "There is no lie in her face or voice. Let us at least listen."

She gestured to a stool. Miriam sat down and fought to hide her own fear. The thin, slender priestess known as Ismene had brought her hand from beneath the table. She was gripping a knife. Miriam held her gaze.

"An attack on me," she added, "will achieve nothing. Let me tell you what I know."

They sat and listened as Miriam began to describe what had happened. The murder of Lysander; the mysterious death of Memnon; the presence of a spy in the Cadmea; the deaths of the sentries; the appearance of Oedipus; and the events of the previous night: the deaths of the Macedonian guards, the violation of the shrine, and the murder of Jocasta. When she had finished, they cried again, but this time more softly, more controlled.

"I speak the truth," Miriam affirmed.

Ismene threw the knife onto the table. "I accept that you do."

"So why did Jocasta leave?" Miriam asked.

Antigone replied, telling her what had happened, how this shadowy figure, undoubtedly Oedipus, had been seen around the house on different evenings, standing just beneath Jocasta's bedroom window. How the old priestess had kept a vigil, waiting for him to come; how last light she had accepted the invitation to go out.

"I thought she was safe," Antigone concluded. "What could an old priestess fear from the god whose shrine she guarded?"

"But weren't you anxious," Miriam asked, "concerned when she didn't return?"

"No. The Macedonians were friendly. Jocasta spoke most kindly about the guards at the shrine. They called her Mother, did everything to help. The officer, in particular; he was most courteous and kind." Antigone smiled through her tears. "Jocasta even called him son. I thought she would go there. She often did. It was her second home, the whole purpose of her life. So why should someone kill her? Treat her so barbarously?"

"Tell me," Miriam said, "did any of you know the password to the temple?"

They shook their heads.

"And before you ask," Ismene spoke up, "we didn't know

how the Crown could be removed; that was a secret passed from one high priestess to another."

"Are you sure?" Miriam asked.

"By the land and the sky," Antigone retorted, "I cannot tell you. Nor can any of my sisters."

"What will happen now?" Ismene asked.

Miriam explained that Alexander wished to keep the matter as secret as possible. That they still had hopes of trapping the murderer and that they were not to leave the house.

"You will be well looked after," Miriam added reassuringly. "The king is firm on this matter. It is to be kept secret until it is resolved."

Miriam got up, walked to the door, and stared out. The grove did not look so green and peaceful now, but dark and threatening. She couldn't see the archers and she realized that it would take some time for Alexander to muster a guard and send them out to protect this place. Antigone joined her.

"What is the matter?" she asked.

"Nothing," Miriam replied. She scratched her head. "Show me where Jocasta saw Oedipus."

Antigone led her out of the house and around to the back. The small wicket gate was unlatched. Miriam went through and stood at the edge of the wood. She could see no marks in the soil. She looked around. The house was built in a clearing surrounded on all sides by the olive grove; the trees clustered thick and close. Jocasta, she thought, must have gone willingly but then, deeper in the woods, the mysterious stranger must have struck.

"A place of death." Antigone spoke Miriam's thoughts. "This used to be so different."

Miriam looked around at her.

"The citizens of Thebes called this the women's place. Before the troubles started, few men came here except when the oath was to be taken and the Crown removed. Now it is a place of the sword, of violent men." Antigone drew close and grasped Miriam's hand. "Who was it?" she asked. "Why did he come every night and stare up at Jocasta's room?" She pointed to the window, the shutters were still flung back.

"I don't know," Miriam replied, "but I suspect that our killer is a cunning and devious man. His presence every night was comforting. Jocasta would have been pleased. Perhaps she thought she was seeing a vision, some form of reassurance from the gods. A promise that, though Thebes had fallen, the shrine would remain. Anyway, once the killer gained Jocasta's confidence, it was easy to entice her down. However he did not want her, but only the secret she held."

Miriam was about to continue when she heard a scream, like the shriek of a bird, from the front of the house. She hastened around, Antigone behind her. The front door was open. Ismene had apparently walked out across the yard to the edge of the olive grove. Now she came back, her hands covered in blood.

"They are dead!" she screamed. "The guards you brought! They are both dead!"

Miriam rushed by her. Forgetting any sense of danger, she crossed the yard to the edge of the clearing. The Cretan archers lay a few paces apart, blood seeping out from the terrible wounds in their skulls.

CHAPTER 9

MIRIAM HEARD A crackling amidst the trees. Someone was lurking, staring out from the tangled greenery. She caught a movement, a figure stepping out from behind one of the thick, gnarled trees. She turned and ran, pushing the priestesses ahead of her through the door of the house and slamming it behind her. Miriam brought down the bar, screaming at the others to shut the windows. No sooner was this done than something thudded against the shutters, and wisps of smoke curled into the house. Miriam had been in enough sieges to know what was happening. Their assailant was in the trees. He had lit a fire, taken the Cretan's weapons, and was now loosening fire arrows at the house. She murmured a prayer of thanks that the building was of stone, its roof of red tiles. But what would happen if there was more than one attacker? If they tried to force the door? Was this the horrid-shaped Oedipus who had already caused such bloody chaos? Or was it a roaming party of Theban soldiers? The priestesses were frantic with anxiety. Miriam shouted at them to keep silent, and she told Antigone to wash the blood from Ismene's hands. What was happening was a result of foolishness and naïveté. Alexander had ravaged the city of Thebes but that damned grove, with its tortuous paths, had not been guarded. From the top of the stairs Antigone screamed. Another fire arrow had hit a shutter on the upper floors. Others followed. Smoke curled in, thick gray wisps as the dry wood caught fire. Miriam noticed water jars in the kitchen. Some were too heavy to move but she scooped water into jugs and cups; the others did likewise thereby drenching the shutters from within. Ismene was beside herself with fear, sitting at the foot of the stairs, hands waving, feet stamping, shrieking like a child. Antigone ran to her, slapping her hard on both cheeks before hugging her close and crooning sweet sounds into her ear like a mother would her child.

"Do you have any weapons?" Miriam asked. "A sword, a spear?" She coughed as the smoke caught in her nostrils and throat.

"Nothing but kitchen knives," Antigone replied.

Miriam noticed the peephole in the front door, a slat of wood that could be pulled aside. She opened this carefully and peered out. The forest edge looked deserted. She was about to sigh in relief until she noticed wisps of smoke along the far wall. She stared in horror as a figure, terrible to behold, stood up. He was dressed in wild skins, a mask over his face. She could see that his hands and wrists were stained in blood but that he was no ghost or specter. With his great horn bow he loosed another fire arrow. What did he hope to achieve? Miriam hastily closed the shutter as the arrow hit the door. She ordered the priestesses to drench this with water and she reopened the shutter. Miriam could see nothing untoward. Then the figure came up again, arrow notched, but this time he paused, looking behind him as if he had heard some sound. The bow was hastily dropped. Miriam closed the shutter and went to sit with the rest as they huddled at the bottom of the stairs. She heard shouts, the clink of armor. She grasped a knife from the kitchen table and opened the shutter. Macedonians had arrived: guardsmen in their plumed helmets, shields and spears in their hands, but the officer directing them looked confused. He could see that the house had been under attack and he was vainly searching for the assailant. Miriam opened the door.

"Over here!" she called.

The officer hurried forward, wiping his sweat-soaked brow on the back of his wrist. He recognized Miriam.

"What is the matter, mistress? We've seen the corpses of two Cretans. They were killed in the same way as the sentries around the camp, skulls staved in, brains and blood spilling out."

"We were attacked," Miriam replied, "by whomever it was that killed the Cretans." She pointed at the charred shutters, the still-smoldering doors. "Though no real harm has been done," she forced a smile, "my legs still tremble and my stomach is pitching."

The officer turned around shouting orders.

"Weren't there soldiers in the grove?" Miriam asked.

The guards officer shook his head.

"There's a rumor," he declared, "that something happened at the shrine. Perdiccas ordered the guards and archers stationed there back to camp to take an oath."

Miriam pulled a face. Of course, that was what Alexander had decided earlier. In fact, she had recommended it. The assailant must have discovered this and exploited the gap between the soldiers leaving and fresh ones arriving. Yet how had he killed those archers? Such men were fierce fighters? They wouldn't have given their lives easily.

"I want a guard around this house!" Miriam declared. "No one is to approach the priestesses unless they carry the personal seal of Alexander."

The officer agreed.

"You are the Israelite, aren't you? Perdiccas told us to look out for you."

He spoke with that lazy, easy charm, a characteristic of Alexander's officers. Once they recognized her, they would do what she asked and, in teasing good humor, offer no objection. Miriam stared back through the open doorway. The priestesses had now regained their composure. Antigone, despite being the youngest, calmed them down, served them cups of watered wine. Antigone was cool, self-assured. During the attack she had acted as bravely as any soldier.

What, Miriam wondered, if there was more than one Oedipus, a group of ardent Thebans dedicated to Alexander's discomfiture? Miriam crossed her arms and walked away, leaving the officer looking nonplussed. Such an explanation, she reasoned, would resolve a number of mysteries. How Oedipus could have been seen inside and outside the Cadmea. And what if this group was both male and female? A lonely soldier would not regard some pretty girl as a threat though a woman like Antigone could wield a club as deadly as any man. Had Antigone encouraged Jocasta to go out? Had someone like Antigone, or indeed her sisters in the order, learned both the password and the secret way of lifting the Iron Crown? Such thoughts ran wild in her mind. One Oedipus? Two, or even a dozen?

"Mistress."

She turned around. The officer was looking at her strangely.

"I'll leave a guard here, as you say. Is there anything else?"

"Yes, yes, I'm sorry," Miriam apologized and walked over to him. "Tell your men not to stay alone or to stand guard by themselves. Treat anyone who approaches you—man, woman, or child—as suspicious, unless as I said, they carry the King's personal seal."

The officer nodded and shrugged. "I would agree with that."

Antigone came out of the house, a blanket wrapped around her, though her feet were still bare. Her eyes were red-rimmed but otherwise she looked serene enough. Miriam recalled her suspicions. Addressing Miriam, she said, "We have allowed no one near this house." Turning to the officer, she continued, "And we will not unless they are escorted by you; that's how it all began."

"What do you mean?" Miriam asked.

"When the city was stormed," Antigone replied, "the king sent an officer with the seal of Macedon to assure Jocasta and the rest that we and the shrine would be safe."

Miriam half heard her; Alexander had done that throughout the city, dispatching envoys to the different temples and shrines to afford them protection. The priestess turned, about to go back to the house.

"Did you leave the shrine during the siege?" Miriam asked.

Antigone whirled round. Miriam saw the flush on her face.

"We have nothing to do with war," she declared, drawing herself up. "The only time was when the elders of the council led by Pelliades came to the shrine to take the oath that they would fight to the death. And, of course, to ask Jocasta to act as the intermediary to swear that Lysander would be returned unharmed."

"An oath they broke," Miriam declared. "Why did they come to see Jocasta?" she continued. "Why not to some other shrine or temple?"

Antigone licked her lips, opened her mouth to reply, but then glanced away. "It was my idea," she answered.

"What?" Miriam drew closer. She took the woman by the elbow and led her into the house.

"I am not what I appear to be." Antigone closed the

door. She peered around Miriam to ensure that she was out of earshot of the rest.

"You are a priestess," Miriam declared, "a keeper of the shrine."

"I am also kinswoman to Pelliades, leader of the Theban council." She glimpsed the surprise in Miriam's eyes.

"Pelliades came here," she declared in a rush. "He was full of what he called great news. Alexander's army had been massacred in the Thessaly mountains. The Macedonian king was dead, the League of Corinth dissolved. Thebes would be free again."

"And he came here to ask Jocasta to intervene?"

"No, no. He came here to see me," Antigone retorted. She rubbed her cheek. "He always did. I'm his niece. He had no children himself and often brought gifts for myself and the other sisters. I'll never forget that morning; Pelliades was almost dancing with joy."

"He and who else?" Miriam asked.

"Telemachus, his confidant, his aide. They were rejoicing. They'd poured oil on their heads and drunk quite heavily. All Thebes, they said, would soon know the news."

"Why didn't you tell us this?" Miriam interrupted.

"You never asked," Antigone replied in mock innocence. "But then again, Miriam Bartimaeus, when Alexander's soldiers are marauding through the city and Pelliades is at the head of their list of wanted men, it is not the time to declare kinship!"

"Did Pelliades tell you" Miriam asked, "how he had learned such news?"

"He was going to but Telemachus restrained him, urging him to caution. He said it wasn't right that I should know but Uncle was insistent. He said they had a spy in the Cadmea. Someone who had Thebes' interest at heart. Telemachus laughed at that. More like Persian gold, he quipped. Pelliades, however, said this man was a friend of Demosthenes and that he had confirmed the news, a closely held secret in the citadel, that the Macedonians had suffered a terrible setback in Thessaly."

"Did he give any indication, please," Miriam grasped her hand, "as to who this person was?"

"He said he was an officer."

"Did Jocasta know all this?"

"Oh yes, she always insisted that she be present when Uncle was visiting." Antigone smiled sadly. "We are all consecrated virgins and Jocasta took her duties very seriously. Moreover, there was a secret agreement between Jocasta and the council that if Thebes ever fell Jocasta was to take the Crown and hide it."

"Then why didn't she?"

"Jocasta was furious with Pelliades. He had broken his oath to her and killed Lysander. She cursed him, told him never to visit this house again. I think Pelliades would have taken the Crown himself but the council would never have accepted such blasphemy."

"And this spy?" Miriam prompted her. "And Lysander?"

"Well, this was before Pelliades broke his oath. He said he wanted to avoid all bloodshed, that he would be happy if the Macedonian garrison left, walked out of Thebes, and never came back. I remember asking him why their spy didn't just open the gates. Telemachus laughed. He reminded me that there was one main gate and a small postern door; their spy had told them that both were closely guarded."

"Of course," Miriam interrupted, "and if the citadel was attacked, the Macedonians would have sold their lives dearly."

"Naturally."

"But if Pelliades and Telemachus wanted the Macedonian garrison to leave, why didn't they negotiate with Lysander instead of killing him?"

"Jocasta never understood that," Antigone replied. "You see, when Pelliades was talking about negotiations and avoiding bloodshed, Jocasta offered her mediation. She was a priestess; she would guarantee Lysander's safety. Pelliades seized on that, claiming it would be very useful."

"But what changed his mind from honorable negotiations to foul murder, displaying Lysander's corpse on a cross?"

"Jocasta said," Antigone went and sat at the foot of the stairs, "she said it all occurred so quickly. As you know, the Thebans had built a palisade around the Cadmea."

"Until then," Miriam asked, "the Macedonians had been allowed to wander through the city?"

"Oh yes, until everything became tense and rumors started to spread. You see, at first, they were just rumors. Alexander dying, his army being defeated, a revolt in the Macedonian capital at Pella. When these rumors were confirmed as fact," Antigone sighed, "The palisade was built, the citadel put under a virtual state of siege."

"Then negotiations were opened?"

"Yes, and you know what happened. Captain Memnon sent out Lysander." Antigone waved her hand. "You asked me why they killed Lysander. Afterward Pelliades came here; he tried to make his peace with Jocasta." She smiled wryly. "He wasn't even allowed in the yard. So I had to go out to meet him at the gate. Of course, I was furious as well. I asked him why he had violated Jocasta's oath, his promise to her and to me. Pelliades was more sober-minded now. He said that when Lysander came out, one of the Thebans councillors had said something that, if Lysander took it back to the citadel, might reveal the identity of their spy. Indeed, Lysander seemed to recognize this; he became alarmed and stepped back. The councillor, realizing his mistake, drew his dagger and, before Pelliades could stop him, plunged it into Lysander's throat. Pelliades claimed that he had no choice but to display the corpse, turn what had happened to their advantage, show the garrison that there was really no hope whatsoever."

Miriam opened the door and stared out. The officer was arranging a guard around the house. She closed the door and leaned against it, a tingle of excitement in her stomach. She had finally discovered a loose thread.

"And you have no idea," she asked, "what this councillor said?"

Antigone looked as if she was going to shake her head.

"Please!" Miriam went and knelt before her. "Pelliades has gone. Thebes is a desert. It's no longer now a question of just Macedon. Jocasta's murder must be avenged."

Antigone put her face in her hands.

"I did ask Pelliades. He was furious at the councillor. Oh, they didn't care very much about Lysander, but their spy in the Cadmea was very valuable. If I remember correctly, the councillor jokingly referred to the spy as *a woman*."

"A woman?" Miriam exclaimed.

"That's what he said. It apparently meant something to Lysander. According to Pelliades, Lysander became pale. He actually spat out, "That treacherous bitch!" She spread her hands. "That's all I can tell you."

Miriam went and opened the door. She called across to the officer and asked him to send a message to the Cadmea demanding that the officers Demetrius, Patroclus, Melitus, Alcibiades, together with Cleon, meet her in the mess hall.

"May I have an escort as well?" she added.

"Of course the officers are ready. And by the way, mistress, my men have scoured the woods, and they can find no trace of the attacker."

"And his weapons?" Miriam asked.

"As I have said, no trace."

Miriam thanked him and closed the door. Antigone still sat at the foot of the stairs, arms crossed, rocking gently backward and forward. Miriam caught her by the arm and helped her to her feet. "You're safe," she reassured her. "Alexander will not lift his hand against you." Miriam walked Antigone away from where the others, now much calmer, sat in the kitchen peering out. "Antigone, I trust you. Is there anything else you can tell me?"

Antigone's dark-green eyes shifted.

Miriam continued, "The other priestesses, could they have been involved in Jocasta's death? Let me explain. Someone is able to move around the Macedonian camp."

"They were all in the house when that man attacked."

"No, no," Miriam declared, "what happens if there's a killer, and a woman, one of the priestesses, is working with him?" Miriam flinched at the hardness in Antigone's eyes. "I have helped you. I have confided in you and for that you have my thanks and Alexander's protection."

Antigone's face softened. "I apologize," she murmured, "but the Crown is gone, the shrine is violated. What happens to us now?"

Miriam patted her on the shoulder. "Alexander will take care of you. There are other temples, other shrines that could use your skills. I beg you to reflect further on what I have said. Is there anything else you can tell me? Be prudent." She stepped away. "And do not leave this house."

Miriam made her farewells and reached the Cadmea just after noon. During her walk back she could see that Alexander had acted vigorously. The revelry in the camp had been cut short. Soldiers and archers now patrolled the olive groves. An entire corps had been deployed around the shrine. At the citadel the garrison had been strengthened, the men standing to arms. Officers and heralds were moving about, proclaiming that no Macedonian was to wander by himself. Any stranger who approached an outpost must be recognized as an enemy. She found Demetrius and the rest waiting for her in the mess hall, lounging on benches; this time there were no grins or sly jokes. They soon assembled around the main table.

"I can see that you have heard the news." She bit her tongue.

"What news?" Alcibiades lisped.

"The dead guards?" Cleon asked.

"And the other business?" Demetrius snapped.

"What other business?" Miriam demanded.

"Oh, we have heard gossip, rumor. Something happened at the Oedipus shrine."

"I have not come to talk about that. Is it possible to have some watered wine, food? I haven't eaten since last night."

Cleon hurried off to the kitchen. He brought back a small bowl of watered wine, cut-up bread, a small pot of honey, and some rather wizened apples.

"It's the best I can do," he apologized.

Miriam thanked him. She nibbled at the food and sipped at the wine.

"I have learned two things," She said, clearing her mouth. "First, before matters became tense in Thebes, you were allowed to wander the city at will?"

"Of course," Demetrius replied. "Beer shops, wine booths, the pleasure of the brothels. You know soldiers, Miriam, no commander likes to keep them cooped up like chickens. But, as I told you, the rumors started, two of our lads disappeared. Memnon ordered us back into the citadel and then the palisade was built."

"But you could go where you wanted before things turned sour?"

"Oh, yes," he agreed.

"What's the second thing?" Melitus asked.

"Ah!" Miriam put the wine bowl down. "I know why Lysander died. I honestly think," Miriam continued, "the Theban council simply wanted to get you out of the Cadmea and well away from Thebes. There was no secret plan to massacre you. They simply wanted you out and their citadel back. Now, in the negotiations between the Thebans and Lysander one of the councillors made a terrible mistake. He referred to their spy as "that woman." Now apart from the servant girls, there was no high-ranking lady or wife of an officer. Yes?" She studied their faces quickly and caught the flicker in Alcibiades eyes. "However, Lysander seemed to know exactly what this councillor was talking about. He reacted. The Thebans realized their spy had been betrayed—"

"—So Lysander was killed." Cleon finished the sentence.

"I suspect," Miriam declared, "that the councillor was referring to a man. I ask you now, on behalf of the king, insulting though this epithet is, why should Lysander become alarmed?" Miriam could tell that the officers were alarmed by what she had said. Alcibiades blushed, Demetrius became agitated. "I'm an Israelite," she declared. "I am not Macedonian. However, I have lived at Philip's court. The old king was killed by Pausanias, one of his bodyguards. Pausanias, how can I put it?"

"He liked dressing up as a woman," Patroclus scoffed. "It was well known. And you are right, Israelite, there are a number of Macedonian officers who sometimes dye their finger nails, paint their faces, and curl their hair." He leaned across the table. "In doing so they only imitate their betters."

"You are referring to the king?" Miriam asked.

"It has been known," Patroclus declared. "And I have seen Hephaestion at feasts and banquets."

Miriam knew he spoke the truth. Alexander and his companions, particularly when in their cups, were known to imitate the rather effete fashions popular in Athens.

"We are not talking about the king or his companions," She replied heatedly, "but a spy responsible for the slaughter of Lysander and possibly the death of Memnon and other heinous crimes against the king."

"We cannot help you," Demetrius intervened. "True insults are traded, gossip is passed round. But I've never heard any of my companions here called a woman, or seen any of them dressed as or act such a part. Indeed," he gibed, "we are as mannish as you are!"

Miriam colored at the insult.

"There's no need for that." Alcibiades spoke softly.

Demetrius wouldn't hold Miriam's gaze. He gestured with his hand.

"No, mistress, there isn't. I apologize. But we have been besieged in this citadel; we held it for the king. Now we are being accused of being spies and killers."

"There is one thing." Patroclus, like Cleon, had remained calm, either because he had nothing to fear or because he could hide his agitation well.

"I never told any one of this," he declared, "because at the time it didn't make sense. It was before the siege began. Or, as you put it mistress, before matters turned sour. We all became lonely and wanted to meet a friendly face as well as grasp a pair of juicy tits or firm, round buttocks. The Cadmea is not the most hospitable place. So we used to stroll down to the city. The Thebans were not happy with our presence but they tolerated us and took our silver. One day Lysander came back. He was slightly drunk. It was late in the evening. He squatted in the courtyard, eating bread and talking to some of the men about his adventures in a pleasure house in the city. How the Theban women were like cats and that he had the scars to prove it. The men drifted away. I went and sat beside him. We got to talking. Lysander, well, he was in his cups; he turned to me and said, 'Patroclus, have you ever wanted to dress like a woman? I mean, not like the court fops or dandies, but in women's clothing, sandals—actually pretend you are one?' 'No,' I replied, 'Why?' 'On my journey back from the city,' Lysander replied, 'I didn't think it was possible, but one of our comrades is a woman.' 'Who?' I asked." Patroclus stared down at the tabletop.

"And?" Miriam asked.

"Well, Lysander was an officer. He became embarrassed and said he shouldn't spread such gossip. At the time I agreed and walked away."

"You never told anyone about that?" Demetrius demanded.

"I didn't think it was important."

"Can you remember the day?" Miriam asked.

Patroclus put his head in his hands and, muttering to himself, began to count back the days.

"You know why I ask? Was there a duty roster?" Miriam demanded.

Demetrius was about to object.

"There must be," Miriam declared. "Where is it now?"

"When Alexander arrived and the city was taken . . ." Demetrius wouldn't meet her gaze, ". . . all such papers were handed over to the scribes in the treasury. They'll have it."

"Is there anything else?" Miriam got to her feet. All five just stared at her, so Miriam thanked them for the food and their cooperation. She left the hall, went out into the courtyard, and stopped. Hecaetus and his boys were there, crouching. At their feet, thick ropes bound around him, was a bedraggled, bloody-faced prisoner. Hecaetus minced forward.

"Pelliades may be dead." He turned with a theatrical gesture. "But look, Israelite, whom we have found!"

"Hecaetus, you should have been on the stage."

"That's what Olympias said. She wants me to take part in her play! Now, aren't I a clever boy? This is Telemachus."

CHAPTER 10

HECAETUS SNAPPED HIS fingers and the prisoner was hustled up into the tower. He was youngish, mousy-haired, with a wispy beard and mustache. He was wounded and scarred from head to toe. Miriam didn't know if this was the work of Hecaetus's "lovely boys" or because the man had likely spent days in hiding.

"A patrol picked him up," Hecaetus smirked, "on the road north. He was mixing with some refugees."

Telemachus opened his mouth; Miriam recoiled at his bloody gums.

"We've tried to make him talk," Hecaetus declared. "So far, he's said nothing, but there are dungeons here. We could spend weeks skinning him alive." He grabbed the man's hair and yanked back his head. "Or we could start breaking his limbs one by one; then he'll talk."

Telemachus looked hunted, wearied, yet Miriam saw a defiance in his eyes. Here was a man at the heart of the Theban councils; he knew the Macedonians would have little compassion for him.

"I doubt if you'll break him easily." Miriam hid her sympathy. "How do you know it's Telemachus?"

Hecaetus shouted at one of his men, who brought across a leather bag.

"A few trinkets, some money, and a letter sealed by Pelliades just before the city fell. Apparently our good Telemachus was to slip out of the city and carry the good fight to another part of Greece." He grabbed the man's beard and viciously tugged at it. "Demosthenes eh? Go trotting to that bald-pated demagogue!" Hecaetus was beside himself with pleasure. "The king will be so pleased. I am sure he'll want to meet you personally, either here or pinned to a cross."

Telemachus brought his head back and spat, the spittle hitting Hecaetus on the cheek. Alexander's master of secrets smacked Telemachus in the face, then kicked him viciously in the stomach. The Theban sagged, groaning and retching.

"I don't think Alexander will wish to see him like this," Miriam declared.

Hecaetus's brows drew together.

"He's a prisoner," Miriam continued. "Thebes has fallen, the blood has cooled. Hecaetus, I don't think Telemachus . . ." She pushed back the prisoner's head and caught the young Theban's stare. "I don't think this man will break because you punch and kick him." She patted him gently and stepped away. "Of course, you could take him to the dungeons, but if he dies, he's no use."

Hecaetus was wiping his cheeks on one of his lovely boys' cloaks.

"Bring him to the hall," Miriam ordered.

Hecaetus was about to object.

"Please!" Miriam added. "And I will tell you all I have learned."

"I know about the shrine," Hecaetus said peevishly. "And the deaths."

"Yes, but I know more," Miriam teased, "and I thought we were going to share Hecaetus, share and share alike, eh?"

Hecaetus agreed. Telemachus was brought into the mess hall as the officers were preparing to leave. When Hecaetus proudly declared that this was Telemachus, Demetrius lunged at him but was held back by Hecaetus's men.

"You'd best leave," Miriam declared quietly. "And Demetrius, I'd like a guard around the hall."

"My boys will also be there," Hecaetus declared.

He dragged Telemachus to a stool and sat him down. Miriam went into the kitchen. Her stomach curdled at the shabby, rather fetid place; she mixed some water and wine, took it back to the hall, and cleaned Telemachus's face and hands. The Theban thanked Miriam with his eyes. She then brought him a cup of beer and held it to his lips. The man winced as he leaned forward, the cords binding his arms to his body cutting into his skin. Miriam picked up a knife and, despite Hecaetus's protests, cut the ropes. The Theban relaxed. Miriam handed the knife to Hecaetus, sat on a corner of the bench, and stared at the Theban.

"Drink the beer," she ordered.

Telemachus sipped at it.

"Why, mistress? Do you want me drunk?"

"No, Theban, I want you alive. My name is Miriam Bartimaeus. I am of Alexander's council, as is our good friend Hecaetus," she added hurriedly. "I want to question you."

"I have heard of you, Israelite. You were supposed to have died with Alexander."

"Thessaly was very cold and hard." Miriam half smiled. "But we survived, as Thebes now knows."

"There's no one left to know," Telemachus gibed. "My

whole family has gone—my wife, . . ." His eyes filled with tears. "Our two children died in the flames. My mother was apparently killed as she fled. God knows where my sisters and brothers are."

"And Pelliades?" Miriam asked.

"Killed in the rear guard that tried to hold the Electra Gate. Most of the council perished there."

"He tells the truth," Hecaetus intervened. "Their bodies were recognized."

"And why didn't you die with them?" Miriam asked.

"When the army broke," Telemachus replied, "Pelliades sealed my commission. He told me to get out of Thebes and reach Demosthenes."

"Why?"

"To continue the opposition against the Macedonian tyrant. I hid out in the woods. I thought it was safe." He shrugged. "You know the rest."

"Why did you besiege the Macedonian garrison?" Miriam asked.

Telemachus took another sip of beer and wetted his chapped lips. He then gargled, swilling it round his sore mouth, and spat it on the floor.

"We really believed Alexander was dead, that the vultures were picking the bones of his army."

"And your spy in the Cadmea told you that this was the truth?"

Telemachus just stared back.

"Why did you kill Lysander?" Miriam persisted.

"He was a Macedonian."

"More than that!" Miriam looked at Hecaetus and winked. "One of your council said something about this spy whom we now call the Oracle; he called him, 'that woman.' " She ignored Hecaetus's sharp hiss of breath but glimpsed the shift in Telemachus's eyes.

"Who was the spy?" She asked quietly.

Telemachus took another sip of beer.

"Listen to me," Miriam urged. "If you tell us, you have my word, by all that is holy, that Alexander of Macedon will have your wounds bathed, give you fresh clothing, gold and silver and a pass to travel wherever you wish. You could find your sisters, your family, begin life again elsewhere. Thebes is destroyed. It is all finished here."

"Or you can die," Hecaetus interrupted. "You can spend a few days with my boys." He pushed past Miriam, his face close to the prisoner. "What's your arse like Telemachus? Do you know what it's like to hang from a cross?"

"If I ever get my freedom," Telemachus replied quietly, "I'll come back and kill you Hecaetus."

Miriam intervened before the war of words led to blows.

"We knew all your names." Telemachus vented the hatred seething within him. "Alexander, Perdiccas, the Israelites! You were all dead, that's what our spy told us." He grinned. "And can't you find him yet?"

"Please." Miriam studied the Theban shrewdly and her heart sank. Outside, this man's city was a sea of devastation. Alexander had told her how the Thebans hated Macedonian rule, so would Telemachus break? Help his conquerors? The men who had slaughtered his family, his wife and children? Perhaps Hecaetus was right, and bribery and soft promises would achieve nothing. Telemachus sipped from the cup.

"We took care of your spies, Hecaetus, those sprinkled about the city. All killed!"

Hecaetus's face stiffened.

"That's why you'll never find their bodies," Telemachus gibed. "We took them out beyond the city gates. We buried them alive."

Miriam jumped to her feet as Hecaetus grabbed a knife. Her cries, the crashing of the bench caught the attention of those outside. The door was flung open. Demetrius's and Hecaetus's men swarmed into the room. Miriam now had her body between Telemachus and his captor. She looked over her shoulder. Hecaetus was white-faced, lips drawn back, teeth bared.

"Demetrius, pull him away!"

"What is this?" Cleon asked.

"Hecaetus!" Miriam seized his hand carrying the knife. "Hecaetus," she whispered, "he is trying to provoke you. He wants a quick easy death."

"Then give it to him!" Demetrius declared. "We know who Telemachus is. Lysander was our companion. Let's blind him like Oedipus!"

"Take him out and crucify him in the same places as Lysander!" Alcibiades shouted.

"Why don't you?" Telemachus sneered. "I hold your lives in my own hand. Is one of you the spy? Eh? Is it you Alcibiades?"

His words created instant silence. Miriam realized how clever he was: Telemachus had quoted a name without looking at the man.

"Or Demetrius?" Telemachus looked at the ceiling. "Or Melitus? Or Patroclus? One of you was in our pay."

The officers stopped mouthing their curses and stared at this prisoner. He had neatly turned the tables on them.

"You knew all our names," Demetrius scoffed. "The council in Thebes did. Every one in the garrison from Memnon down to the stable boys. Don't threaten us!"

"Ah, yes," Telemachus smirked, "and we must not forget dear Memnon trying to fly from the top of his tower! You can take me out and crucify me," he taunted, "but I'll die screaming one of your names. Perhaps two. Alexander of Macedon will always wonder who the real spy was!"

"Take him away," Miriam urged. "Hecaetus, don't hurt

him! Take him downstairs, keep him in a store room closely guarded, never by himself."

Alexander's master of spies was going to object.

"He should be taken from here," she urged. "The king himself must see him."

Hecaetus nodded at two of his men. Telemachus's hands were grasped and bound behind him, he was shoved from the hall, Hecaetus following.

"We are in great danger," Demetrius murmured. He picked up the knife and threw it angrily onto the table. He glanced pleadingly at Miriam.

"He's going to confess nothing. I wager, mistress, he'll try to cause much chaos and confusion before Alexander tires of him and nails him to a piece of wood. He threatens us all."

"I know." Miriam rubbed her eyes. "He could mislead us deliberately." She stared at the door. But something had happened here. Her mind was too tired to grasp it. Was it what the officers had said? Telemachus or Hecaetus? She brushed by the men and went out into the courtyard. The day was drawing on, the weak sun was beginning to set. Hecaetus joined her.

"Share and share alike, Israelite."

Miriam led him away to a bench propped against the yard wall; she told him everything that had happened and what she had learned. Hecaetus sat, arms crossed, head bowed, now and again whistling between his teeth.

"You've learned a great deal Miriam." He patted her hand. "And I'm sorry for what happened in there. But I had some lovely boys left in Thebes." His eyes filled with tears. "Merry lads, all of them gone. They knew the risk, but to be buried alive." He got to his feet wiping his eyes.

"Let's take the bastard into the camp!"

"Do you think he'll talk?" Miriam asked.

"No, I don't," Hecaetus retorted. "Telemachus is a brave man who hates Macedonians. If he talks it will be a web of lies and deceit. We'll never know the truth; he will only muddy the waters." He chucked Miriam under the chin with his fingers. "You are not fit for camp life, Israelite. Your face is pale and the dark rings under your eyes are not paint." Hecaetus shouted across at one of his men to bring the horses.

Grooms led these around, harnessed and ready. Telemachus was bundled up onto one of them. Hecaetus helped Miriam onto a gentle palfrey beside the prisoner, and with Hecaetus's men around her, they left the citadel. Darkness was falling. Miriam noticed how many of the fires had now gone out. Thebes was nothing but a wide sweep of ruins, broken walls, blackening stonework, and over all hung the dreadful stench of death. She glanced sideways at Telemachus. He was fighting back tears.

"Nothing," he whispered. "There's nothing left! A terrible price, Israelite? A warning to all Greece, eh?"

Miriam didn't reply but grasped her reins more tightly. She wanted to be back in the camp. She wanted to be away from Thebes. Above all, she couldn't bear the horror-stricken look in this man who was certainly doomed to a hideous death. Darkness enveloped them. Ahead the fires of the camp rivaled the stars now breaking clear in the velvet blackness above them. Miriam became aware of how silent this devastated city had become. Time and time again the Macedonian soldiers had combed it, looking for items of plunder that their predecessors had overlooked. Now it was a place of ghosts, of shades wandering from the shadows of Hades looking for their homes, signs of their former lives. Telemachus had his head down and was quietly sobbing at the full horror and degradation of what had happened.

Miriam recalled her father's lamentations over Jerusalem. She had never seen the holy city, but her father used to tell her about the temple, the incense-filled courtyards, the streets, olive gardens, and cypress groves. About how the invader had brought it all low by fire and sword, reducing her people and culture to nothing but a sea of ash. The exiles had now returned. Miriam had vowed that one day she would join them, go to the holy place, and pray for her parents. She and Simeon had often discussed it though not in detail. She glanced sideways and wondered what Alexander would do to Telemachus. Suddenly a bright light caught her eye and she whirled round. They were passing what had once been a narrow alleyway in the poor quarter of Thebes; from the ruins a torch was tossed. It landed in their midst, creating chaos and consternation. Hecaetus shouted orders, horses whinnied and reared. Thankfully, Miriam was on the other side and she was able to steady her docile mount. She heard a sound like the whirr of a hunting hawk swooping from its perch. One of Hecaetus's men threw his arms up and screamed. Something whipped by her face; there was a loud cry followed by a moan. She turned her horse around. Some of the riders had dismounted. One of Hecaetus's men was lying on the road, his face visible in the pool of light thrown by the pitch torch. He was dead, eyes open, blood pouring out of his mouth. Miriam quickly dismounted, using her horse as a shield. An assassin was on the loose! Hecaetus's men were already drawing swords, running toward the ruins. Her horse moved and she saw Telemachus; the arrow had caught him deep in the chest. He lay, his head half buried in a mound of ash. She scrambled over to the corpse. In a way she was relieved. Telemachus must have died instantly, the stout, feathered Cretan arrow having pierced him directly in the heart.

"You will tell us nothing now." Miriam tried to close his eyes with her hand. She heard shouts and cries. A torch was picked up; Hecaetus crouched beside her.

"Whoever it was," he grasped, "has gone. Very clever, very quick, eh Miriam?"

He got up and kicked the corpse. "Now his mouth is sealed for ever." He shouted into the darkness, calling his men back. They had suffered two casualties: one of Hecaetus's men was dead, the other had a slight arrow wound to the shoulder. Hecaetus thrust an arrow into Miriam's hand.

"It's one of ours," He declared.

"It was taken from a Cretan this morning," Miriam explained. "You know; I told you."

Hecaetus had the horses collected, the corpses slung across, and muttering that the king would not be pleased, led them back into the camp.

Miriam found that the attack on the shrine and the deaths of the guards had already made itself felt. Alexander had moved the camp to military preparedness, as if they were in a hostile country expecting to do battle. No longer solitary sentries, but groups of men, gathered around camp fires within sight and earshot of each other. Deeper in the camp, groups of cavalry mounts were ready to take up any pursuit. The haphazard nature of the encampment had also been changed, avenues and paths laid out. Around the royal quarters in the center, a three feet moat had been dug, spanned by makeshift bridges.

Hecaetus would have liked to talk. Miriam explained that she was too tired and would be reporting all to the king. It was not so much Alexander's questions she feared but Olympias's. If the queen was in one of her moods, she would talk and talk until Miriam's legs buckled under her. Simeon was waiting for her in their tent, seating cross-legged on his cot bed, carefully rewriting drafts of Alexander's orders. Miriam threw herself down on her own bed, ignoring his questions. She realized how tired and grubby she felt.

"Don't ask me any questions, Simeon." She hardly bothered to raise her head. "My legs ache. My belly has had nothing but paltry food and all I have seen today is murder."

Simeon came over with a goblet and told her to sit up. She sipped from the wine, wrapping her blanket round her. She felt warm and sleepy.

"Don't disturb me." she begged.

Simeon grinned. "Olympias has sent for you. She wishes to begin her play tomorrow."

"Then she'll have to do it without me!" Miriam snapped. "Simeon, do me a favor. Let me sleep. But go to the chief scribe in the king's writing house and ask him if he has any records, manuscripts from the garrison at the Cadmea. Will you do that?"

Simeon promised he would, but Miriam was past caring. She put her cup down on the ground, pulled the army blanket over herself, and fell into a deep sleep.

She woke early the next morning clearheaded and refreshed but ravenously hungry. Simeon was snoring on the bed opposite. On the camp table she saw a mound of greasy yellow papyrus parchment; Simeon had kept his word. Shivering, moving around to keep warm, Miriam quickly stripped and washed herself with the water, a rag, and some oils that Simeon had laid out. She put on the thick-gauffered linen dress Alexander had given her as a present from an Egyptian merchant, picked up a military cloak—the heaviest she could find—and wrapped this around herself. She put on some leggings and a pair of stout military boots and went out into the camp. A heavy mist had rolled in. She could scarcely see in front of her, but she followed her nose and found a group of cavalry men cooking oatmeal and boiling a chicken. They declared, in round-eyed innocence, that they had been given it as a present. Miriam guessed they had filched it either from some deserted, outlying farm or from the quartermaster's stores. They allowed her to join them, indulging in gentle teasing and banter. They gave her a bowl, first slopping in thick oatmeal mixed with honey and, when she had eaten that, pieces of chicken white and tender, chopped up and mixed with dry rye bread and olive oil. She ate quickly, listening to the men's chatter.

"There were no incidents last night?" She asked.

The officer in charge shook his head.

"We don't know what's going on," he moaned, "but the orders come down." He peered across the fire at her. "You are a member of the royal circle. You should know more than us."

"I'm just like a soldier," Miriam replied. "I follow orders as well."

Someone muttered a joke about Alexander's bed. The officer, his mouth full of food, shouted that he would have no offensive remarks when a lady was present.

"How do you think this will go on?" he asked. "I mean, who has been killing these sentries? And the business down at the shrine. They say the guards were killed and the Crown stolen."

"Have you never been on guard duty?" Miriam asked abruptly.

The officer smiled, licking his fingers.

"More times, mistress, than I like to think."

"Well let's say you were guarding a house and someone came toward you; what would you do?"

"If she had big breasts," one of soldiers declared irrepressibly, "I'd run down to meet her!"

His words were greeted by guffaws and laughter.

"So if a woman approached you," Miriam declared, "you would not find it threatening?"

"Well, of course not," the fellow replied. "I mean, I'd only draw my sword if a stranger approached."

"How would you know it was a stranger?" Miriam asked, "if it was dark or, like this, misty?"

"Well, you'd call out, wouldn't you!" the officer declared. "And if there was no answer, you'd strike first and ask afterward!"

"So," Miriam continued, putting her bowl down, "if you were on this so-called duty and a Macedonian approached you? . . ."

"I wouldn't give it a second thought."

"But how would you know it's a Macedonian?" Miriam insisted.

"Well, by his armor, his speech."

"But there are Thebans who could take Macedonian armor, and Alexander's armies include men from all over Greece, not to mention Asia."

Miriam got to her feet.

"What's the matter, mistress? Something we've said?"

"No, no," she replied absentmindedly. "It's more something I've said. I'm looking at this the wrong way, aren't I? I mean, you accepted me into your circle because you know who I am."

"We were pleased to see you," one of the soldiers declared. "You're not that ugly, and all soldiers like to hear a bit of gossip."

"Thank you," Miriam declared. "I'm glad I'm not that ugly."

"No offence, mistress."

"None taken."

Miriam thanked them and walked back to her tent. She sat on the edge of the bed and recalled Aristotle's lecture, "A True Philosopher." Her teacher had declared, "Always look at things differently. The sophists put the question, 'Is there a God?' I would answer: 'Why shouldn't there be a God?' My question is as valid as theirs!"

"And the same applies here," Miriam whispered to herself.

She thought of those soldiers outside the shrine of Oedipus. They had been lounging about, chatting to each other. If that terrible figure had appeared, they would have sprung to arms, as they would have with any stranger. Accordingly, their assailant must have been a Macedonian, seen as friendly and no threat. It was the same with the guards on the outskirts of the camp. They could call out, and the person would reply. Now a solitary guard would be easily dispatched once his suspicions were lulled, but a guards officer and a group of men? How could they be attacked and killed so expertly? Miriam recalled Telemachus's death the previous night. I think we've seen the last of Oedipus, she thought. The Macedonian army is now on the alert. Nobody will go wandering about, garbed like the figure she had glimpsed; in a way it was becoming more dangerous. The assassin, the spy, the Oracle had now turned silent. He would hide and lurk, strike without warning. Hecaetus had wanted to discuss the prisoner's death but Miriam knew the truth. The assassin must be a member of the garrison. One of those five officers, frightened that Telemachus under torture might break and reveal more. Yesterday evening all the soldiers would have left the citadel, drifting back toward the camp. It would have been easy for one of them to run ahead, to lie in wait with a bow and arrow. Throwing the pitch torch had been a clever idea; it startled their horses and allowed the assassin a good glimpse of the prisoner. Of course, it would be easy to flee under the cover of night. She wondered if Hecaetus should question Demetrius, Cleon, and the rest about their whereabouts. But what would that prove? Telemachus was dead, and his secrets had gone with him. But there was something he had said. Something about Memnon flying from his tower.

Miriam rubbed her arms and looked at the pile of documents Simeon must have collected from the chief scribe. She lit an oil lamp and, sitting on a camp stool, began going through them. Most were lists of stores, similar to the documents she had studied in Memnon's chamber. At last she found the duty roster. It was divided into night and day. Memnon never took a watch; that was understandable, but each of the officers was listed. She jogged her memory and found the day Demetrius had mentioned, when Lysander had come back from visiting one of the pleasure houses in the city. She grimaced in annoyance. All four had been absent; the only one left was Cleon. Miriam tossed the documents aside.

"They are of little use," she murmured.

Miriam lay back on the bed, pulling the blanket over her, half listening to the sounds of the waking camp. She tried to impose some order on what she had seen and heard. She rolled over onto her side. The breakfast she had eaten had made her sleepy again. Images flitted through her mind: Antigone telling her about Jocasta, the visits of Pelliades and Telemachus. "That's where it all began!" she murmured. She heard the sound of the tent flap being opened.

"Oh no, Hecaetus!" Miriam groaned. She felt a flicker of cold and jumped up. She was sure that the tent flap had been opened. Surely someone had entered the tent?

"Simeon!" she shouted. Then she saw it resting against the leg of a stool, a leather ball. Miriam scrabbled under her pillow for the dagger, then relaxed as she heard a voice.

"Mistress, it's only us. We wondered if you were awake?" She recognized the two pages from the Cadmea.

"Come in, my lovely lads," she called. She glanced across. Simeon hadn't even stirred. The tent flap was raised and the two page boys scrambled into the tent.

"Why are you here?"

"Two reasons," Castor declared rubbing his stomach. "We are very, very hungry, and we would like to talk to you about old Memnon."

CHAPTER 11

MIRIAM WENT OUT and brought back bowls of hot food for the pages. By the time she'd returned, Simeon was awake, sitting heavy-eyed on the edge of his bed, staring at the two imps.

"They haven't moved," he said, as Miriam came into the tent.

"I wager they've got sticky fingers."

The pages ignored him as they grabbed the bowls and began eating, dipping their spoons into the hot porridge, blowing to cool it, then pushing it into their mouths. The porridge and bread Miriam had brought disappeared in a twinkling of an eye. Both pages burped and sat, eyes wandering round the tent.

"I'll leave you to it," Simeon moaned. He wrapped an old blanket around him and left.

"What do you want to tell me about Memnon?" Miriam asked. "Or was that just an excuse to get some free food?"

"We are very hungry," Pollux replied. "It's now scraps of food from the kitchen."

"Well, in future you can stay in the camp," Miriam replied. "My brother will have a word with the quarter-master."

"Oh, he's your brother?" Castor asked. "We thought he was . . ."

"Don't be crude!" Miriam snapped.

"Old Memnon," Castor hastily added. "We said he liked taking wenches into his bed."

"He did," Pollux declared, "but we also think he had a boyfriend."

"What makes you say that?"

"Late one evening," Pollux replied, "I was climbing the tower; I was looking for food. Now old Memnon didn't like us wandering about. I heard footsteps and hid. A figure passed me; the head and face were shrouded, but I smelled perfume, really rich and strong."

"So it was a woman?" Miriam asked.

"No, no, as the person passed, I glanced down; it was a man! He was wearing military sandals and had hairy legs, not like any woman I've ever seen."

"And where was this person coming from," Miriam asked, "Memnon's chamber?"

"It could have been. But then again, all the officers have their chambers in the tower."

"Not all of them," Pollux intervened. "Cleon had his over the stables."

"That's right," Caster agreed.

"You've been listening at keyholes."

Castor and Pollux nodded solemnly.

"We listened to you when you were talking to the officers yesterday and when you were talking with that man with the cruel eyes."

"Hecaetus?"

"Yes, that's right, Hecaetus, who brought the prisoner in. We heard what was said about the spy being a woman."

"That's impossible," Pollux continued. "Only serving wenches were in the Cadmea, and they knew nothing. When the garrison was besieged by the Thebans, the serving wenches were dismissed."

"And when did you see this man pretending to be a woman?" Miriam asked. "Was it before the Thebans locked you into the citadel or afterward?"

"Oh, before," Castor replied. "I got the impression he or she was going out into the city."

"But you mentioned Memnon?" Miriam asked.

"Well, we talked about it last night," Castor declared. "We think this person was going out disguised as a woman to move among the Thebans would not be recognized as one of the garrison."

"Ah," Miriam smiled, "I see what you mean. Is there anything else, lads?"

Both pages shook their heads. Miriam went over to the makeshift writing desk. She scrawled a short message on a piece of papyrus.

"If you do remember anything else, come back. Take this to the quartermaster. He's a big fellow with a balding head. His name is Solomonides. Tell him you have spoken to me. He'll give you food, but you'll have to work for it."

"I hope he doesn't like boys," Pollux declared, scrambling to his feet.

"Just to eat." Miriam smiled.

The two pages left. Miriam lay back on the bed. She heard the tent flap pulled back, and Alexander walked in quietly, followed by Hecaetus. Both nodded and sat down on the opposite bed. The king looked clear-faced and bright-eyed.

"I retired early," he joked. "There's nothing like Mother

to spoil a good feast. Hecaetus has told me what happened. Pity, I would like to have met Telemachus," he added wistfully. "I am sure he could have told us a great deal." He played with his wrist guard. "Hecaetus has also told me what you learned yesterday. The waters are becoming more muddied; I can make little sense of it all."

"The spy, the Oracle, is in the Cadmea," Hecaetus intervened. "My lord, if I were you, I'd arrest all five officers."

Alexander snorted. "I've thought of that. Tell me, Miriam, why I shouldn't arrest all five, confine them to quarters?"

"First, you've no real evidence," Miriam replied. "Second, I wager some of those officers have powerful friends and ties with leading Macedonian families; their confinement will be seen as an insult, particularly if no charges are leveled."

"Go on," Alexander insisted.

"Third, the soldiers regard them as heroes. Whatever happened to Memnon or Lysander, those officers did not lose their nerve. Despite the most frightening rumors about your death and the destruction of your army, they held the citadel until you arrived. It seems a poor reward to place them under house arrest. Last, the army is preparing to march on the Hellespont." Miriam continued, "You don't want any divisions and you don't want to give comfort to your enemies by lashing out, striking out against those around you."

Alexander clapped his hands.

"Well done, Miriam!" He sighed and looked at Hecaetus. "And, if I put them under house arrest, what will happen?"

"Well, at least this Oedipus won't go around killing people," Hecaetus retorted.

"Oh, I think he'll stop that," Miriam declared. "It's becoming too dangerous for him. He's made his mark. He killed Telemachus because he had to. He'll only strike again if he can get away with the crime. After all, he's got the

Crown, he's caused confusion and chaos. I think he'll sit, wait, and watch."

"Is that all you can say?" Hecaetus sneered.

"Oh, we could put them under arrest," Miriam continued. "One of them could be guilty, two could be guilty, or it might be all of them. Let's review what we do know or what I suspect. We have a spy, a high-ranking traitor, a very skillful and subtle man. He knows the Cadmea, the city, and the shrine of Oedipus. He is a master of disguise. He can dress up as Oedipus. I suspect he can also disguise himself as a woman. Now, he may have used the latter ploy to attack our sentries or to go around the camp and approach the shrine. He certainly used that disguise to slip into the city of Thebes before the Cadmea was ringed off. Disguised as a woman, he could meet people like Pelliades and the other Theban leaders and give them all the information they needed before slipping back to join his companions. Now in the main, he was successful, except on two occasions. First he was glimpsed by Lysander, who probably uncertain about what he saw and a good officer, kept his mouth shut. Second, he was seen by one of the pages coming down from the tower and going out into the city. Now, before the Thebans cut the citadel off, people were allowed to go in and out of the citadel at will. Memnon wouldn't have objected, would he have, my lord?' She paused.

"I know what you are going to say, Miriam." Alexander replied. "He was to do nothing to antagonize the Thebans."

"The Thebans also," Miriam continued, "seemed to prefer such haphazard arrangements." She paused. "I've said something." She put her finger to her mouth. "I've said something. . . ." She scratched the back of her head. "I don't realize the significance of it. Anyway," she continued, "Matters changed when the siege began. There were no further strolls in the city. Instead the spy communicated with his

Theban friends by fire arrow: the tip soaked in oil, the message tied to the other end. It would be shot to a specified location and the Thebans would then collect it. The spy, the Oracle, as you call him, also tried to unnerve Memnon: this business of Oedipus being seen around the citadel."

"You said he was also seen beyond?"

"Oh, that was a Theban trick," Miriam replied. "While the Oracle played the Oedipus in the Cadmea, some Theban played the role outside. It was to disconcert Memnon."

"Why should they do that?" Alexander asked.

"You attacked Thebes," Miriam replied, "because they rose in rebellion. They really thought you were dead and that the bones of you and your army were whitening in some mountain valley in Thessaly. It was a lie, a trick. The Thebans really believed the rumors and the spy did everything to encourage it. Whether he believed it himself, or whether he just wished to stir the Thebans up, we don't know. In fact, the war was being fought in the mind and soul, especially of poor Memnon. The Oracle hoped our commander's nerve would break, his spirit fail. Fearful of the Thebans, deeply anxious about Alexander and the army, Memnon might have been stupid enough to capitulate and ask for terms. Indeed, he was almost there, sending out Lysander to negotiate. Now I don't think the Thebans wanted to kill Lysander. However, one of them foolishly said something that may have revealed the identity of the spy, so Lysander was killed and his corpse gibbeted to show how confident the Thebans were."

"And, of course, Memnon's state of mind would grow worse?" Alexander asked.

"Oh yes, but he was a tough old dog," Miriam continued, "so the Oracle somehow killed him!"

"You don't think he committed suicide?" Alexander queried.

"No, I don't," Miriam answered. "But how he died is a

mystery. Only the gods know what would have happened if the Macedonian army hadn't appeared. However, it did, and Thebes fell. Now, the spy could have fled but he has impudence and cheek second to none." She paused. "He's taken the Crown. He's killed Macedonian guards." Miriam went cold.

"What it is, Miriam?" Alexander asked.

"Who ever it is," she replied slowly, "is devious and cunning. He certainly hates you Alexander. I just wonder . . ."

"Whether he will strike at the king himself?" Hecaetus asked.

Miriam nodded. "He'll either do that," she concluded, "or disappear."

"And the Crown?" Alexander asked, ignoring the threat. "How did he kill the soldiers? How did he take the Crown?"

"I don't know." Miriam closed her eyes. "My lord, I really don't know." She opened her eyes and stared at the king. "Antigone will not suffer, will she?"

Alexander shook his head.

'Good! Because I think I am going to need her help. I have your permission, my lord, to return to the shrine? I would like to take her with me."

Alexander nodded. "Tell Simeon to draft a letter to the captain of the guard, a pass to let you in. You'll find the shrine changed. I've had the two pits cleaned."

"Why?" Miriam asked.

"The snakes were a danger and I can't stand them," Alexander declared, getting to his feet. "I also wanted to check myself, or Hecaetus did, that there were no secret entrances, passageways, or tunnels."

"And there were none?"

"None whatsoever." Hecaetus said with a grin.

Alexander moved to the tent flap, beckoning Hecaetus to him.

"I understand your concern, Miriam." Alexander smiled. "But I don't think this assassin wants my life."

"Why not?" Miriam asked.

"If he wished to strike at me he would have done so," Alexander said. "But that would be very dangerous for him. Instead he's created chaos and stolen the Crown. He's done that for a purpose. He intends to sell the Crown to someone." Alexander walked back toward her.

"Demosthenes? The Athenians?" Miriam queried.

"We thought that at first," Hecaetus smirked, "so I've had Timeon and his delegation carefully watched; they're not involved. Timeon is acting like a good little boy; he never leaves his tent. And the news from Athens is that Demosthenes has fled without a coin to his name."

"It's true," Alexander confirmed.

"So that leaves one person," Miriam replied. "His Excellency, Darius III King of Persia."

Hecaetus smirked. "Then the rumors about Alexander's death and the destruction of his army must have been started by Persian agents in Greece. The actions of the Oracle confirmed this. He may have deceived the Macedonians but he also deceived the Thebans and brought about their destruction."

"That's why he killed Telemachus, isn't it?" Miriam asked.

Hecaetus nodded.

"If Telemachus had been kept alive long enough, if he'd been forced to reflect, he may have realized that the Thebans had been most cruelly tricked."

"But surely the Thebans realized that when the Macedonian army appeared?" Miriam asked.

"They still had doubts," Alexander replied, "that I was with them. Again, the work of the Oracle. Can't you see, Miriam, if Telemachus had survived, he would have had to concede to a dreadful nightmare—that he and his entire city had been duped into revolt."

Alexander left, followed by Hecaetus. Simeon came back; he sat on the edge of the bed and looked mournfully at his sister.

"A busy morning?"

Miriam picked up her belt and threw it at him but he ducked and grinned mischievously.

"You are supposed to help me," She said crossly.

"What help can I give?" he countered. "And what will you do now?"

"This Oracle, the assassin," Miriam replied, "is both confident and cunning. Why is that Simeon, eh? Thebes is in ruins, the Macedonian army controls Greece, and yet he acts with impunity. I mean, . . ." She paused.

"What?"

"Well, Telemachus may be dead but what happens if another Theban is also picked up by Hecaetus's net?" She paused. "Of course!" she breathed.

"Don't be enigmatic, sister."

"The Thebans know as much about the Oracle as we do," Miriam added. "The spy communicated with them when he was disguised as a woman, or by arrows shot out of the Cadmea. I wager you a jug of wine, brother dearest, that if we had subjected Telemachus to the most horrific tortures, he would only have confessed to being approached by a spy, but never to having known who that spy was."

"So the Oracle thinks he's safe."

"He's certainly safe from the Thebans. Most of the council are probably dead, and if there were any survivors, they wouldn't be able to point the finger."

"So why kill Telemachus?"

"I don't know," Miriam murmured.

"Perhaps to protect someone else?"

"Or to buy time," Simeon added, "till he manages his escape."

"Perhaps," Miriam pulled a face, "the Oracle wants to keep us guessing, stumbling in the dark. If we had learned that Telemachus knew as little about him as we do, it might have opened other paths of inquiry."

"He'll also need help to escape."

"If it's the Persians," Miriam replied, "our spy has got nothing to fear. Thebes stands on a tongue of land surrounded by the sea; it would be very easy to leave by merchant ship or to be picked up by some galley in the pay of Darius. I suspect that this is what is going to happen." She got to her feet and finished dressing; using a piece of polished bronze, she applied some paint to her face. Simeon rose.

"Don't go away," she warned. "You've got a sword belt; wear it. I need protection. I also need a warrant to get into the shrine of Oedipus. So, if you could draft it and have it sealed?"

Simeon reluctantly agreed. Miriam tidied the tent, her mind distracted by what she had learned. She pulled back the flap and looked out. The mist had lifted, the camp was now fully awake, the soldiers going about their usual tasks. We'll have to move soon, she thought; the army can't stay here forever and our friend the Oracle knows that. He's waiting for chaos, for confusion to break out; then he'll slip away. She idly wondered if Hecaetus's suggestion was correct? Perhaps the officers should be confined to house arrest, but there again, how long could that last? The Oracle would simply bide his time and leave when it suited him. She let the tent flap fall. She walked back, opened a small coffer, took out a silver chain—a present from Alexander—and absent-mindedly put it around her neck.

"Miriam Bartimaeus?"

She started and looked over her shoulder. Timeon, the Athenian envoy, was standing in the mouth of the tent. He looked nervous, shuffling from one foot to another.

"To what do I owe this honor?" Miriam asked.

"May I come in? I wish to speak."

He didn't wait for an answer but scuttled in. Miriam gestured to a stool.

"The king is angry," he began.

"He has good cause," Miriam replied. "His guards are killed." She was about to say that the Crown had disappeared but caught herself just in time.

"I know what's happened." The envoy clawed at his straggly mustache and beard. "The Crown has disappeared from the shrine." He continued, "Oh, the king won't say that but the gossips are busy."

"And you know how dangerous it would be to spread such gossip?"

"I know," he stammered.

Miriam watched those deep, watery eyes.

"So, why are you here, Timeon of Athens? At the banquet the other night you were more sure of yourself, issuing challenges. Now you've come here all atremble, wanting to speak to me, the Israelite woman." Miriam studied his pallid face. "You've had fresh letters from Athens, haven't you? The news of Thebes' destruction has reached there. The pro-Macedonian faction is now in power; they don't want you to do anything to upset Alexander now that Demosthenes and his demagogues have fled."

Timeon just blinked.

"And, of course, you are wondering about yourself. After all, you were appointed official envoy when Demosthenes was cock of the walk in the Agora of Athens."

"They say you have a bitter tongue."

"Do they now, Timeon, so why are you here?"

"They also say you are fair and can't be bribed."

"You want me to act as mediator?"

Timeon nodded.

"If you could," he paused, "if you could assure the king that what has happened in Thebes is not the work of Athens or its envoys."

"Well, of course I will," Miriam retorted coolly, "I mean, if that's the truth."

"It is, it is!"

"Then why are you so nervous?"

Timeon spread the fingers of his right hand.

"All of Greece has changed," he murmured. "The wolf was bad, but the cub is even worse." He lifted his head. "When Philip died we thought the power of Macedonia would collapse with him. There would be the usual blood-letting and Alexander would disappear. Now it's all changed. Demosthenes was wrong. I do not wish to be crucified. And the Athenians don't want a lake of ash where their city once stood."

"Athens is safe." Miriam hid her excitement. This treacherous envoy was going to offer her something. He wouldn't dare go to Alexander or his companions: their moods were unreliable, their tempers savage.

"Everything has a price Timeon," she declared. "And, as Aristotle said, even the gods can't change the past. What I am interested in is what you are going to tell me. You are going to offer me something, aren't you? I've read your playwright Aristophanes; he says you cannot make a crab walk straight. Perhaps he should have written, 'you cannot make an Athenian tell the truth.' "

"And the wisest of the wise may err," Timeon snapped back.

"Aristophanes?" Miriam asked.

"No, Aeschylus!" Timeon made to get up.

"Sit down, man!" Miriam soothed. "You've come here to buy Alexander's good will, yes? To give him reassurance that you are not involved in what has happened, whatever that may be!"

Timeon pulled his cloak around him and nodded.

"And you've come to me," Miriam continued, "because what you've got to say is very dangerous, isn't it?"

Timeon breathed in rapidly.

"I have your word of honor?"

"You have my word," Miriam declared.

"In Athens," Timeon spoke hurriedly, "the news arrived that Alexander was dead and his army destroyed and that Olympias was facing a revolt in Pella. Demosthenes was ecstatic. The Thebans sent envoys and our council met with them in the dead of night. The Thebans said they had a high-ranking spy in the Cadmea, that they were going to throw off the Macedonian yoke, expel or kill the garrison, and rise in revolt. Wiser minds in our council urged caution. The Thebans were furious. We asked for proof, for the name of this spy. The Thebans were most reluctant. Demosthenes didn't have it all his own way. Again the demand was made, and the Thebans replied that the Athenians would know the name well. When questioned further, the Theban envoy simply replied, 'Haven't you heard of Socrates' pupil?' "

"Socrates' pupil?" Miriam queried.

"That's all they said. The envoys left and the council voted. Demosthenes wanted to send troops immediately to help Thebes but we were not so certain."

"So you adopted a wait-and-see policy?"

"Of course we did," Timeon retorted, "as did all of Greece."

"And there's more?" Miriam asked.

"Yes, there is." The Athenian looked anxiously about. "Could I have a cup of wine?"

Miriam poured one and thrust it into his hands.

"When Alexander lay siege to Thebes, Demosthenes sent me here with strict instructions to keep Athens closely informed. Of course, I did. After all, I am only an envoy."

"Of course," Miriam echoed.

"Well, you know what happened. Thebes fell, the face of Greece changed for ever. Demosthenes lost control in Athens. Two days ago I received a mysterious message. I left the camp accompanied by one of my squires. We had to meet the sender in the olive grove near the shrine of Oedipus."

"Why did you go?" Miriam interrupted.

"The note, which I've destroyed, simply said it was in the interest of a son of Athens, for had not both Sophocles and Oedipus found refuge in this city? We met at dusk; it was easy to slip out without Hecaetus noticing. The figure was shadowy; I could smell woman's perfume on him."

"How did his voice sound?"

"More a whisper, a hiss, as if he was holding something over his mouth. Despite the perfume, the voice was unmistakably male. He asked two things. One, was the city of Athens still interested in the Crown of Oedipus?" Timeon shrugged, "I said I didn't know. And two, more important, would the city publish the truth if it was stolen? Again I replied that I didn't know."

"What happened then?" Miriam insisted.

"I told him that Athens was still a member of the League of Corinth and owed allegiance to Alexander of Macedon. The stranger became very angry. I wanted to question him further, but he disappeared; that's all I know."

"Is it?" Miriam asked.

Timeon held his right hand up.

"I swear by Apollo, by all that is holy, that that is all I know."

Simeon pulled back the tent flap and entered. Miriam beckoned for him to leave. She could tell by the look of concern on Timeon's face that he wanted no witnesses. The Athenian leaned forward.

"If Alexander learned this from any other source," he hissed, "he would have my head, but Athens had no hand in it and does not wish to be involved." And pulling up his hood, Timeon left the tent.

Miriam waited for her brother to reenter.

"We have a name," she declared. "The Thebans believe that the Oracle was a 'true son of Athens,' a disciple of Socrates."

"In which case," Simeon replied, "Alexander should arrest Aristotle or Plato or dig up all the corpses. Miriam, that means nothing! Socrates and his circle have been dead for years!"

Miriam sat, eyes closed. She recalled the histories of Athens.

Simeon's jaw sagged.

"Of course, Miriam! Alcibiades was one of those whom Socrates was accused of corrupting. He became a power in Athens during the war against Sparta. He led the disastrous expedition to Sicily and later sought exile in Persia. The Oracle wasn't referring to the historical Alcibiades but to Memnon's officer."

Miriam tried to control her excitement. Alcibiades could provide the explanation for everything, she thought: He was foppish, petulant, probably a transvestite. It would have been easy for him to go around Thebes pretending to be a woman and attending secret, shadowy meetings with members of the Theban council.

Miriam recalled what the page had told her. How he had

glimpsed a man dressed as a woman coming down the stairs of the tower. Was he the same one Lysander had glimpsed?

"Brother," she urged, "send a courier to the Cadmea. Tell those officers I want to meet them again, urgently. Oh and this time let us bring some soldiers."

Simeon tossed her the scroll sealed in the royal chancery. "This is your pass into the shrine."

Miriam followed him out of the tent, stretched, and took a deep breath. The sun had now broken through, weak and watery. She became aware of the din in the camp.

Alcibiades, she thought; it was so simple! She recalled the words of Aristotle: "Miriam, you don't have to search for the truth. You usually stumble over it." She went back into the tent and got her cloak, took a sheath dagger from the chest and stuck it into the cord round her waist. Simeon returned, four soldiers trailing behind him. They all set off at a brisk pace through the camp, up the hill, and into the citadel. The officers and two pages were in the hall, lounging about on benches. They greeted her arrival with dramatic groans and moans. Cleon offered her some wine but she refused. Miriam stared around quickly. Alcibiades was missing!

CHAPTER 12

DEMETRIUS WAS ABOUT to argue, but one look at Miriam's face and he answered her question.

"Alcibiades shares a chamber with me," he declared, "and I haven't seen him since, well, since yesterday evening."

Immediately a search was organized. The tower and the rest of the citadel were scoured. When they all returned to the mess hall, Demetrius wore a woebegone expression.

"He's gone!" he declared, "and some of his possessions with him: his war belt and saddle panniers. I have," he drew a breath, "I have talked to a groom. Late last night Alcibiades took a horse from the stables. He said he was on business for the king."

"Quick!" Miriam snapped her fingers at one of the pages. "Castor, run to the camp as fast as you can. Search out Perdiccas and Hecaetus. Tell them Alcibiades has fled!"

The page ran off. Miriam tried to hide her disappointment. She sat on a bench and glanced across at Simeon.

"We failed," she declared. "Alcibiades could have ridden inland and hidden or he could have hastened down the coast to some prearranged spot where a Persian galley, or one of the ships in their pay, could take him off."

"What are you saying?" Demetrius came and sat on the bench opposite. The rest gathered round him.

"What does it sound like?" Simeon taunted. "Alcibiades is the spy known as the Oracle."

"But that's impossible!" Cleon declared. "Alcibiades is one of us, a Macedonian soldier, an officer! Why should he betray his compatriots?"

"Persian gold," Miriam declared, "probably sacks of it, as well as the offer of asylum, a pleasant house and gardens, and treatment as a noble in Persopolis. He'll hand Oedipus's Crown to Darius and the Persian king will taunt Alexander for all he's worth. Tell me all you know about him. No, no." Miriam shook her head, "I will tell you about him; if I'm wrong, you will correct me. Alcibiades was a transvestite, wasn't he? One of those Macedonian soldiers, brave as a panther in battle, but in private, his ways were foppish."

Demetrius was about to object, but Miriam stamped her foot on the floor.

"Don't lie!" she yelled. "If you had all told me the truth earlier . . ."

"Alcibiades had his strange ways."

"Yes, Demetrius and you knew about them. You were his lover, weren't you?"

Demetrius blinked.

"And when Alcibiades was assigned to the citadel," Miriam continued, "he became bored, didn't he? He liked to dress up as a woman, go out into the city. What you didn't know was that he used this as a disguise to meet Thebans."

Demetrius shook his head.

"Alcibiades had his eccentricities," he murmured. "And yes, sometimes he would dress like a woman, but it wasn't as you said."

"Well, how was it?" Miriam asked.

"Some men," Demetrius explained, "and I have met them, believe they have been born the wrong sex. Yes, Alcibiades was my lover. Sometimes he did dress as a woman. But this was ribaldry." He glanced away. "Alcibiades hated women."

"Why didn't you mention this?" Miriam insisted, "when I met you earlier, when I mentioned that the spy had probably disguised himself as a woman?"

"I couldn't believe it was Alcibiades."

"The same is true of all of us," Cleon interrupted. "We all knew," he smiled, "about what Demetrius calls Alcibiades' eccentricities."

"Whatever," Patroclus declared, "it still doesn't explain how Commander Memnon died."

Miriam gazed around the hall. Everything that had happened made sense. Alcibiades must be the spy, yet the more she sat listening to the men, the more her doubts festered. It's too precise, she thought, too easy. Alcibiades could act the traitor. He could have betrayed his king, his compatriots, for Persian gold, but Patroclus was right. How was this connected to Memnon's death, the other killings, and the theft of the Crown?

"Since the fall of Thebes," she asked, "had Alcibiades acted strangely, gone out by himself?"

"We all did that," Demetrius replied, "having been cooped up here for weeks. We joined the rejoicing in the camp. Now the matter's over. Isn't it?" Demetrius got to his feet. "If Alcibiades is the killer and he has fled, there's no longer need for any questions, is there?" And not waiting for a reply, he spun on his heel and walked out the door.

Miriam glanced at Simeon and raised her eyes heavenward.

"We'd best be going. Is Memnon's chamber and the little garret above it unlocked?" she asked.

"Of course," Melitus replied. "We received orders from headquarters to clear the citadel within a week and rejoin the rest of the camp. Alexander intends to burn the Cadmea to the ground."

Miriam left the hall and went up the steps. On each stairwell the chamber doors were open. Memnon's room had already been stripped; only a tattered leather belt lay in a corner.

"What's wrong, sister?" Simeon came up, closing the door behind him.

"What's wrong, brother, is that I thought Alcibiades was the spy, but now I'm not too sure."

She heard a rap on the door. Simeon opened it, and Pollux came in looking sheepish.

"I heard what you said, mistress, about old Alcibiades. He could be a bit of a lady." He grinned, "but . . ."

"But what?" Miriam asked.

"Demetrius isn't a liar; it's true what he said. Alcibiades dressed up more to make fun, to cause a laugh, and he didn't do it very well. I mean, paint on the face, a veil over his head . . ." Pollux did a mincing walk that made Miriam laugh.

"He could swing his hips and look at you coyly."

"But you don't think he was a spy?" Miriam asked.

"No, I don't," the page replied. "I have heard what goes on, mistress. I listen to the chatter."

"And at keyholes?" Miriam asked.

"Yes, mistress, and at keyholes. Alcibiades was dull, more interested in his belly. A good soldier. More important, I don't think it was him I saw going down the steps of the tower."

Miriam looked at him.

"Why do you say that?"

"Because of the way the figure looked and walked."

"But you said it was dark?"

"No, there's something else. You see, mistress, that night the tower was deserted. The person who crept down the steps came from the very top."

"He what?" Miriam asked.

"I've got good hearing, mistress. At night, when the tower is deserted, it's like a tunnel; it echoes. The chamber Alcibiades shared with Demetrius is much lower down; that night, I am sure, the person who passed me came down from the very top."

"From Memnon's chamber?"

"Perhaps, or even higher."

"You mean the garret?" Simeon asked.

"I think so. I went up the steps. I was going to see General Memnon. When I knocked on the door, his dog barked and I opened it. Memnon was lying on the bed. Oh aye, I thought perhaps the General had had a visitor, but he looked as if he had been asleep for some time. There was no, well, I couldn't smell any perfume in the room or see that anyone else had been there."

Miriam opened the purse that swung from her girdle and thrust a silver daric into the page boy's hand.

"Keep your mouth closed!" she warned. "Don't tell anyone. Simeon, go downstairs, use your authority, bluff, anything you want. Ask Demetrius to send out a search party."

"For whom?"

"For Alcibiades."

"What are you saying, sister?"

"That Alcibiades hasn't fled. I think he's been murdered and his corpse hidden away."

"But it could be anywhere."

"Ah yes, brother, but Alcibiades left on a horse. Now, the killer is not going to bring the horse trotting back, is he? I suspect that if we find the horse, Alcibiades' corpse will be nearby. Now go on, both of you!"

She heard their footsteps outside and, slipping out of the chamber, walked farther up. The small garret room was off unlocked. Miriam pushed it open and went inside. The chamber was dusty and dirty. She opened the shutters and stared abound. A table and stool stood in the corner. She went and sat down, scrutinizing the tabletop. She saw stains in the woodwork, as if someone had spilled ink over it. She leaned down, sniffed, and caught the faint fragrance of perfume. On the floor beneath was what looked like sealing wax, a dark red stain.

"It's henna!" she murmured. "This is where our spy dressed. But wouldn't Memnon have objected? Wouldn't he have heard this person moving about upstairs? Is that how he died?" She glanced at the narrow window, but she was wrong. She had been tempted to think that Memnon had come up, having left his dog downstairs, and that he was killed, his corpse thrown through the window. Of course, the door to Memnon's chamber was locked and barred with a guard outside, but the window in the garret was far too narrow. Miriam sat and put her face in her hands.

"I look at the things the wrong way," she whispered. Of course, she thought, the Oracle is eloquent and cunning. She went to the window and stared down, a sheer drop into the courtyard below. Demetrius was already organizing a search party. She saw horses being led out from the stables and she heard shouted orders. Miriam went and closed the door. She brought the bar down and sat on the floor with her back to the wall. She recalled a childhood game in which she would chant the verses her father taught her.

"What do we have?" she whispered. "A spy, not paid by the Thebans or Athenians, but by the Persians. What's wrong with that?" She paused. Persian gold flooded into Greece but who would pay the spy here in the Cadmea? At first it had looked as if the Oracle was in collusion with the

Thebans, but that was wrong. In the end the Oracle had inflicted more destruction on Thebes than on Macedon; that was why Telemachus had had to die. "Right," Miriam said. "We know there's a spy paid by Persia. He disguised himself as a woman so he could move about the city?" She paused. "Persian agents and spies," she spoke aloud to herself, "were spreading rumors easily seized upon by Alexander's enemies that Macedon was no more. The Oracle confirmed this. How?" Miriam steepled her fingers. "Of course." She continued speaking to herself, "He was an officer, he could claim that Memnon had received special intelligence. What now?" Miriam folded her arms across her chest. "Thebes rose in rebellion. The citadel was cut off. The only way the spy could communicate was probably by arrow. He probably painted a dire picture of the garrison. To a certain extent that was correct. Memnon was becoming more and more estranged." Miriam stared at the sunlight streaming through the window. Thebes was destroyed, she thought, but the spy worked on to create more mayhem and chaos. A born actor, he stirred up agitation by slaying the guards and then seizing the Crown. "But how did he achieve all this?" Miriam clambered to her feet. She dusted off her gown, opened the door, and went down the steps.

Simeon was waiting for her in the courtyard, talking to their escort. Miriam waved them over and walked toward the gate.

"Where are you going, sister?" Simeon caught up with her, hugging his writing satchel to his chest.

"Out to the priestess," she declared. "I have some questions for Antigone."

"I'm glad I'm with you," Simeon declared. "Olympias is busy organizing her play."

Miriam paused and glanced back at the citadel.

"You don't think it was Alcibiades, do you?" he asked.

"No, I don't." Miriam smiled. "Forgive my arrogance; at first I thought, perhaps. Yet it's too neat and leaves too many unsolved questions."

She walked on and reached the grove.

"There seem to be as many soldiers as there are trees." Simeon stared round. "It's a pity Alexander is closing the stable door after the horse has gone."

Miriam didn't answer. Now and again she was stopped by officers, but she produced the pass and eventually reached the white chalk path that led up to the shrine. This, too, was lined with soldiers. The officer in charge allowed them through and up to the priestesses' house. Again, more soldiers though the priestesses were composed, relaxed. Antigone was in an upstairs chamber busy over a spinning wheel.

"I always have difficulty with the thread," she declared. "My eyes have never been strong." She got to her feet. "Would you like some wine and honey cakes?"

Miriam looked around the chamber and noticed the packed saddle bags.

"Are you leaving?"

Antigone turned at the door.

"Why not? My sisters and I have decided that there is nothing left for us in Thebes. We will go our separate ways. Look, I have a present for you." She picked up a small square of blue silk and handed it to Miriam.

"It's a shawl," she declared. "Very costly. It comes from the east. It was a gift; I give it to you."

Miriam shook the silk out. It was blue like summer sky and shimmered in the light.

"It's like touching water," Miriam murmured, "so soft and smooth."

"You won't refuse it?" Antigone smiled. "You have been most kind. Please." Her eyes softened. "Accept it as a gift."

Miriam blushed. Antigone took it out of her hands and

placed it around her neck. "It's very rare and very costly," she whispered, "but please take it."

Miriam, rather embarrassed, thanked her. Antigone helped fold it up.

"Where will you go?" Simeon asked.

Antigone shrugged. "Athens, one of the cities. My sisters have friends, relatives in Greece. You Macedonians will march away," she blinked back the tears, "and in a year Thebes will be nothing but weed-choked ruins." She smiled. "Why have you come?"

"I have a pass to enter the shrine of Oedipus," Miriam explained. "I would like you to accompany me there."

Antigone stepped back, hand to her throat. "Must I?" she asked. "The shrine is empty. Jocasta is dead, the Crown gone. It has nothing for me but painful memories."

"You don't have to," Miriam countered. "But just for a short while? I'll explain later."

Antigone agreed. She told the other priestesses, took her cloak from the peg, and followed Miriam and Simeon out of the house into the courtyard. At the gate the soldiers were holding back Castor, teasing and taunting him. The young page, red-faced was holding his own, and the air was rich with his jeers. Miriam hurried ahead. The soldiers goodnaturedly let Castor through.

"What's the matter," asked Miriam, "has Alcibiades been found?"

Castor shook his head.

"No, mistress, not that. I bear orders from the king. Tomorrow morning Queen Olympias will stage her play, *Oedipus*. It is the king's wish," Castor winked, "that all be present."

Miriam groaned. Castor smiled mischievously.

"Alexander said his most beloved of mothers was insistent on that."

"Of course. She would," Miriam responded. "There's nothing that Olympias likes better than an audience."

The boy's eyes strayed to where Antigone and Simeon were standing behind her. He narrowed his eyes and gnawed at his lips.

"Is that all?" Miriam asked.

"Ah, no." Castor's eyes become pleading. "I have one favor, mistress. When the army marches, will you take us with you? We can cook, clean, sew . . ."

"Aye, and lie and steal!" Simeon intervened.

Castor lifted his hand, middle finger extended to make an obscene gesture, but then thought differently about it.

"I'll think about it," Miriam declared. "Now go back to the camp. Tell my lord king that I will be there."

Castor sped off. He ran the gauntlet of jeers and shouts from the guards. Just before he disappeared into the trees, Castor stopped, bent down, pulled up his tunic, and showed his bare arse to the soldiers. That was followed by another obscene gesture, then Castor disappeared into the olive grove.

"A lad of spirit," Antigone observed.

She followed Miriam out the gate and into the trees. "I've heard you mention Alcibiades. Wasn't he one of the officers in the Cadmea?"

"He's disappeared," Miriam explained. "Some people think he's the spy responsible for the theft of the Crown. Why, did you know him?"

Antigone shook her head.

They reached the path and walked up to the shrine. Antigone pulled the cowl of her cloak over her head and kept her face down. She seemed nervous around the guards lounging on the steps. Their officer brusquely examined the pass.

"Do you want us to accompany you?" he asked.

The officer was in full armor. His great Corinthian helmet

with its blood-red plume made him look like a giant, eyes glittering behind the metal rims.

"No." Miriam thanked him. "Just open the doors. Lock us inside."

The officer agreed. The outer and inner doors were opened then closed behind them. The shrine was dark, cold, and empty. Antigone crouched in the corner while Miriam examined the pits. The charcoal had been raked out and, beyond the spikes, lay nothing more than a stinking trench.

"What happened to the snakes?" Antigone called out.

"Alexander hates them," Simeon replied. "I suspect they were raked out and put in sacks."

"They were sacred," Antigone countered.

"Not to Alexander," Miriam snapped. She walked up to the pillar and looked at the metal clasps. They had been intricately made by some blacksmith many years earlier. They were hinged. One part was riveted to the pillar; the other could swing backward and forward. There were three clasps in all; at the back of the pillar protruded a wooden peg on which the Crown had rested. Miriam scrutinized this carefully. She walked back, taking care when she crossed the row of spikes dividing the two pits.

"It's nothing more than a dirty chamber, is it?" Antigone declared, getting to her feet. "The glory and the power are gone."

Miriam knelt and stared at the pillar.

"Antigone," she pleaded, "can't you help us? Didn't Jocasta ever tell you how the Crown could be removed?"

"It was a secret," the priestess replied, "handed down from one high priestess to another."

Miriam sat, the iron bar with its protruding plate at the end nestling against her waist.

"Tell me," she said, "the Crown was removed on certain occasions?"

"Aye, on great feasts no more than two, three times a year." Antigone replied absentmindedly.

"So." Miriam made herself comfortable. She grasped the iron bar; it was cool in her sweaty grasp. "The high priestess came in here by herself?"

"Yes," Antigone replied. "Everyone else would wait outside. Once she was ready, Jocasta would unlock the bronze doors and release the bar. The doors would swing open. Everyone would file in, and Jocasta would hold up the Crown. Whatever the occasion was, the taking of oaths or pledges, the leaders of the council would touch the Crown held by Jocasta with the tips of their fingers. When the ceremony was over they would retire."

"Was the Crown heavy?" Simeon asked.

"Oh, no," Antigone replied, "it looked much heavier than it was. In fact, it seemed very light."

"But where was the secret kept," Simeon persisted, "I mean, if the high priestess died suddenly?"

"I don't know," Antigone confessed. "You saw the pectoral that Jocasta wore; that was her symbol of office."

Miriam stared down at the floor. She recalled that awful, half-burned cadaver. "The pectoral wasn't there!" she murmured. "When Jocasta was killed, I am sure the pectoral was gone!"

"Perhaps her killer took it," Antigone replied, "or the soldier who found the corpse?"

"No, no he wouldn't have taken it," Miriam countered. "Such looting would mean crucifixion." Miriam moved and, as she did, felt a tug, as if the dagger in the sash around her waist had been pulled. She moved away from the iron bar.

"What on earth?" She took the dagger out and crouched down. She pushed the blade close to the iron plate on the end of the bar; the dagger stuck to it.

"Simeon, here, look!"

Her brother hastened across. She did it again, the dagger stuck hard against the side of the plate.

"It's a magnet," Miriam declared, springing to her feet. She crouched down on hands and knees, moving along the iron bar. The clasps that held it to iron stands riveted into the ground were not soldered fast and could be pulled back. Miriam, assisted by Simeon, now pulled these loose and lifted the bar up. It was as long as one of the great pikes carried by the guards regiment in battle and, like them, surprisingly light.

"It's hollow," Simeon exclaimed.

Miriam lowered the pole; it swayed precariously in her hand. She recalled how soldiers managed their pikes in battle. She turned slightly sideways and, coming to the edge of the charcoal pit, lowered the pole. At first she was clumsy but eventually, helped by Simeon and watched by round-eyed Antigone, they lowered the pole so that the magnet at the end caught the iron clasps. These were easily pulled back. She tried each one.

"The clasps are well oiled," she murmured. "They come away, and because of the wooden peg at the back, the Crown would remain firm." She thrust the pole into Simeon's hand, went across, placed her dagger on top of the pillar, and going back, lowered the pole again. The magnet caught the dagger. She lifted this up, pulling the pole back as if it were a piece of rope, and with a cry of triumph, she snatched the dagger from the end. She turned, face bright.

"That's how it was done! That's the secret! Using the plate on the end of the pole you can release the clasps and then, with the magnet, simply lift the Crown off!"

"It's even easier than that." Simeon examined the iron

plate, pointing to how it tapered to a sharp end. "If you are unsure of the magnet, you can use this to prize the clasp loose and then hook up the Crown."

"That's how it was done," Miriam exclaimed. "The high priestess kept to the ritual; she did not bring anything into the shrine."

Antigone stared, mouth half open in surprise.

"Jocasta knew that," Simeon confirmed, "but the one who stole the Crown. How would he know?"

"The pectoral," Miriam declared. "That's why the assassin burned Jocasta's corpse. He wasn't trying to hide any sign of torture but to disguise the fact that he had taken the pectoral. Don't you remember?" Miriam continued excitedly, "the pectoral had a pendant in the center."

"Of course," Antigone added, "it must have been some form of locket that contained instructions on how to remove the Crown."

"In the end the secret wasn't so hard to figure out." Miriam declared. "It's just that we never realized that the iron guard rail was really a rod, with a hook and magnet on the end." She laughed. "It was more a puzzle than a mystery."

"Yet you are no further to reclaiming the Crown!"

"No, I'm not," Miriam replied. "And, for all I know, it may now be many miles from Thebes." She heard a rapping on the door. "Lift the bar," she urged.

Antigone did so. "Come in!" she called.

The officer entered, helmet cradled under his arm.

"Mistress Miriam, Demetrius is outside. He has something to show you."

Miriam followed him out. Demetrius was holding the bridle of a horse; across its back, covered with a bloody, dirty sheet, was the corpse of a man. Miriam glimpsed a blood-stained head on one side and the military boots dangling down over the other.

"You were right." Demetrius cheeks were tear-stained. "It didn't take us very long."

Miriam went down and lifted the corpse's head. A deep gash gouged one side where the skull had been staved in; the rest of the face was covered in dust.

"We found the horse about eight miles from Thebes," Demetrius exclaimed, coming around. "It was off the main highway, cropping some grass. There was no sign of Alcibiades."

"Wouldn't the assassin have driven the horse away?" Simeon asked.

"He would have tried," Demetrius explained, "but it's a cavalry mount. It would always return to where its rider had left it."

"So how did you find Alcibiades?"

"We searched through a rocky outcrop. We found bloodstains, signs of a newly dug grave." Demetrius gently touched the corpse. "I'm taking you back to the Cadmea," he murmured, his face tight. His eyes had a wild angry look.

"He was no traitor, Israelite. He was a soldier, a good companion. He would get drunk, and, yes, he had his weaknesses, but he was a brave Macedonian. I won't hear differently. I'll build a funeral pyre; he deserves a hero's end."

"Do that," Miriam replied. She clasped Demetrius's hand. "He was no traitor. He was probably lured out to some meeting and then killed." She looked up at the lowering sky and felt the rain on her face. "But don't build the pyre tonight," she murmured, "we are going to be drenched. Tomorrow perhaps." Miriam thanked Antigone and, followed by Simeon, took the path through the olive grove back toward the camp.

"You now believe Alcibiades was innocent?" Simeon asked.

"I do." Miriam paused. "I am sorry for Demetrius. He has lost a lover and the rain will prevent a funeral pyre." She smiled at Simeon. "But look on the bright side: at least Olympias will not be able to stage her play!"

CHAPTER 13

THE RAIN FELL in sheets, drenching the camp; it seemed as if the heavens themselves were stretching down to complete the picture of devastation around Thebes. Miriam sat in her tent half listening to the heralds postponing the play that was supposed to take place the following morning. She looked at Castor standing before her.

"You are sure?"

"Mistress, as I am that I am standing here. The staircase was dark but the cloak the man was wearing was very similar to the one that that priestess wore."

"But it was not the priestess herself?"

"Oh, no," the boy said hurriedly. "But I remember that it was thick and gray, the edges trimmed with red stitches."

Miriam glanced at Simeon.

"Very observant," her brother replied. "That's what Antigone was wearing but such cloaks are fairly common."

Miriam gave the boy a coin and watched him go out, splashing in the mud.

"Brother, pass me Antigone's gift."

Simeon tossed it across. Miriam pressed it against her face and sniffed carefully. She could detect nothing, so she unrolled it. Near the middle, where it had been draped around the priestess's throat, she sniffed again.

"Brother, here! Smell this; can you catch a fragrance?"

Simeon took the cloth and sniffed at it. "A slight one," he said, "of perfume."

Miriam took it back and sat holding the piece of silk.

"Everything is wrong," she murmured. She recalled Antigone squatting in the temple, watching them make their discovery; the table in the garret above Memnon's chamber and the fragrance she had detected there.

"But that's impossible!" she exclaimed.

"What is?" Simeon demanded.

"I smelled some perfume on a table in the Cadmea. It's the same as on this piece of silk."

"Perfumes are common," Simeon replied, "as are cloaks. You don't think Antigone is the Oracle, do you?"

"No." Miriam shook her head. "I've spoken to virtually everyone who used that tower. Never once were any of the priestesses seen in the citadel. But, it is a coincidence."

"Antigone couldn't kill a man," Simeon declared.

"No, no she couldn't."

The flap was pulled back and Alexander, accompanied by Hecaetus, slipped into the tent. The king shook himself like a dog and sat on Simeon's bed, staring across at Miriam. He had lost his look of exhaustion; the skin around his eyes was smooth. He wiped the rain from his face.

"I'm so glad the weather's broken," he declared. "It's kept Mother in her tent. She hates the rain. She even talks of going back to Pella sooner than she'd planned. Hecaetus, would you like to go with her?"

"Don't threaten me, my lord. You know I would be

dead within a month. Olympias would kill me just for the sport of it."

Alexander laughed.

"Mother hates rain." He leaned forward. "Her face gets wet, the paint runs, and she hates to look old. That's why she stopped campaigning with Father and why we moved to Pella. There's supposed to be less rainfall there. Miriam, I want you to pray to your known God that it rains until the army marches. Yap! Yap! Nag! Nag! Anyway, I received your message about the Crown."

Miriam told him what she had discovered. Alexander sat, fingers to his lips, listening attentively. When she finished, he stretched toward her and gripped her hand.

"You were always better at logic than I. I never dreamed that black iron bar was the solution. However, it won't bring back the Crown. It won't capture the Oracle, and Memnon's blood, as well as Lysander's, still cries to the gods for vengeance."

"Does it really matter?" Simeon asked. "Soon the army will move; Demosthenes has fled from Athens. You are undisputed captain-general of Greece."

Alexander clapped his hands.

"You are right. What happened here will soon be forgotten. Until I cross the Hellespont. Then Demosthenes will scurry back to Athens." His face grew tight. "And do what he is very good at—whisper, gossip, gossip! Say that Alexander is cursed! That the removal of the Crown was a sign of the gods' anger toward me! So, I want that Crown! I want the Oracle crucified!"

"This spy . . ." Miriam turned to Hecaetus. "Before all this began, you knew there was a spy in the Cadmea?"

"I knew for two reasons," the master of spies replied languidly. "First, the rumors in Thebes itself. Second, we intercepted a letter from Demosthenes to his Persian paymasters."

"What did it say?" Miriam demanded angrily.

Hecaetus closed his eyes and swallowed hard.

"The actual quotation was, 'So you have been informed that there's a spy in the Cadmea to harm Macedon's interests?' "

"Why didn't you tell me this?"

"I did tell you, in as many words!"

"Say it again."

Hecaetus repeated the phrase.

"So, the spy could be working for anyone: Demosthenes, the Persians, as well as the Thebans?"

"So it appears to me. Anyway," Hecaetus added crossly, "it's the same thing. Thebes relies on Athens, and Athens relies on Persian gold."

"But bear with me." Miriam held her hand up. "This was a letter from Demosthenes to the Persians?"

"Yes."

"And he is repeating information received from the Persians?"

"I suppose so."

"And why do you call him the Oracle?"

"It's a word Demosthenes uses in the next sentence, 'This Oracle,' " Hecaetus closed his eyes, " 'Could be of more value than the one at Delphi.' "

"So," Miriam persisted, "The spy could be working for the Persians?"

"Of course."

"But who would have informed the Persians?"

Hecaetus blinked.

"What are you saying?" Alexander asked. He loosened the tight strap on one of his sandals and rubbed the top of his foot against his leg. He cocked his head sideways, a common mannerism whenever he was puzzled.

"It's possible," Miriam replied, "that one of the garrison

simply opened negotiations with Persia. However, that's very dangerous; he would probably have had to use someone in Thebes, or even more perilous, someone in Athens."

"And the more people know, the more dangerous it is."

"Naturally."

"So?"

"There is another alternative."

"You mean?" Hecaetus broke in, "Persia already had a spy here, who, in turn, bribed a member of our garrison?"

"It's a possible interpretation of Demosthenes' letter."

"And?" Alexander asked.

Miriam heaved a sigh.

"And nothing, my lord; that's as far as I can go. But, I beg one favor. Have the soldiers on the shrine and at priestesses' house doubled. Tell the officers to be most vigilant. The priestesses are not to leave."

"I can't very well stop them." Alexander got to his feet. "I gave them my word that they would be protected and given safe passage."

"It's raining," Miriam replied. "Surely, my lord, priestesses cannot travel in such weather?"

Alexander came back and ruffled her hair.

"Let me know what happens, and by the way, Miriam, hide that piece of blue silk. If mother sees it she'll want it."

Hecaetus would have stayed but Miriam insisted that she wanted to be alone. When her visitors had gone, she picked up the blue silk, lay down on the bed, and laid it across her face. She used to do this when she was a child. Different colors meant different worlds. She'd make up stories or pretend the piece of cloth was a magic mirror that would let her see her mother or Jerusalem. Now she saw the Cadmea, that grim citadel, and its lonely tower. Outside the Thebes had ringed it: Lysander's corpse was rotting on the cross. Memnon was hiding in his chamber, wondering if he was hearing ghosts. And that garret above. The figure on the stairs dressed as a woman. Lysander squatting in the courtyard, surprised at what he had seen. Images were jumbled in her mind. She couldn't make sense of them, and even if she did, what sort of proof could she offer? Every line she followed had proved futile.

"Let me go back," she murmured.

"Miriam, you are talking to yourself!"

"Shut up, brother, I am thinking!" She recalled the different conversations she'd had with the officers, the pages, and Antigone. She recalled Telemachus, defiant yet driven with anguish at what had happened to Thebes. And what was it Telemachus had said about Memnon flying from the top of the tower? But he hadn't fallen from the top. He'd fallen from his window. So why had Telemachus said that? Why hadn't he said he'd been pushed? Miriam pulled the piece of silk away from her face and sat up. "Because he did fall from the top!" she shouted.

"Sister, what is the matter?"

"Memnon didn't fall from his window," she declared.

"From where, then?"

"Telemachus talked about Memnon flying from the top of the tower. I think it was the only mistake he made, but that's why he was killed. He could have made other slips, though I am just beginning to wonder how much Telemachus really knew. You see, brother, Memnon's chamber was locked and guarded, his war dog was with him. No one could go through the door, and, if anyone tried to come through that window, the dog would have attacked and Memnon would have fought for his life." She paused. "We must turn the problem around. No one came through the window. I now believe Memnon climbed through it, probably with the help of someone else."

"Where was he going?" Simeon asked.

"He was climbing to the top of the tower!"

"Like a fly?" Simeon teased.

"No, he was being helped. Someone persuaded Memnon to leave that chamber. Someone persuaded Memnon that he was in great danger."

"Which is why he was dressed?"

"Of course. He climbed the rope and reached the top of the tower."

"But Memnon would have still struggled."

"No, brother, Memnon told his war dog to stay silent. He left, climbing the rope, but as he reached the top, the person who was supposed to be helping him, instead of grasping his hand and pulling him over, pushed him away. Memnon, shocked and surprised, fell to his death. The assassin pulled up the rope and disappeared."

"But who was the assassin?"

"I am not too sure. It's one of those officers. Simeon, go find the pages!"

Simeon reluctantly agreed. A short while later, he brought a bedraggled Castor and Pollux into the tent. They looked nervous, slightly wary but Miriam assured them all was well. They protested that they'd already answered her questions, but Miriam said it was important so the two pages, sitting on a rather tattered, woollen rug, repeated their earlier conversations about the officers and their private lives, what scandal and gossip existed. After they'd been paid and left, Miriam got up, put a pair of battered boots on and fastened her cloak around her.

"Where are you going?"

"You are coming with me, Simeon. I want you to do exactly what I ask."

They went out of the tent—Miriam talking, Simeon protesting, but at last he'd agreed. He went down to the quartermaster's stores and came back. Miriam, meanwhile, had seen the captain of the guard and, with a squad of soldiers behind them, set off for the priestesses' house. It was cold and growing dark. All those who could had found shelter either in the camp or in the ruins of the city. The olive grove was a popular place, the men sheltering beneath the trees, clustering around camp fires. The air was thick with the odor of sweaty leather and cooking. The priestesses' house was well guarded but lights in both the lower and upper windows showed that the women had not yet retired. Merope answered their knock and took them into the small dining chamber. Antigone came downstairs, her fingers stained with ink.

"I've been making inventories," she apologized.

"Could you take me to Jocasta's chamber?" Miriam asked.

Antigone looked surprised.

"Please!" Miriam insisted, "it's very important!"

Antigone shrugged and went up the stairs. Miriam quickly stepped into the kitchen, where the other priestesses were seated around the wooden table. She asked them a few questions then broke off as Antigone called from the top of the stairs.

"I am sorry," Miriam apologized, joining her. "I am curious as to where you are all going."

Antigone had already lit the lamps in Jocasta's chamber.

"It's rather warm despite the rain," Miriam declared. She opened the shutters and stared out. She saw Simeon standing below, dressed in a military cloak. Antigone came behind her and gasped.

"It's only my brother," Miriam confided. "But this is where Jocasta stood the night she was killed isn't it? You were with her, remember?"

"Yes, yes, of course."

Miriam turned so that her back was to the window.

"You loved Jocasta?"

"Like a mother." Antigone became wary.

"She was old," Miriam continued. "My mother died in childbirth, but I tell you this, priestess, I would not have let her go out in the dead of the night to meet a ghoulishly dressed stranger standing under the olive trees."

"What are you saying?" Antigone's hands fell to her side. "What are you implying?"

"I just think it's very strange," Miriam repeated. "Here you are, Thebes is devastated, a killer on the loose. Jocasta sees this possible killer from her chamber window."

"But she ignored my advice, she wanted to go," Antigone broke in. "Jocasta really thought it was Oedipus, or at least a friend."

"Shouldn't you have accompanied her? And when she didn't return, why didn't you become alarmed? Why not send a messenger to the camp or even gather the others and go looking?"

"But it was common knowledge that Jocasta went out and visited the shrine."

"At the invitation of a stranger?" Miriam snapped. "There's a contradiction, Antigone. I asked your sisters downstairs. They thought Jocasta had gone out to the shrine that night. I wager they didn't know she had left with a stranger; if they had, they would have become alarmed. I just find it overstrange, that you let your so-called mother wander off into the darkness and never turned a hair, at least not until we arrived with the dreadful news."

"Jocasta was a law unto herself," Antigone retorted. "She was high priestess."

"We'll leave that for the moment."

Miriam sat down on a stool, Antigone on the cot bed. Miriam noticed that her hand was out, just touching the rim of the bolster.

"You gave me a lovely gift." Miriam forced a smile. "A piece of blue silk. I could smell your perfume on it. I detected the same fragrance on a table in the citadel, but you didn't visit there, did you?"

"Of course not!"

"And that page boy who brought the message from the camp yesterday. He claimed to have seen a woman dressed in a cloak similar to the one you wore coming down the steps of the Cadmea. He was intrigued because, although the cloak was a woman's and the fragrance was certainly not worn by any man, the figure was definitely a male."

"I'm not responsible," Antigone's gaze didn't waver, "for what went on in the Cadmea."

"Oh but you are," Miriam declared. "Do you know, Antigone, that I think you are a killer, a murderess! With your shaven head, your slender form, your doll-like eyes, and, above all, your blunt speech, you could deceive Olympias, that queen of serpents!"

"Are you going to say that I am the Oracle?" Antigone accused. "The spy in the citadel?"

"Everything to its own," Miriam murmured, "and in its own time. You say you were Pelliades' niece?"

"Of course."

"And Pelliades came out here to visit you often?"

"Naturally, I was his kinswoman."

"And you and he would just talk, would you? Is that why a leading Theban councillor came to the shrine, to see his beloved niece? Or was it something else? Do you know, Antigone, I believe you seduced one of the officers in the citadel. If you painted your face, lost that reverential look, and donned an oil wig like the women of Egypt wear, you'd be very beautiful, quite ravishing."

"I thank you for the compliment," came the cool reply.

"You seduced one of the garrison officers, a man open to

bribery. He became the Oracle. You told him what to do. Rumors were sweeping Greece that Alexander was dead and the Macedonian army no more. In Thebes, Pelliades and Telemachus fanned these sparks to a flame, especially when they received confirmation from a Macedonian officer."

"So I deceived my uncle?"

"Oh, don't look so round-eyed, Antigone, you know you really should act in Olympias's play. The queen would take to you like she does to one of her vipers. You didn't really care about Pelliades or the Thebans. And it wasn't very difficult for your lover in the citadel to confirm the rumors, started by other Persian spies, that Alexander of Macedon was no more."

Antigone's brows knit together.

"But I don't understand, Israelite. You talked about my uncle's visits here and yet the spy was in the citadel?"

"That was the transparent beauty of your scheme." Miriam shifted on her stool. "Until the siege began, the Macedonians were able to wander where they wished. That's how you enticed the officer, wasn't it? A man who came here to see the shrine, susceptible to your charms and to the wealth and prospects you offered. At first he may have been reluctant, but eventually, like all traitors, he embraced the whole treason, just as he embraced you, body and soul. You played a very treacherous game. You told your uncle that one of the garrison had come to the shrine. Oh, you . . ." Miriam shook her head, ". . . you wouldn't tell him that he was your lover, no more than you'd reveal that you were a Persian spy, but you would tell him that he'd confessed to you some dreadful news, that Alexander and his army had been destroyed. Pelliades and Telemachus, eager to throw off Macedonian rule, would scarcely believe such marvelous news. However, thanks to Persian gold, similar rumors were seeping through all of Greece, so they accepted it as a truth revealed by the gods. They would often come out here to see how much more you had learned and you would tell them about the garrison. How some of the officers were weak but that the two leaders Memnon and Lysander, well, they were Alexander's men, body and soul, and they wouldn't frighten easily." Miriam paused. Antigone was now watching her like a cat, head down slightly, glaring at her from under her eyebrows. "Pelliades," Miriam continued, "encouraged you further; that's why you used Jocasta and the priestesses here to open negotiations with the Macedonian in the citadel."

"But Jocasta was her own person," Antigone snapped.

"Jocasta loved you," Miriam retorted. "I could see that. She would do whatever you asked. Go out into the night to meet a stranger, or act as the broker of peace for your uncle. Now we come to Lysander." Miriam brushed the hair from her brow. "I really thought you were telling us the truth behind Lysander's death, about one of the Theban councillors almost betraying the identity of the spy in the citadel. It was all a lie. The spy never went into Thebes. He never met Pelliades, Telemachus, or anyone else. The only person he met," Miriam pointed across the chamber, "was you, somewhere in the olive grove. He'd come here disguised as a woman, wouldn't he? I suppose that was your idea? You lent him the perfume, the paint for his face, the gray cloak. You told him what to say and what to do. To any onlooker, you'd be two women talking."

"Do you have proof of all this?" Antigone intervened.

"Logic is better than proof. Antigone, why should a Macedonian officer dress up as a woman to meet Thebans? They'd see through the disguise and it would afford him little protection. One member of the Macedonian garrison nearly stumbled on the truth: poor Lysander. One day, by chance, he came into the grove. He glimpsed something extraordinary, one of his compatriots dressed as a woman, slipping through the trees. Now, Lysander probably dismissed this as some sexual escapade. He may not even have been sure who the man was. What he didn't know was that the spy had also glimpsed him. Frightened about what Lysander might eventually do, you persuaded your uncle to open formal negotiations and entice Lysander out. You were very persuasive. Pelliades would listen. If you could entice Lysander, even Memnon, out of the citadel and kill both of them, your spy in the Cadmea would be protected and the others might be persuaded to surrender. In the end, Pelliades had to accept Lysander alone."

"But he needn't have come." Antigone said softly.

"Oh no, it was very clever," Miriam declared. "You asked for Memnon and Lysander. Anyone who knows soldiers would realize that Memnon couldn't possibly come but would send his lieutenant."

"And Jocasta swore an oath to guarantee his safety?"

"Another reason for Lysander to come out. Jocasta swore this oath at your insistence. Poor Jocasta was deceived. She had to die, didn't she? In time she may have come to reflect, question the advice you had given her. In the end you were successful. Lysander came out, and once he was through that stockade, he was killed. There was no argument, just brutal murder. Pelliades was acting on your advice. The garrison had lost an outstanding officer and now they could display his corpse to lower the morale of the soldiers inside. At the same time, your lover began to play upon poor Memnon's mind. Memnon, however, was made of sterner stuff. He didn't break, so he had to be murdered."

"And Memnon never knew who the spy was?" Antigone leaned forward.

"It was a skillful piece of treachery," Miriam declared. "Before the siege ever began, the Oracle told Memnon that he, in fact, had found a spy among the Thebans, that he was receiving secret information. Memnon, of course, accepted this and allowed his officer the use of the garret above his chamber so he could dress the part."

"And you say Memnon accepted this?"

"Of course he would! As commander of the citadel, he'd be deeply interested in collecting information about Thebes."

"Wouldn't he tell the others?"

"Why should he? The spy answered to him and when matters turned ugly, just before the siege began, this officer would hint that he was also hunting a spy among the Macedonian garrison. So, why should Memnon reveal that?"

Antigone smiled, thinking.

"The two of you played the Macedonians and Thebans like musicians would flutes, piping the tune everyone wanted to hear."

"But Thebes fell," Antigone declared. She sat farther up on the bed, close to the bolster.

Miriam wondered if she had a dagger concealed, but Simeon was downstairs and the house was surrounded; she did not feel afraid but satisfied; Antigone's reaction was proof enough of the accusations leveled against her.

"You didn't give a fig if Thebes fell," Miriam replied. "What did it matter to you? But let me hurry on. Thebes did fall. The Macedonians swept in and the garrison was relieved. Now you had two tasks. To spoil Alexander's victory as much as possible and to steal the Crown. First, there was the usual whispering campaign. I suppose the envoys from Corinth and elsewhere became aware of the gossip. You and your lover dressed as Oedipus, a charade both of you had played before. At night the two of you would approach lonely sentries. The Macedonian soldier, cold and disgrun-

tled, encountered this beautiful woman coming out of the
night carrying a small jug of wine and some honey cakes.
He'd relish the chance to gossip. Perhaps tease and flirt. You
were safe. If any officer approached, you would hide in the
shadows till he passed, and no soldier would confess to being
distracted by such a beauty during guard duty." Miriam
paused. Antigone's head was back, a faint smile on her face.
"The soldier would be off his guard, shield and spear down.
He'd hardly hear your lover come up behind him. And with
a swift blow to the head, the man was dead. But that was just
a minor part of the drama to dull Alexander's victory. Your
real intent was to steal the Crown."

"I didn't know how the Crown could be removed,"
Antigone intervened. "And, even if I did, how could I get
through lines of soldiers?"

"Oh don't be so coy, Antigone! It was quite easily done.
You'd work on Jocasta. She would give you the password.
But, there again, perhaps she didn't, because it wasn't really
necessary, was it? What we have are a squad of soldiers outside the shrine of Oedipus. They are truly bored. The shrine
is quiet, the olive grove a sea of darkness around them. From
the camp they can hear the sound of revelry as their fellow
countrymen celebrate their great victory. They would be
slightly resentful. Thebes was no more. Why should they
waste their time guarding a deserted shrine? You played the
same game again. If Jocasta could slip out at night, why not
you? You could make up any excuse. You wanted to see that
everything was safe. Or to walk through the trees. Or to
take the night air. Why should Jocasta object? The high
priestess had been given the solemn word of Alexander of
Macedon that she and all her household were safe. I am
speaking the truth, aren't I?"

Antigone, tight-lipped, just stared back.

"Don't you object?" Miriam asked.

"I am a priestess," Antigone replied. "But I do love a good story, Israelite. So far you've no evidence."

"Oh, but I have." Miriam leaned forward. "More than you know." And, at last, she saw her opponent's confidence slip—a quick blink, a licking of the lips. "He's told me."

"You're a liar! He'd never say." Antigone's hand went to her lips.

"Who'd never say, Antigone?"

"I cannot and will not betray myself," the priestess replied. "You have me tangled, trapping me with words. You come here with a story and now you are going to allege that I, who did not know the secret, persuaded Macedonian soldiers to let me through their lines."

"Ah, yes," Miriam replied, "so let me tell you about the honey cakes and wine."

CHAPTER 14

"IMAGINE . . ." MIRIAM FELT as if she were telling a story to Simeon. "Imagine the soldiers on guard outside the shrine of Oedipus. Suddenly a young priestess, your good self, comes out of the olive grove. You carry a basket of food and drink, those honey cakes and that delicious wine you serve your guests. You claim it's a present from the chief priestess. The soldiers eat and drink and, as they do so, consume the sleeping potion with which you've laced both the drink and the food. I can't imagine a soldier on earth who'd refuse such a gift, and what threat could a young priestess pose? They are soon unconscious. Your accomplice then appears from the trees. The key is taken, you open the main doors of the temple and go into the vestibule." Miriam paused. "Now, I don't know if you used the password, pretending to be Jocasta, or just persuaded the soldiers inside to lift the bar. After all, if the officer in charge had let you through, why shouldn't they?" Miriam glanced over her shoulder at the window. She wondered if Simeon had the sense to leave his post and come into the house.

"Your accomplice hid in the shadows of the vestibule. The front doors of the temple were locked, the soldiers inside would think their commanding officer had locked you in. They would certainly suspect no danger. Again the gifts were offered. The potion you gave them would work quickly. In a short while they were asleep, and then you took the Crown."

"But I didn't know how to! That was a secret."

"No. There are two possibilities. First, like me, you could have discovered that the iron bar was the means to remove the Crown. Second, by that time Jocasta was dead. Her pectoral had been removed, the clasp undone, and what was inside? A piece of papyrus that revealed the secret? Jocasta's dream suited your purposes: there would be no question about you slipping out of your bedchamber. And if anyone had noticed it, in the chaos and turmoil following Jocasta's death, they would have thought you'd simply gone looking for her. Anyway, you removed the Crown, and your accomplice, with his club, smashed in the brains of the soldiers sleeping inside the shrine. You then relocked the door and did the same to the guards outside. You took the remains of the food and drink you'd brought and fled back to the priestesses' house. Your accomplice returned to the olive grove where he burned Jocasta's corpse before returning to the citadel. No one would have noticed you had left, and until the theft and Jocasta's death, Macedonian soldiers were at liberty to wander where they wished."

"And if what you say is true," Antigone demanded, "why should I have done all this?"

"Because you've got a soul as dead as night! Because you are bored, but above all because you are a Persian spy!"

"That's nonsense!"

"No, it isn't. Persian spies are as many as sparrows in a tree. They work throughout Greece, particularly in the principal cities, places like Thebes and Athens where resistance to Macedonian leadership is the most intense. Persia didn't care whether Thebes stood or fell. In fact, Darius would have been delighted that Alexander was provoked into devastating a principal Greek city. He will be even more pleased when the Crown of Oedipus arrives in Persopolis. How he'll crow with triumph! How lavish his rewards will be for this spy who achieved so much, who soured Alexander's great victory! He could fabricate some story." Miriam waved her hand. "How the gods of Greece gave this Crown, which so mysteriously disappeared, to the king of kings in Persia."

"Why would the Persians use someone like me?"

"Oh, they probably met you through Pelliades. Priestesses hear all the gossip. They can influence events, especially one like you who, perhaps, had grown bored with tending a small shrine and living in a house with priestesses you didn't give a fig for. The Persians must have been delighted with your work, particularly when you ensnared an officer in the garrison at the Cadmea."

"But you have no proof." Antigone stretched out her hand. "Where is the proof? Who is this accomplice? Where is the gold the Persians are supposed to have given me?"

"Oh, you'd collect it as you travel," Miriam replied. "And it would be nothing to what you'd receive in Persia. Alexander will question you—well, not in person; Hecaetus the Master of the King's secrets will do that. And then, of course, your accomplice."

"What, Alcibiades?"

"Oh, no," Miriam retorted. "He was your protection. I am sure your uncle asked who the spy was. You gave the enigmatic reply, 'a disciple of Socrates,' a reference to Alcibiades. A good choice, a man well known for his liking of women's clothing. Poor Alcibiades would protect your lover and, at the appropriate time, divert suspicion—"

"From me? I had nothing—"

"From you," Miriam continued softly. "Your lover did that by slaying the two Cretan archers; he came back to the grove and caught them unawares. His attack on the house was cunning; he might kill me and end my snooping as well as divert any suspicions that there was any collusion between himself and a priestess."

"Give me his name," Antigone gibed.

"No, why don't—" Miriam stopped. Antigone had taken a knife from underneath the pillow and was balancing it in one hand.

"What are you going to do?"

"We were talking here," Antigone replied, "and this secret assassin, this shadow known as Oedipus, came through the open window."

Miriam got to her feet, rolling her cloak around one arm. In the grove of Midas both girls and boys had been taught to fight, but she always felt so clumsy. Antigone was now balancing on the balls of her feet, and she held the knife expertly. Miriam backed to the window.

"Simeon!" she screamed, "up here!"

She picked up a stool and threw it. Antigone sidestepped. It crashed into the wall as Antigone struck, lithe and swift as a cat. Miriam sidestepped but stumbled. Antigone turned. Miriam caught the hand holding the dagger and desperately struggled to grasp the other, which was pummeling her stomach and chest. All she had to do was stop the dagger from coming down. Antigone was strong and agile. Miriam found it hard to press the dagger back. She heard a pounding on the door, the latch rattling but Antigone must have locked it behind her. The dagger came down. She was aware of Antigone's glaring eyes but she watched the blade, feeling the muscle ripple in the wrist. Miriam freed her other arm, smacking the heel of her hand into Antigone's chin.

Antigone staggered back. Miriam was now aware of the crashing against the door. Simeon must have arrived with the soldiers. Antigone stood upright, even as the lock began to splinter. One minute she had the dagger out and the next she turned it, driving the blade deep into her own heart. All the time her eyes watched Miriam, a faint smile on her lips, even as the blood bubbles appeared. Miriam stood tense; she found she couldn't move. Antigone came toward her, one hand out, the other still grasping the dagger hilt; her eyes rolled up and she crashed to the floor. Miriam crouched down beside her, watching the blood pump out of her mouth.

The door snapped back on its leather hinges. Simeon was beside her, soldiers milled about. She heard the other priestesses wailing on the stairs. Simeon put a cloak around her.

"Is she the Oracle?" he asked.

"No, but she was his lover," Miriam replied. "And tonight's business isn't finished. I was foolish to come up here alone. Very, very foolish."

Simeon led her downstairs. He wanted to take her into the kitchen but Miriam glimpsed the white faces and staring eyes of the other priestesses.

"Not here!" she urged.

They went out of the house and across the yard into the olive grove. An officer caught up with them. Miriam was aware of sitting down beside a camp fire. She laughed softly when honey cakes were passed to her followed by a deep bowl of watered wine. She couldn't eat the cakes, but she sipped at the wine. Simeon kept questioning her but it was hard to concentrate. At last the wine and the heat of the fire made her relax. Secretly she was glad that Antigone had taken that way out. It made things easier, both for her and for what was to happen in the citadel. She looked up through the branches. The night sky was showing the first pinpricks of light. The rain clouds had broken, though rain still dripped through the trees and the ground was damp.

"Simeon, send a message to the citadel! Tell Demetrius and the officers to assemble in the mess hall. This time I want a corps of guardsmen, in the tower and outside."

"Will you be all right?"

"Please!" Miriam grasped his hand. "Just do as I ask."

Two hours later, as the sky lightened, Miriam entered the Cadmea and made her way across to the mess hall. Patroclus, Demetrius, Melitus, and Cleon were present, sharing a jug of beer and a platter of oat cakes. Miriam sensed that they knew this was important; the one she suspected looked pale-faced and heavy-eyed, nervous and fidgety. Men from the guards regiment stood around the hall: grim, stark figures in their bronze armor, the great plumes on their helmets making them bigger, casting long shadows. Outside, in the courtyard and passageways, other guards stood in silent vigil as Cretan archers patrolled the ramparts. Miriam took her seat at the head of the table, Simeon sitting on her right; she joined her hands before her and stared at Demetrius.

"First, I've come to apologize. I understand that later today Alcibiades' body will be burned?"

"As befitting a Macedonian hero."

"Quite so," Miriam replied. "And I myself will sprinkle incense on the pyre. Alcibiades was a good soldier, a loyal officer. He was foully murdered by the man we know as the Oracle. But," she added quickly, "there is not one spy but two. The first," she didn't falter in her story, "is Antigone, a priestess at the shrine of Oedipus. She has been closely questioned by Hecaetus, and we know who her accomplice is."

The one she suspected pushed back his stool slightly.

"No one can leave." Miriam stared at a point on the far wall. "Anyone who attempts to do so will be arrested."

"In which case," Demetrius added dryly, "we had best wait and listen to your story, Israelite."

"There are certain things I cannot tell you, though I'll be as succinct and as clear as possible. Alcibiades was loyal and so was Lysander." She waved her hand. "Forget this nonsense about the woman. The Oracle never met Thebans. Disguised as a woman, he met the priestess Antigone. So, if they were seen together in the olive grove, people would simply dismiss them as two priestesses taking a walk. Of course they would meet deep in the grove where no one was supposed to go."

"Except Lysander," Demetrius intervened.

"Lysander did go there, and he saw something untoward." Miriam replied. "But he could make no sense of it. The man he glimpsed disguised as a woman did not have a reputation for such practices. Perhaps Lysander, as a good officer, discussed the matter with Memnon?"

"Yes, he would," Melitus broke in.

"Memnon, however, had an answer," Miriam declared. "You see, Antigone was a spy for the Persians. She had recruited an officer here in the citadel. They met secretly. Lysander had noticed this. He may, as I have said, discussed it with Memnon." Miriam paused. "And this shows the cunning of our spy. Memnon probably told Lysander that the man he'd glimpsed was meeting a spy working for the Macedonians, possibly a priestess who could tell them what was happening in the city. Lysander would have accepted that. However, the Oracle could afford no mistakes. He was probably relieved and pleased that Lysander was later killed by the Thebans."

"But you told us earlier that one of the Thebans may have betrayed something."

"No, no." Miriam shook her head. "I told you to ignore

that. The Thebans wanted to kill both Lysander and Memnon so that the garrison here would surrender." Miriam shrugged. "We all know what happened. Now the Oracle, once Lysander had been removed, tried to unsettle Memnon. First, there was the nonsense about the ghost of Oedipus. That would certainly cause a shiver, a sense of haunting, particularly on a commander who had just lost his loyal lieutenant, a commander who had received rumors that Alexander and the Macedonian army had been destroyed, a commander who was now besieged by Thebans."

"But Memnon was as tough as a donkey," Demetrius spoke up.

"Yes, yes he was, but he was also suspicious. He knew there was a spy in the citadel, and his confidant played on these fears, perhaps raising the specter that one of his officers, or all of them, could be involved in such treason."

"Yes, that was true," Demetrius said. "Memnon hardly met us."

"Now the spy was very astute," Miriam continued. "He offered to be Memnon's man, to spy on his colleagues. Memnon accepted this. After all, the same man had braved his life in recruiting a so-called spy among the Thebans. Before the siege began, Memnon had allowed this man to disguise himself as a woman in the small garret above his chamber, well away from anyone else's view."

Miriam heard a sound outside and stopped. She hoped that Hecaetus had not arrived and, by his blundering, do more harm than good.

"This spy," she continued, "persuaded Memnon that his officers were going to kill him on a particular night. They would assassinate him in his chamber and hand the citadel over to the Thebans."

"What proof do you have of this?" Patroclus asked angrily.

"Oh, I have none," Miriam countered. "But think of

Memnon! Frightened about Alexander, grieving over Lysander, realizing he was in charge of a small Macedonian cohort besieged by a powerful city."

"That was true," Melitus intervened. "Especially the day before he died."

"This spy mustn't have thought much of us," Patroclus declared languidly.

"Oh, I think he did; that's why he was so clever; isn't that right, Cleon?"

All heads turned to where the young officer sat pale-faced, hands clutching the table.

"You are the spy," Miriam continued quietly.

"But Cleon always claimed he was hated by the Thebans," Demetrius spluttered. "His family had been killed by them."

"I couldn't think of a better reason," Miriam declared. "Would he worry if Thebes rose in a futile revolt and was destroyed? What did he care about Macedon? He was infatuated with the priestess Antigone, the prospects of limitless wealth, and a life of luxury in Persia. He persuaded Memnon." Miriam held Cleon's eyes, "that he could go out and spy among the Thebans disguised as a woman. He was actually given a cloak by his lover, perfume and paints. He used to dress in that garret above Memnon's chamber where no one else could go. He was seen by Lysander and must have been relieved when the Thebans killed him. He, through Antigone, confirmed the rumors that Alexander of Macedon was dead. He was the candle flame that lit the oil and made it flare further. He didn't care if Macedon was defeated or Thebes destroyed: either way he would be victorious."

Cleon just stared rigidly ahead.

"Before the siege," Miriam continued, pointing at him. "he had Memnon's permission to slip out of the citadel in disguise. Once the siege began, he'd certainly support Memnon's decision to send Lysander to deal with the Thebans. After Lysander's death, whenever this tower was deserted, Cleon would pretend to be the ghost of Oedipus while his lover played a similar role beyond the palisade."

"And he would communicate with her by arrow?" Melitus asked.

"Yes, Cleon would fire the occasional arrow, marking the spot for his lover to collect the message, though, I suspect," Miriam smiled thinly, "that they didn't need to tell each other very much. Perhaps the fire arrows were simply a diversion, another means to unsettle Memnon and the garrison. Now, Cleon," she continued, "serpentlike, began to talk to Memnon, reassure him of his loyalty, warn him of plots among you officers. In this he was successful. Memnon would trust Cleon, a man who had good reason to hate Thebes. On the night Memnon was killed, Cleon told him some fable, that you were about to storm his room, kill him, and surrender the Cadmea to the Thebans."

"But we were guarding his room!" Demetrius exclaimed.

"Cleon would only use that to heighten Memnon's suspicions. He persuaded his commander to leave his chamber and climb a rope to the top of the tower so that when the mutineers broke down the door there would be no one there. Cleon would use such a story to unmask the traitors as well as to protect his captain."

"You mean," Patroclus intervened, "Cleon had persuaded Memnon that on that particular night we were going to kill him?"

"Of course. You can only feed uncertainty for so long. If nothing happened, Memnon's suspicions might shift. Moreover, if Memnon was killed, there was always a chance that the rest of you might lose your nerve and surrender the Cadmea. Cleon lowered a rope from the top of the tower. Memnon, in full armor, left his chamber by the window. However, when he reached the top, Cleon struck him, sending him spinning down to the yard below. The rope was removed and Cleon hid until the following morning when everyone clustered outside Memnon's room, wondering what had happened."

"But we were on guard," Demetrius declared. "We would have noticed Cleon going up and coming down."

Miriam shook her head. "You told me Memnon could not abide anyone using the garret above him. But that night, as on those days before the siege when Cleon used to disguise himself as a woman, Cleon had Memnon's permission to be there."

"True," Melitus declared. He wagged a finger at Cleon. "Your quarters were not in the tower. No one paid much attention to your comings and goings. You answered to Memnon for what you did."

"Is she safe?" Cleon abruptly asked. He leaned forward. "Is she hurt?"

"You whoreson bastard!" Demetrius would have lunged across the table but Melitus held him back.

"Once the Macedonians had arrived," Miriam continued, "the game shifted. This time fear was spread among the Macedonian army: the guards were killed by this precious pair, the shrine raided, and as Cleon knows, the Crown stolen."

"How was all this done," Demetrius asked.

"Oh, quite easily," Miriam answered. "I will tell you later. However, Cleon was very busy with his lover; they had the run of that olive grove. Cleon could wander at will, be it frightening me here in the tower or leaving messages in my tent."

"And Telemachus?"

"The Theban had to die: he knew about Memnon's death and other matters, but not the identity of the Oracle. Nevertheless, these scraps of knowledge could be dangerous: what if Telemachus knew about Antigone? Pelliades, who was her uncle, may have said something. Telemachus was killed by Cleon only because of what he may have known."

"And Alcibiades?" Patroclus asked.

"That was a very astute ploy. All the business, about Telemachus and the Thebans thinking one of you was dressed like a woman, was arranged to point the finger at Alcibiades, whose private pleasures were public knowledge."

"You murdered Alcibiades," Demetrius declared.

"Yes, he did." Miriam added, "Alcibiades was to be the cat's-paw, the diversion to our thinking that the matter was ended." Miriam held Cleon's gaze. "Of all your stratagems, that was the most cunning. Alcibiades, right from the beginning, was chosen as a victim, a sure means of protection should things go wrong, as well as a scapegoat to dull suspicion and provide the means for a leisurely escape."

"How did you do it, Cleon? Lure him to some meeting?" Demetrius asked.

"He was always partial to a young boy," Patroclus declared.

"You lured him out," Miriam continued, "killed him, and buried his corpse. You and Antigone thought that would give you time, and when the army marched, both of you could slip away to meet your Persian masters. It may have taken months, even years for Alexander to find out." Miriam gestured at the accused. "Arrest him and hold him fast!"

Cleon didn't struggle when the soldiers dragged him to his feet. The officer had taken a piece of rope and was going to bind his hands; Miriam ordered him not to. She walked around the table. Cleon's face was so surprised, he could muster no defence; he was more concerned about Antigone than anything else.

"Can I see her?" he asked.

"I have spoken the truth, have I not?" Miriam asked.

"Can I see her?" he whispered.

"The truth?" Miriam asked.

"The truth, Israelite." Cleon regained his wits. He smiled slyly. "You are right. What do I owe to Thebes? What do I owe to Macedon? I love her! I loved her the first time we met. I went out to the shrine and she was sitting on the steps. She talked to me." He shrugged. "It made sense. She asked if Alexander was dead. I told her we had heard rumors. But she held my hand as we talked; from that touch everything flowed. How did you know?" He paused.

"Perfume," Miriam replied. "Antigone gave me a gift of blue silk. I smelled the same perfume on the table upstairs in the garret. Then I recalled the gossip of the two pages. All your colleagues here, the other officers, are lovers of men, but they never once mentioned you. Who I asked, who could be seduced by the beauty of a woman? The logical answer was you; each time I put that piece into the puzzle, everything fit."

"He should be crucified!" Demetrius spat out. "He should be nailed to a cross and allowed to die."

Cleon was studying Miriam closely.

"She didn't confess, did she?"

Miriam shook her head. "She killed herself."

The change in Cleon's face was dreadful. His composure disappeared. He closed his eyes and gave the most heart-rending groan.

"All that is left," Miriam declared, "is the Crown. Where is the Crown of Oedipus?"

Cleon was still shaking his head, muttering to himself.

"Is the Crown gone?" Miriam insisted. She took Cleon's face in her hands, forcing him to look at her. "It's over," she murmured. "It's all finished."

"Why should I give it back?" Cleon brought his head up. "Why should I give it to you, clever Israelite?"

"A quick death," Miriam replied, ignoring the exclamations of the others. "The Crown," she insisted.

"Do I have your word on that?" he demanded.

"You have my oath," she declared.

"The garden," Cleon smiled, "at the back of the priestesses' house. Dig deep beneath a stunted rosebush in the far corner."

Miriam looked at the officer, who rattled out an order.

"Simeon," Miriam declared, "Go with them! Have the prisoner taken away."

Chaos broke out as the guards pushed Cleon to the door. Demetrius and the others jumped up. Patroclus tried to lash out with his fist but the guards officer knew his business. He pushed them away and, with Cleon shouting insults, bundled him out of the room.

"Is this acceptable?" the officer asked, coming back. "Shouldn't my lord the king? . . ."

"All the king wants is justice for the murders and the return of the Crown," Miriam replied. "Nothing else. We could nail Cleon to the walls of the citadel and the Crown could lie undiscovered for ever. If he speaks the truth, then I'll keep my word."

Miriam sat down and put her face in her hands. Patroclus brought some wine but her stomach curdled, so she refused it. On the one hand she felt relieved, on the other a sense of exhaustion. It had been so close, Cleon and Antigone so clever. If the priestess hadn't given her that gift, that piece of blue silk, or had the Fates ordained that? Had Antigone made a mistake because she liked her? She looked around the mess hall. Miriam wondered if the officers would intervene—seize the prisoner and carry out their own dreadful punishment? She got up and went out to the courtyard. She was sitting on the steps when Simeon came hurrying back. He thrust a soiled leather bag into her hands.

"It's there, undamaged!"

She undid the cord and took out the Iron Crown. Although it looked heavy, it was surprisingly light. Its blazing red ruby sparkled and flashed. Miriam resisted the urge to put it on her head and moved it around in her hands. Was it iron, she wondered, or some alloy? She recalled a lecture given by Aristotle on how the Dorians had first used iron.

"You know, Simeon," she murmured, "it's all a charade! We call this the Iron Crown but I think it's made of some alloy. If there was a real Oedipus, I doubt very much that he ever wore this. But as Plato said, things are not what they are but what people make of them. Tell the officer to come out. Ask him to lock the hall door behind him."

Simeon hastened off and the officer came down. He towered above Miriam, his harsh young face staring through the slits of the armored helmet. He stood, one foot on the step beside her, one hand grasping the hilt of his sword.

"I have the Crown," Miriam declared. "You heard me. I gave my oath. Let it be done quickly! Before the others know."

The officer shouted to two of his men. Miriam heard them go down the steps to the cellars below, heard the sound of doors opening. She sat holding the Crown, staring up at the sky. She would be glad to be gone from Thebes, away from destruction and death. She still marveled at Antigone's cunning.

"Simeon, will you do me a great favor?"

"That's what I'm here for sister, to do your bidding."

Miriam smiled at the gentle sarcasm. "If Antigone had

governed Thebes," Miriam declared, "the city would never have been ruined. She was shrewd and calculating, a woman of great strength. I'll always wonder if she loved Cleon as much as he loved her."

"You asked me for a favor?"

"This will all be over soon. I don't want Cleon's and Antigone's bodies thrown to the dogs. Put their corpses together in the olive grove. Take some of the guards and pay them well. Let the corpses be burned together! Please!"

Simeon nodded and stepped back as the soldiers returned. Miriam glimpsed one of them wiping his sword on some straw before sliding it back into his scabbard.

"It's done," the officer declared. "He fell on a sword."

"Did he say anything before he died?"

"Antigone."

Miriam nodded and got to her feet.

"It is what I expected."

A few hours later Alexander—beside himself with glee, ready to accept what Miriam had done, and loudly telling Hecaetus not to sulk—stood on a great dais in front of the Macedonian army, Olympias beside him. In the presence of his armed host and of the representatives from all over Greece, Alexander lifted the Crown of Oedipus and placed it gently on his own head. He stood, hands extended, as thousands of swords rattled on shields. The Macedonian king was hailed as victor, captain-general, and soon-to-be conqueror of Persia!

The Owen Archer historical mysteries of

Candace M. Robb

from
ST. MARTIN'S DEAD LETTER MYSTERIES

The Apothecary Rose

Christmastide, 1363—and, at an abbey in York, two pilgrims lie dead of an herbal remedy. Suspicious, the Archbishop has Owen Archer masquerade as an apprentice at the shop that dispensed the fatal potion.

_____ 95360-7 $5.99 U.S./$7.99 Can.

The Lady Chapel

During a summertime feast, a prominent wool merchant is murdered in the shadow of York's great Minster. Owen Archer must unravel threads of greed, treachery and passion that run all the way to the royal court...

_____ 95460-3 $5.50 U.S./$6.50 Can.

The Nun's Tale

A ghostly pale woman claims to be the resurrected Joanna Calverley, a nun who died of a fever some months before. Owen Archer is called to investigate the murders that seem to follow in her wake.

_____ 95982-6 $5.99 U.S./$7.99 Can.